NARC

FROM
DAY TO DAY

FROM DAY TO DAY

BY

FERDYNAND GOETEL

TRANSLATED FROM THE POLISH BY
WINIFRED COOPER

WITH A FOREWORD BY
JOHN GALSWORTHY

THE LITERARY GUILD

NEW YORK   MCMXXXI

4688

FOREWORD

I WOULDN'T go so far as to recommend people, as a rule, to read a foreword by me, but I do advise them to read this; it is short, and if they intend to peruse this very remarkable book it will save them time and perhaps a little mental effort.

The book is written in what I believe to be the totally new form of a diary by the leading character, in which he incorporates the text of a novel as he writes it. His diary describes, day by day, his present spiritual state and material surroundings in the Polish city of Cracow, to which he has returned from the war, and the novel describes his past experiences as a Polish prisoner of war in Turkestan. The diary, of his present, is printed in Roman letters, and the novel, of his past, in italics, so that there is no possibility of confusion between the two.

I ventured to suggest, publicly, not long ago, that every literary experiment must be justified by the nature and needs of the theme. Applying that test to this book one finds that it has been passed. For the task the author set himself was this: to disclose how a certain episode, detached in time and space, in the past of his hero, has lingered on into and coloured his hero's present. At a certain point far advanced in the book the novel fades out, and the legacy, as it were, from the novel drops into and blends with the diary. Incidentally, it was a stroke of genius to bring this mingling about through the child of the diary and the child of the novel. The form of the book, in fact, is most ingenious, though very difficult to handle, and it is a triumph for Ferdynand Goetel that he has used it with such conspicuous success. I would certainly not advise an inexperienced writer to follow his example. The ingenuity of the method perhaps only becomes fully apparent when one tries to think of any other way of doing exactly what has been done here. It would have been, for instance, quite useless to have written the book in a stretched-out straightforward line, describing first the past in Turkestan and then the present in Poland. The effect would have been lifeless and far too disjointed. As it is, the book is knit together into a whole which pulses with life.

This is the first work of the Polish writer Ferdynand Goetel to be given to the English public. A leading Polish author, a man of charm, energy, and experience, a traveller, a mountain-climber, a writer of great gifts, whose work has been acclaimed in Poland, France, and Germany, he now comes before the English reader in a truly admirable translation by Miss Winifred Cooper. It was high time.

JOHN GALSWORTHY.

TRANSLATOR'S NOTE

THE DIARY is written in Cracow in post-war Poland, independent and united; whereas the events described in the novel take place in Turkestan during the war, when Poland was still partitioned among the three Powers—Russia, Germany, and Austria.

The Polish colonists in Turkestan, of the novel, are naturally from Russian Poland. They are Roman Catholics, and there were of course Catholic parishes in the towns colonized by Poles. The Polish priest in the book is therefore a Catholic and not an "Orthodox" priest.

The prisoners of war are Poles from the Austrian part of Poland, have been fighting in the Austrian army, and have been captured by the Russians.

CHARACTERS

PEOPLE IN THE DIARY

STANISLAW	(*Stanislav*) diminutive "Stach." (Tadeusz in the Novel.)	*The Writer*
ZOSIA	Diminutive of Zofia, the Polish form of Sophia	*His Wife*
EVA	(*Eyva*), Evka, Evunia	*His Daughter*
FELIX	(*Feylix*), (Ignacy in the Novel)	
PROFESSOR KLAPA		
HELENA KLAPA		
THE MOTORIST		
SZMID	(*Shmid*)	

PEOPLE IN THE NOVEL

MARUSIA RADZIEJOWSKA	Diminutive of Marja (Mary). (*Radgeyovska*). Polish surnames ending in ski are adjectives and take -*a* for the feminine	*Daughter of Colonel Radziejowski, a Polish Colonist in Turkestan*
MADAME KAMILA		*Her Stepmother*
JUREK	(*Yourek*) diminutive from Jerzy, in English George	*Her Brother*
IRENKA		*Her Sister*
JUDGE SZAROTA . .	(*Sharota*)	
THE POLISH PRIEST		
BARAT . . . . °		*A Native of the Sart Race in Turkestan*
TADEUSZ	(*Tad'eyoush*) (Stanislaw in the Diary)	*Polish Prisoners of War from the Austrian Army*
IGNACY	(*Ignát'sy*) (Felix in the Diary)	

ix

FROM
DAY TO DAY

FROM DAY TO DAY

September 10th.

Well, I am at the starting line again. The nicest moment of the entire process of literary tillage, which somebody, goodness knows why, has called "creation," is the beginning. You strut about swelled out like a lion, you roar, shake your mane, and drive fear into the simple. You dream of unheard-of deserts, you reckon up the yield of the bloody harvest, to crawl at last into a cage where, in reward for foolish antics put on to oblige the Public, a piece of carrion is pushed through to you by the tamer who finances you—in other words, by your publisher.

But we won't exaggerate! That headlong leap which must be taken into the uncanny depths of experience before you can start work is not an everyday act; nor is it easy. A certain rehabilitation is also due to those "foolish antics." The grimace must be convincing—worse, it must be "real"—to take effect. And after all it is indifferent whether it be performed in the publisher's lair or under the blue cage of God. The principal thing is that the lion be not an ass sewn up into a lion-skin.

But why in the world am I writing all this? I regret that paragraph. It is more suitable to a novel than to a diary. If it

I

has crept in here, it must be to bear witness to the uncertainty that always takes possession of me before starting a new work. Especially today. I feel that I'm beginning something which I ought to leave untouched. But I can't help it. It oppresses me too much. It must be written, and then there will be an end of it. Oh, bother all this meditation!

So—how did I think it out? Let us re-create the "skeleton." But, to be exact, what skeleton is there in it? She . . . well, one can't call her by her name, though it really is difficult for me to imagine her with any other name and surname than her own. Think of something "suitable"? Well, I've plenty of time for that. We'll have it in the rough copy as it was in reality, and we can change it later. So: Marychna, or, as in Russian, Marusia. That has an idyllic sound, truly—but what matter? All the more that she was in reality an idyllic type. Her soul was translucent as amber, refracting everything in its clear heart. Yes! . . . "refracting everything in its clear heart!" I haven't come across a stupider expression for ages. You see to what depths of idiocy one can descend? Let's leave the "skeleton" alone. I lived the whole thing, I absorbed it, I have it in my blood. I'll get it written . . . and then we'll see.

. . . . .

Marusia had never seen her fatherland. Born and brought up in the steppes of Asia. . . .

. . . . .

What the devil! Am I writing her *curriculum vitae* for a situation in a municipal office? No! I'm decidedly not in the vein for writing today. I'll go and build pyramids with my little daughter.

We always come to grief over pyramids. At first the child is pleased and I laugh. Then I begin to build while she looks on. Then she wants to build too, and I won't let her because she'd spoil my work. And the end is wrath and tears. You old donkey! Did you buy the bricks for yourself or for the child? Well, of course, a pedagogic moment. Development of the sense of harmony, symmetry, logic . . . go on further with this, Stanislaw, and your daughter will be a first-class stone-mason!—In the meantime she's howling and I can't write. I must hurry up and tell her some story about daddy-paddy or our stupid Kundy-pundy, the cook. However you may look at it, Kunda is a sort of cactus in the house. A strong and decided personality, dubbed by all of us, most frivolously, "the slattern." She makes me think of some household antique. You would often like to ask it what it is thinking about, but you never do so because if the thing so much as creaks you get gooseflesh all over you. But our Kunda differs from a piece of old furniture in having a whole series of dogmas which she does not attempt to conceal and which no human power can dislodge. The mightiest among them is horse-radish sauce, and with this she has completely brought me to her feet. I admit it, careless as to whether my memoirs will ever be printed. After all, there is no real depth of difference between horse-radish sauce and trout in aspic, and if I had written "trout in aspic" no one would have thought the worse of me. On the contrary, such a phrase in a biography would sound rather well:—"the maestro's favourite dish was mountain-trout in aspic!" . . . Down with humbug! Up with horse-radish sauce!

September 11th.

"So you'll stay on at the farm, Marusia?"

"Yes, Father."

"You won't go back home?"

"No!"

"And you won't give up the children?"

"No!"

"Is that your last word?"

"Yes, my very last!"

"And I must write that to your father?"

The girl's head drooped helplessly. "Please do. . . . Or perhaps I'd better write myself."

"Yes, write yourself!" cried the priest. "And if you'll take my advice, don't write for a day or two. Think it well over, my girl. Be considerate. Remember, you've broken your father's life."

Marusia turned pale. "It wasn't I!" she contradicted hotly. "I didn't break it. I"—her voice changed—"I"—she fluttered, her eyes filling with tears— "You know it wasn't I!"

The priest glanced at her agitated face and regretted his harsh words. Anxious to make amends, he went up to her and stroked her hair benevolently. "Come, come! You must calm yourself, my child. Don't cry! It is her fault, I know. Everyone knows it! And everyone sympathizes with you. . . ."

"I don't think they sympathize," whispered the girl resentfully. "Why, they're trying to force me to go back to her. They persecute me, they reproach me. Even here at the farm I've no peace. You're not angry, are you?" She looked at him beseechingly.

"No, child!" said the priest gravely. "Nobody can drive

you back to your stepmother by force. But from you one may expect sacrifices. While she"—*he waved his hand in resignation.*

"Sacrifices! and isn't this a sacrifice?" She pointed to the humble furnishings of the room. "I left her the whole house, everything—even Mother's own belongings."

"Well, well, that'll do, Marusia. So you'll write yourself. And I ask you once more—write considerately. Don't forget that it isn't very nice for your father at the front. And he isn't well besides."

She stirred uneasily. "Has he written?"

"No. His wife told me, your mother—I mean to say, your stepmother . . . Madame Kamila."

"Oh yes!" and Marusia's face assumed its usual reserved expression.

"Well, my dear!" sighed the priest, rising heavily from his seat, "I must be getting on."

"Won't you stay to tea?"

"I can't. You know it's a goodish drive to the railway. And I wanted to call on the way to see the volostny[1] and the aryk-aksakalla,[2] to make sure that they let no harm come to you."

Marusia shot a quick glance at the priest from eyes that had grown suddenly happy. "I knew you wouldn't abandon me!" she said, kissing his hand. "If you don't mind my asking, would you remember about the books for the children?"

"All right, all right. But you must be patient. It's very difficult to get school books. May God give you happiness

[1] Volostny: head man of a country district.
[2] Aryk-aksakalla: Superintendent of the irrigation system. Aryk means canal or dike.

here"—he turned on the threshold—"since there's no other
way to it! Shall I see the children again?"

"I don't know, unless you can wait a little longer. They're
at work at something near the aryk. Our fields were flooded
yesterday."

"Well then, another time. Won't you take me as far as
the river? You used to like riding."

"Oh, of course! I ride every day."

The priest lingered on the terrace of the homestead to cast
an anxious eye over the farm buildings. Then his glance
swept round the steppe, lighting for a moment upon a clump
of trees that concealed a native village, and discovering in
the distance the hazy outlines of a neighbouring farmstead.
The steppe enclosed Marusia's property with a ring of waste
land, while on the other side of the river it was cut off by a
wall of thick-grown reeds.

He sighed. "You won't find it easy, my girl, in such a
desert."

"I shall manage all right!" she said cheerfully. "Barat
lived here all alone and kept the place going more or less.
Now there are three fresh hands for the work. And in a few
days I shall have two Austrian prisoners, some of those who
are taken for field work. . . ."

"Did you ask for them?"

"No, but when the volostny was making out the list, he
put me down too."

"Aren't you afraid of these foreigners?"

"Why? Everyone says they're peaceable and quiet."

"You're doing a crazy thing, girl! Crazy!" The priest
shrugged his shoulders as he went over to his tarantass.

Marusia ran to the stables, reappearing in a moment with her horse saddled in the Cossack way.

They started off at a good pace, though the sun had barely passed the zenith, and the white ribbon of road curving over the flat surface of the steppe puffed fire and dazzled with its glare. The priest tried to fling a few words more to his companion, but after swallowing the dust thrown up by the horses he wrapped his travelling cloak about him and abandoned himself to the rhythmic motion of the carriage. At the place where the road, which had run at first along the riverside, described a wide curve before darting off into the far distance, the priest smiled at Marusia and waved his hand in farewell. She responded warmly, checked her horse, and her eyes followed the carriage for a long while as it rolled in its ball of dust over the steppe.

Then she looked about her and rode slowly back towards the river. She reached its first channel by a narrow track beaten in the reeds, and went through it to an islet overgrown with brambles. Her horse she tied up to the one willow growing on the bank, and threaded her way through the thicket, till she arrived at a small clearing not far from the ravine of the river. This was the beloved goal of her lonely rambles. Its shutters of thick-woven leafage opened on nothing save the still mirror of the water or the deep blue of heaven. Tired out with the heat and the ride, she fell face downwards upon the ground. The pulse beating in her temples grew quieter under the spell of the surrounding silence. A light wind blowing down the ravine enfolded her now and again in a soothing caress. With closed eyes, she seemed to be on her mother's bosom. . . . Very quiet . . . and

*safe. . . . Nobody asking anything and knowing everything
. . . everything.*

．　　　．　　　．　　　．　　　．

There—that's enough for today. Quite a bit of work, for
me. I didn't expect to get swept off my feet like this. How
alive those memories of captivity are in me! For never were
my eyes more widely opened upon the world. From the moment when, ordered to be nothing, I was sent like a labelled
parcel beyond the confines of my world, I was given that
wonderful independence of soul, never tasted before or
since. Least of all today, when my "powerful," "promising,"
"undeniable," "lyrico-epic," and "brutally subtle"—God
have pity!—literary talent turns me into a monkey on a tight-
rope. I protest, it is true, but not always successfully.
"You've nothing of the literary man about you," my publisher tells me—adding at once: "All the same, when you
begin to get a swelled head, I shall want to see you!" And he's
right. Whatever I may do in self-defence, nobody takes my
writing for granted. Even my own wife's attitude towards
me has undergone a great change. She seems to be amazed,
and even scared that I write books, that others print them,
read them, and—most of all—pay for them! Pay better and
better and more and more punctually. For there was a time
when I had but one pair of trousers and fraternized with the
peasants, and not long since I thought of becoming—by
"vocation"—a village schoolmaster. She can't understand
whether I'm completely dotty or whether she herself's been
a fool all this time. So in this quandary she gives way more
and more, while I spread myself on every position she
abandons. What is to be said for my family, who turn a

strange eye upon me? They think prosaically: "Well, well! His first and second books have come off, but in the end he'll come a cropper, and take a job in a municipal office, for that's his real calling." But it's not so—is it, Marusia? You'll help me out, you poor dear!

September 12th.

Nothing, for ages past, has drawn me to my desk like this Marusia story. What can it mean? Is it the unpaid reckoning with the past? In that case I had better leave it alone. Nonsense! I don't reckon with others, but with myself. I've a right to that. The worst of it is that I must hide this manuscript from my wife. Yes, Zosia, I must hide it from you, or, to speak more accurately, from your feminine flair. I hope I shall manage it, for I'm no conspirator. But manage it I must, if these reckonings are to be brought to a close. Then—then, when it is finished and printed, I shall have to face the music. . .

To work, to work! It's late. Eva is saying her bed-time prayers. "God bless Granny and Mummy and Daddy and all my relations." Good night, baby, good night.

• • • • •

The priest's visit was a last attempt to dissuade Marusia from staying on at the farm. He had carried it out as a sacred duty, but at the bottom of his heart he sided with the girl against her stepmother. In common with the entire older Catholic colony in Turkestan, he did not take to the lady from Warsaw who, on a holiday visit to relatives one summer, had made such a conquest of the newly widowed Colonel

*Radziejowski that he led her to the altar within a year of his
wife's death. This had greatly astonished the whole colony,
since the Colonel had been an exemplary husband to the dead
woman, and had been frantic with grief on losing her. And as
he was regarded as a man of stern and blameless character,
people racked their brains to discover how he could have let
himself be caught by this unknown stranger about whom
various stories were told. Following the universal opinion, the
priest had several times even given the Colonel to understand
what was the reputation of his new acquaintance, and when
asked to publish the banns he actually made a serious objection. The Colonel then declared shortly that he was taking
the step for the sake of his children, who needed the guiding
hand of a civilized and sensible woman. They wouldn't go
on living in those wild steppes for ever! He was contemplating selling his property in Turkestan and moving to Poland,
where his father and grandfather were born.*

*Startled by all this, the priest protested no longer and even
regretted his spoken word. It was only on the wedding day,
when he saw the Colonel's young, elegant, and pretty bride,
that he grew sad and uneasy again.*

*And the history of the Radziejowski family after the
Colonel's new marriage exceeded the priest's worst forebodings. On the wedding day itself it transpired that Marusia,
who was sixteen and the eldest of the Colonel's children, had
left home and gone to her mother's outlying farm, on purpose
to avoid greeting the pair on their return from church. The
Colonel, leaving his wife in the sulks, went off after the girl
straight from the wedding feast, and it was said that he
fetched her home by force. This was more than the truth, for*

Marusia yielded to her father's will and came of her own accord, after shedding an ocean of tears on the paternal bosom. The Colonel was touched by the tears, forgave his daughter's action, and grieved exceedingly to see the boding shadow between his children and their new mother.

After this incident apparent peace reigned in the house. Marusia had promised to be correct towards "Madame Maman," and she kept her word. Madame Radziejowska promised to be kind to the children, and displayed a generous impulse now and then, although she was more occupied at that time in reforming the household and giving éclat to the honeymoon. The house she really did put, as she expressed it, on "a European footing." Old pieces of furniture were relegated to the children's quarters, to garret and storeroom; old customs vanished together with old servants and long-standing friends. New visitors, hitherto unseen and smarter than those of former days, descended upon the Radziejowskis in noisy crowds. The old family library was opened, and part of the books removed to the lumber room to clear the shelves for new ones from the publishing house, "Europa."

The Colonel consented to everything, and even in his soul approved of some of the changes. He went once a day with a kind word to his daughter's room, and brought his wife flowers. For the rest, he looked on and waited. As soon as he judged the new order of things to be more or less settled, he conferred with his wife about the children's education. She took up the subject with enthusiasm, and it was decided that Marusia should be sent to the best college in Petersburg, while a tutor should be brought from Warsaw for the children. When Marusia was ceremoniously informed of the

decision, she refused to go to Petersburg, and declared her
intention of teaching the children herself. Asked by the
Colonel the reason for her attitude, she answered that she had
promised her mother on her deathbed not to leave the children until they were grown up. And that she was there to
help her father and not to be an enormous expense to him.
The Colonel said nothing, kissed his daughter, and dared not
reject the offer. But Madame Kamila took up the gauntlet.

From that day, silent but inexorable combat became a daily
factor in the life of the Radziejowski household. Madame
Kamila came to understand that complete dominion over her
husband was an unobtainable dream unless she could win
influence over the children. Pained and repulsed by Marusia,
she turned her attention to the younger members of the
family. But here too she met with a baffling resistance. Jurek,
the twelve-year-old boy, took his sister's part with a ruthless
and silent determination which developed at times into gross
impudence. Irenka, who was younger, submitted to her
sister's influence and her brother's tyranny in all decisive
matters, although she was more yielding and greedy for the
presents her stepmother showered upon her. Discouraged by
her failure, Madame Kamila tried falling back on the authority of the father to wrest the children from the strong hand
of their sister. The Colonel flogged his son for his mulishness
and disobedience, and scolded Irenka. Then he summoned
his wife and Marusia and informed them that he would not
hear a word of any domestic quarrels. And with that he contented himself.

With time the home of the Radziejowskis developed into
three separate camps. In one wing lived Marusia and the

*children, taken up with their lessons and with the orchard;
in the middle were the Europeanized apartments of Madame
Kamila; while the Colonel always shut himself up in his study
after returning from duty. They all met twice a day at table,
to eat their dinner and supper in stern silence. Even the most
care-free visitors were frightened away by the cold and
gloomy atmosphere of the house. And the energy of Madame
Kamila was quenched in consequence. The uncompleted arrangement of her European dwelling was carried through
anyhow, and the new home usages fell into neglect and died
out. The lonely woman began to pay calls on her former visitors, and dropped here and there an embittered word. Informed of this, the Colonel forbade her to tell tales in the
town about what happened at home. So she was forced to
content herself with books and newspapers sent from Warsaw, and with tears and headaches.*

*The Colonel realized that the position won by long years
of hard work in a foreign land was crumbling, and began to
meditate upon carrying away his family before the roof fell.
New strength revived in him at the idea of a return to his
native land. He got into touch with relatives in Poland, and
this emboldened him to start preparations for the sale of his
possessions in Turkestan. No easy matter, since his property
was very considerable and of various kinds. He owned the
house he lived in and another let to tenants in the town, the
farm in the steppe left him by his dead wife, a cotton plantation which was on lease, and shares here and there in manu-
facturing concerns. Shut up in his study, he added and sub-
tracted and cautiously interviewed prospective purchasers,
cheered by the thought that he was about to sever at one blow*

*the horrible tangle of his present life, seeing his children at
school, his wife in more suitable surroundings—when suddenly came the war.*

.   .   .   .   .

I can't go on with this. And perhaps there's no need to.
Everybody will say to himself: "The Colonel went to the war,
and there wasn't room for those two women under the one
roof." Anybody but a donkey would guess that. But—and
this is more to the point—ought I to write about such recent
events, profiting by the fact that some of the people are already in their graves and others as good as in theirs? And this
business of taking models from real life? Models? No, if they
were merely models I shouldn't be so shaken by it all. Why
do I run off the rails again on a hopeless line of research?
The question is: have I the strength to write this or have I
not? I have!

September 16th.

For a few days past a cataclysm has been upon the house:
the wash! By the same token my wife is in a bad temper from
morning to evening, Kunda looks black as night, and Eva
cries. And I—I can't write, of course, and am furious in consequence. I even made a terrible scene, for I really do not see
why my writing-table should be a repository for soiled linen.
And why should it be for me to decide whether the laundress
ought to be given bread and butter or bread and jam? In my
opinion she should have cake and caviare and lobster mayon-
naise, but since I can afford neither the one nor the other, let
Zosia, who doesn't agree with me, decide for herself. Ergo:—

I have flung the washing out of my room, snubbed Zosia, slapped Eva, locked my door—and it profiteth me nothing. I can't possibly write with Zosia upset and Eva dissolving in tears. For ... I'm really in the wrong. What right have I to hold myself above the doings of my own household? I thought out my best short story once when I was cleaning my boots, so why can't I write this tale in the steam of the wash-tub? Or, for instance, under a railway-bridge if my house is too small for me? Why ever should that child's heart be afflicted and deprived of its sacred right to caresses? Well, well! I'll go and mollify Zosia and tell Eva a fairy-tale and give Kunda money to buy slippers and take the whole lot of them to the movies this evening.

... It didn't come off! They turned from me, looked despitefully upon me. Eva alone was magnanimous enough in the end to give me a kiss. Perhaps only because she is a child? Oh, well, let's get back to Asia and the steppe.

· · · · · ·

This farm of Marusia's had been her mother's marriage portion. It lay at the extreme edge of an oasis, and the life-giving network of waters reached it only with a meagre and elusive stream. The small stretch of chequered soil that was always in tillage lay along the banks of this stream, but the farm land included an enormous expanse of steppe that had never been ploughed all over. It was cultivated here and there, and was harvested if rain fell. The work of tillage was carried out by Barat, half tenant, half servant, steward if that was to his mind and if he was able to get his own way in spite of the sun and the spring floods. The farm buildings were extensive, to meet all contingencies that might arise. Wandering bands of mardakieri¹ arrived from time to time and leased a piece of the land, turning over half their harvest into the farm granaries. In the gamble with sun, steppe, people, and God, the big draw of a lucky year redeemed munificently the lean years of poverty. Then Barat's wagons wended their way to the town, beating out the track anew over the foundered wheel-ruts on the steppe. The Colonel recollected that, in addition to his many other belongings, he possessed this piece of land in the steppe, and now and again he bought fresh stock for his servant-tenant-steward. Then it left his mind. For him the farm was merely a reserve station, lying at the furthest base behind the front of life.

But the farm was the core of his children's ardent dreams and longings, a kingdom of every kind of fancy for those young hearts reaching out towards life. The one or two summers they had spent there with their mother had engraved in their souls the memory of a Paradise in which no tree was forbidden. And after her death the place was linked up with all their pining for the boundlessness of a mother's heart, which gives without measure and asks no return. There Marusia fled for shelter on her father's wedding day, and there the lad once escaped after being punished by his father. When Marusia decided, on the Colonel's departure for the front, to go there with the children, she met not the slightest opposition on their part.

Barat greeted them with grave dignity, and displayed no surprise at their arrival.

¹ Mardakier: (Sart) field labourer.

And now I too have my farm, to which I can escape until
it is reduced to ashes. If it depended on me, I should like to
exchange it for a desert in the heart of the naked steppe. But
one must keep oneself in hand. Tempers have a bad effect on
my pen. That passage ought to be far broader and stronger.
I'll change it sometime when I can sit down to work with less
loathing for the world. Or no! I won't change it at all. Let
the story have its bad tempers too. It's late, and I'm off to
bed. I'll go and kiss Zosia, so that everything may be in the
style of today's day.

September 17th.

Nonsense! Life has no style whatever! Zosia wasn't asleep,
and when I kissed her there was a great reconciliation. It's a
crazy world! A few seconds of harmony, and years of misunderstanding. When I'm affectionate, she's angry—and by
the time she's thought it over and grown tender, I have managed to get cross. And then comes just such a chance moment
when we are both in a mood of unwonted harmony. What
was so nice yesterday was that the affair passed over without
quarrel or sulkiness. In view of that reserved and, I may say,
systematic inflexibility of Zosia's character, it was a strange
and unprecedented phenomenon. She simply overwhelmed
me with a torrent of real kindness, to which I, of course, most
willingly responded—to confess today, old duffer that I am,
that I had no notion of such possibilities in my wife. And I
start off writing about people and flatter myself that I write
"with truth"! If in my "romances"—yes, romances, for the
bait to catch the swarms of the reading public must always

be a romance—if, then, in my romances—no, not romances! A romance is, as I have rightly said, the bait, but only the bait. The chief thing is the hook upon which they are caught and afterwards held. So—if in my creations—but how the devil can one write in such a piffling way about oneself! I shall soon be addressing myself as "maestro." I had better asseverate that I was—and am—a writer. To have let oneself be put off for ten years by one's nearest and dearest with false coin of heart and blood, only to discover later that she could have given a hundred times more! And worst of all, to be unable even to understand why it has happened so.

One detail struck me yesterday, it is true. When we began to talk in that extraordinary friendly way she asked me what it is I am writing now. I said that it was, as always, something from . . . from over there, from my captivity. A theme partly made up, partly based on my own and others' experiences. Of course I was lying. It is an absolute record. Then she declared at once that even if I was writing my "real" adventures, she didn't mind. Didn't I know that she had not the slightest claim on my years of imprisonment? Seeing that I had passed through so many "frightful things"—and here came a new attack of tenderness. I think she was lying too. But not so badly as I had done.

In any case she had some reason for asking. Either she has read by stealth the beginning of the story, or else my dear colleague, Felix, who is going to be Ignacy in my novel, keeps her informed as to my experiences as a prisoner. A queer fish! One would think him a close friend—oh, very much so! On every question at least he is of the same opinion as myself. And, as if that were not enough, he wants to have everything

in life that I have. Only he doesn't succeed. He's somehow
always too late with everything. Years ago, when I became
friendly with Zosia, he wanted to be her friend as well. He
was too late, as usual, for in the meantime I had managed
to become engaged to her. Before he had succeeded in falling
in love with her, she had become my wife. We went to the
war together, and together were taken prisoner, I from the
front and he from his hospital. During our captivity he followed me about like a shadow. I remember that we started to
make a collection of insects together. That is to say, together
and not together, for he never showed me his specimens. He
outdid me. It didn't matter, as I had left off bothering about
the grubs and things and had given my cases to a professor
from Tarnopol before he mustered up courage to come in
with his collection. He fell in love with Marusia, but had no
luck in that quarter. And today he is the friend of the
family. Oh, and he writes, too—but without success. I suppose that the man often dreams of wiping me off the face
of the earth. But before he makes up his mind to do it I
shall have died. And after my death he will go to the dogs.
Meanwhile he has become a habit, for by associating with
him I always know what it is that I no longer need. And
Zosia likes him, or perhaps she only says so to frighten me.
I ought not to call him Felix in the novel, so, as I said, I
shall call him Ignacy.

September 19th.

*Marusia had nevertheless some trouble in convincing Barat
that her sojourn with the children at the farm had a different*

significance now from what it had meant in the old days. The Sart was not altogether ignorant of the strife at home. He had heard this and that about the war and the Colonel's departure, and after listening to Marusia's frank but incomplete confession he understood what had brought her to the farm. But he could not understand the connexion between all that and the ardent desire to work shown by Marusia from the moment of her arrival.

"There's the horses," he explained to her kindly during one of their talks about the management of the farm. "If you like, you can go for rides along the river or out on the steppe or over to the bazaar. There's a gun for Jurek and a fishing-net. I'll buy a donkey for Irenka if you like. What is it you want, Marusia? God gave us a good harvest last year, there's enough and to spare. We shall have labourers coming to do the sowing, and there'll be the harvest again. Keep quiet and don't dream of working, or the Colonel will be angry when he comes home from the war."

"That's just what he won't be," objected Marusia. "Father can't bear idleness. And you know that I don't want to take anything from him. That's exactly why I came out here, Barat. Don't you understand? We shall be here goodness knows how long."

"Barynia! stay as long as you need to. I'll go and get some farm-hands in a week's time, and we'll have the land sown right down to the river."

"But that's not what I mean! Each of us must have work to do apart from that. Jurek must take charge of those fields near the aryk. Irenka must look after the garden and I . . . I'll help you in everything."

"*Very good, barynia, very good! As you like,*" consented
the Sart.

But next day he gave the lad a gun and showed him the
pheasant coverts and took Irenka down to the meadows by
the stream. He himself escaped from Marusia into the fields
and toiled there till dusk. After listening, in the evening, to
her reproaches, he got out a plough and worked till late at
night.

After a few repetitions of this, Marusia realized that it
left her nowhere, and she made up her mind to act differently. She spoke sharply to the children and gave them definite work to do, reserving for herself the hardest untilled
field, and trying besides to forestall Barat in every job about
the farm. The Sart suffered in silence all one day and the
next, then spent a few days walking about, observing,
musing, and shaking his head; at last he came to Marusia
and asked her straight out what were her orders for him and
what was to happen in the oncoming summer.

Delighted at her victory, the girl settled that next day,
after getting through the usual work about the house, they
should ride round the entire property and decide what was
to be done and how to do it. At his ardent request she took
her brother with them.

But she came near to drawing back helpless when, out
upon the fields, she tried to look at them with the eye of a
husbandman. The huge expanse of untilled land intimidated
her. What did it matter that everything, on all sides as far
as eye could reach, was "*ours*" or nobody's, since "*our*" hands
could barely suffice for the orchard surrounding the homestead and for the adjacent fields? The deeper they penetrated

into the steppe, the further they rode along their boundaries, the greater grew the fear in her heart that she had undertaken a task beyond her strength. She began to understand her father's indifference towards the farm, and the resigned "if it please God!" of Barat. But the boy's eyes glowed with pride and eagerness as his gaze ran over the vast circle of the steppe. He reckoned up, measured out, wove far-reaching plans that embraced the no-man's land and dragged in the wildest thickets, for he had even thought over these already and had decided to make use of them. Marusia looked at him with astonishment, with a certain quiet rapture. Usually silent and reserved, here he was talkative, excited, speaking straight from the heart with all the disarming simplicity of youthful faith and conviction.

Compliant in spite of herself and for love of the boy, Marusia consented to prolong their ride till late afternoon, and raised no objection when on one of the river meadows he begged that their grand day might be celebrated by an open-air supper. The moment she gave her consent he galloped off to the farm for Irenka, a kettle, and provisions.

"He's a hero, your Jurek!" cried Barat, as the lad vanished through the bulrushes. "There's a farmer for you! The steppe likes that sort!"

"But he's so young," sighed Marusia. "Only fifteen. He ought to be at school."

"Well, that's all right. When your father comes home he'll go and get his schooling and then he'll come back here."

"There's no knowing. You see, Barat, Father wants to sell the farm. We are to go to Poland."

"He'll go to Poland and come back again. Tell your father

*not to sell the farm. The steppe will wait, and nothing will
change here."*

*Marusia made no answer. Her mind was strangely divided
between the Poland she had never seen, where they were to
go, and this steppe, which would wait on and on and know
no change. She suddenly felt a longing to make no altera-
tions at the farm. Let the years go by and let it go on for ever
the same. Some one belonging to her, or she herself, would
always find peace and shelter there.*

*"I like this place, Barat!" she whispered, her eyes wander-
ing over the meadow. "I'm glad we are going to spend the
evening here."*

*"Ah, Khozaika! Your mother loved this place too. But
Jurek seems to be coming back!" He bent to catch a distant
crackling among the reeds.*

"What! Already?"

"Here he is! don't you hear him? He's in a hurry."

*The crackling changed to the sound of rushes trodden
down at a gallop, then the water boiled up beneath a horse,
and Jurek appeared on the meadow, riding like the wind.*

"What's up, Jurek?" called the girl.

"Men coming to the farm!" he panted.

"Men? What men?"

*"I don't know! a soldier with a bayonet and two men be-
sides."*

"Didn't you speak to them?"

"No! I just saw them on the road and tore back for you!"

*"How extraordinary! . . . a soldier?" replied Marusia.
"Oh, it's those prisoners, for sure. Oh, you tiresome boy! You
ought to have taken them up to the house. Well, there's no*

help for it, we must go home." She got on her horse and turned sideways through the marsh, anxious to catch up with the strangers before they reached the farm.

At the place where the road took its last curve towards the homestead, they came suddenly out of the rushes and almost rode down three men toiling on foot along the track. The meeting was so unexpected that riders and pedestrians came to a halt, gazing at each other in astonishment.

Only now did the girl understand her brother's excitement. These men formed upon the background of the steppe a picture so inconceivably alien that it stabbed the eyes. In front a solitary soldier in war kit, and behind, two men in close-fitting clothing of singular cut, with figures and gestures that were somehow odd. From their faces, grey with dust, eyes arrogantly curious and importunate were fixed upon her.

Without knowing why she pulled back her horse till she was on a line with Barat and Jurek.

"You people," the soldier's voice made her jump. "Are you from the farm?"

Nobody answered.

"Well, you!—are you deaf? is that your farm?"

"Yes!" she said, through her clenched teeth. "I—I—the farm is mine."

"Well, thank God! I've brought you your prisoners, barynia. Take them up to the house, for—by God!—my gentlemen are done for."

She recovered herself, and noticed that the men were bent double by the weight of huge bundles on their backs. She remembered that, on that sultry day, they must have come

over an enormous track of the steppe without a roof or a
tree or a well. She saw the thick layer of dust on their clothes
and hands and faces.

Following her heart's instinct without a moment's reflection, she drew near them.

"Please—please!" she said kindly—"it's not far. Please
take off your packs, we can put them on the horses . . .
please!" she encouraged them with gesture and word and
smile.

The strangers looked at one another and then again at the
girl.

"Merci," said one of them.

And then the bent figures quivered, straightened up, and
dusty hands were raised to foreheads to make her a short
and barely perceptible salute.

But that salute acted on Marusia like a thunderbolt.

.   .   .   .   .

And there's the drama begun.   After coming to grief over
the stepmother's mediation, the devil from beyond seas ap-
proaches the girl under a new form foisted upon him by the
demon of war.   The man he uses will think, feel, act independently, commit consciously a hundred good deeds, and
once will sin unwittingly. And by that once will destroy
everything and . . . escape. But the girl . . .

September 20th.

I've had another scene with Zosia. The cause: those unlucky five-o'clocks. Not so much a cause as another move
in the game of blind man's buff we have been playing against
each other ever since my return from captivity.

Let's recollect:—when I turned up after several years, stripped and down and out, she welcomed me affectionately. Oh, yes! without reservation, affectionately. If, at the same time, she shed tears over herself too—well, she's a woman. But after that affectionate greeting she took me under observation. She had to swallow a pill at once, when I refused to take over my uncle's business. Nevertheless, she defended me fiercely against the attacks of my family.

When, shortly afterwards, I went into a government office, she said that she did not understand me but that she was not going to interfere with my affairs. Nonetheless she read my first literary scribblings attentively and could not contain her impatience to know the end of the story. When my first book came out the fabulous activity and energy she displayed were invaluable. It was the same with the second. She fitted me up a study in which I feel rather uncomfortable, and subscribed to papers which I do not read. The most difficult moment came later on: she couldn't help noticing that though I pass for a man of letters and write "sublime things," I have nevertheless the tastes of an ordinary fellow descended from a poor but honest family and a *milieu* of a like kind. She resigned herself to that, for when all's said and done she does care for me. And now she is fighting for appearances or illusions—God knows! Truth to tell, I don't wonder at her. As she hasn't many illusions left, she wants to console herself at least with the illusions of others. A grievous fate! For a year she was the wife of an absolvent of law,[1] for six years in mourning for a war prisoner, half a year sick nurse to a

---

[1] Absolvent: a law-student who has passed out of the University but has still to pass a Government examination to get his diploma.

repatriated man, and the following two years caretaker of a budding author. She's had enough of it and is now pining for some life. And I do nothing to help. It's always "Really, Zosia dear," or "I haven't time, Zosienka."

To return to those "five-o'clocks." Our house, it appears, has got to become a centre for "eminent" people. *Wie heisst?* Our house has not yet become a centre for the four people living in it, and these "eminent" ones are the circle of mannequins called today, rightly if beyond expression miserably, the "working intelligentsia." This original epithet doubtless means that the "intelligentsia" darns socks, cleans saucepans, develops hæmorrhoids on office stools—and sighs for the days when the "intelligentsia" was not a "working" one, but created something or other. By what rhyme or reason should our house become a centre for these poor devils? The lame vagabond who sells cigarettes opposite my window interests me a hundred times more than all that Parnassus with its worn-out brains. Corpses, damn it, the whole lot of them!

In spite of which I consented to a tea-party for the corpses, and even promised Zosia to be entertaining. And I was. I talked like a mill-wheel, kept them all there till the right moment, and then got them properly tight.

It was no common spectacle! Professor Klapa, very much on, sang—yes, sang something about "one (?) white breast" to the editor's wife. The editor—I swear it—twice forgot himself with our deaf Kunda. The priest-orientalist gabbled incomprehensible things. Weird shudders passed through the statuesque Klaponcia. They ate without blinking the supper sent in from a restaurant. And at last they all started singing in chorus "The Water Drips in the Well," with great unanimity and heartiness and with no less great lack of harmony (Felix sang "seconds"). They would have stayed till morning if I had not run away to Eva, who was awakened by this chorale. As it was, they left at midnight. Felix was the last to go, holding it fitting, as the friend of the family, to linger a moment and assure us that "our" evening had been a success.

They are all furious with me today, no doubt, after getting up and thinking it over. Looking at Zosia's set face this morning, I had a foretaste of what they are feeling. I descended to greater depths of iniquity when, hoping to avoid her bad temper, I declared casually that though our evening had been a real success, it was not yet quite "it." Another time we would have, not a "five-o'clock," but an "orgy" beginning at 11 p. m. That was what ought to issue from us, and not any kind of *blasé* "five-o'clock." She looked at me somewhat incredulously, but it was evident that the shot struck home and rankled. She has something to think over for a week now, and I shall have peace. But how long is this game to last, and is there no other way to it?

Aha! something else. Kunda has asked me who the nice gentleman was in the light waistcoat, that sang so beautifully. I advised her to go and get shriven at once, for he has a wife and five children. For the first time since we have had her in the house she looked upon me with a baleful eye.

September 21st.

I may be wrong, but I have an idea that Zosia cries of nights. A moment ago a faint—a very faint—sob reached me from her room. And not for the first time. I can't catch her at it, for every time I go near her bed she pretends to be asleep, and that puts my back up. In the face of that pretence all my heartfelt intentions go for nothing. I come back to my pen and—I can't set to work again. For here, close beside me, is being spun a thread of suffering which I am powerless to prevent. These mysterious sobs alarm me. I tremble before the faint sighs that besiege me of nights. And not only from my wife's room. My little girl sometimes sighs in her sleep as though a mountain-load of grief were falling from her heart; and that Kunda of ours, besides, wanders about the kitchen till all hours like a ghost. I haven't yet managed to plumb the depths of the sufferings I am depicting here, and already fresh sorrow is drawing near me from every side. In a day or two I shall shake it off, not listen, forget—until some thunderbolt falls and rends me asunder. For I cannot prevent everything, even if I would.

Even if I would. And I should try in vain. Zosia will have her cry out and wake up in the morning and start thinking about something or other—say, about the "orgy." Eva will pull the fur off her new Teddy, and Kunda will run to market and get her bosom friend to come and have "just one"—at my expense, of course. And I shall go to the office and work till dinner-time.

That office is my second fortress, after my writing-table—and who knows if it isn't the safer of the two? When I get there and open the first envelope containing an official document, I at once fall under that mystic influence of the paragraph which hypnotizes me all through office hours. When I'm reading these things I seem to see the interior of an enormous cellar draped with a pall. In the middle, behind a catafalque in which, during office hours, repose the souls, hearts, and brains of all the officials and "functionaries" of this august Republic, the masked Grand Master of the official lodge sits and writes. From time to time he strikes a gong and hands a roll of papers to other lesser masters, who run off to smaller cellars, make of this roll a dozen smaller rolls, and deal them out to the brethren. The brethren make the dozen into a dozen dozen and take them out, by paths entangled in the twisted prevarications of the paragraph, to gates opening upon the four corners of the earth. There await them porters of the fourth degree of pay.

At one of the gates I see our Mr. Michal, with his twenty years of service, his medium-sized family, and his copper cross of merit. The solemn emotion depicted on his face is undisturbed by the thought as to whether the next rise in prices will take into consideration his love for pigs' trotters. At a given moment the doors open noiselessly, and Michal receives an official packet. Or he doesn't. In that case he comes to me and announces spitefully, though he may be carrying a sheaf of private correspondence: "Nothing today" —or, with sympathy, "Nothing ministerial again!" and hurries away.

But when he brings in stuff of the more important kind, he stands silent behind me till I open it. That unrelenting shadow at the back of my neck used to make me wild. I tried various ways of getting rid of him. Once, for instance, I sprang up delightedly, shook hands with him, and said "I congratulate you! At last they have granted us credit for a dynamocompensator!" The joke missed fire, for Michal ac-

cepted the congratulations with dignity and stood by longer
than usual at the opening of the post next day.

I've got used to him by now, and to a good many other
things as well. I pass for a model Government official. And
that is no irony of fate. I appreciate my office's good points.
First and foremost, for six hours a day no one has any right
to me—except the law itself. This gives me a god-like feeling
of independence which I experienced only once before in my
life—when I lay in prison.

. . . .

*When Tadeusz [that's myself] was sent into the steppe
for army work he did not rage or complain, as others did. He
had learnt much from his war experiences. The hurricane
which had flung him so many times to the ground to cast him
up again upon some unknown shore could now startle him no
longer. The first harbinger of disaster had been the Austrian
mobilization order. A slip of paper had come, and he, a Pole,
an absolvent, the father of a family, a citizen, an active member of society, had become nothing in the twinkling of an eye.
Or so it seemed to him, at least, when, wept over by wife and
family, he pulled on the uniform of a cadet of an army he
despised. He went to the front with a storm in his heart, a
storm that went on raging as long as, allotted to a field hospital behind the line, he listened to the groans of men ripped
up by bullets. But when the cannon thunder out-muttered
these, when he was hurled, in command of a company, into
one battle after another, he felt he was something again, came
to grips with the Moloch of war, fraternized with bullets,
with entrenchments, with the rattle of flying shrapnel. A star
dropped upon his collar, and on his breast a cross, another*

cross; but he did not ask whence they came or why, taking it all for granted.

Till one day a shell, bursting in the hut where he was quartered for the night with his men, decorated his breast with a new ribbon of bright blood. Cossacks came galloping, rounded up the living and wounded—and again he felt himself to be nothing. Or so it seemed to him, at least, when he dropped from the shoulders of a lousy Cossack upon the muddied floor of the last Podlasie field-hospital, and when a field surgeon raked his chest with a weeding-knife in the hope of extracting a fragment of iron from between his shattered ribs. Gangrene, or at best inflammation of the lungs, menaced him for a certainty; but he did not care, though his heart ached because he was nothing.

In spite of that, he journeyed a few months later, patched up and well, to the Turkestan steppe with the first batch of prisoners. On the way he endured misery that surpassed his conception, and on arrival saw a world that surpassed his dreams. That was something again—he felt sure of it.

Longing for the new something to appear as quickly as possible, he scorned his officer's rank, with the pay and confinement it involved, and was one of the first to enter his name for army work. His friend and inseparable comrade, Ensign Ignacy [this is Felix], did likewise. They were sent, with the company of prisoners allotted to them, to a place near the town to work at repairing a neglected highroad.

But this time fate did him an ill turn. He soon grasped the real meaning of the primitive toil, and, perceiving that the repaired road would continue to be, as heretofore, useless, he lost all interest in the work. And he then gave his mind to the fellow-sufferers that had been entrusted to his charge, using his slight authority to win back for them some part at least of the gifts of life now withheld from them. He got permission to build separate huts instead of the hateful barracks where they all lived in common; he provided a doctor, set up a canteen, and began to think about games and amusements.

These attempts, however, led to nothing. The camp was a core of the rancorous suffering, dumb or stupefied, of men hurled by force beyond the parentheses of life. Behind the barrier built against the world by their misery and abnegation lay an abyss of pain that aimed its shafts at heaven. Whoever knocked at that wall turned away horrified and impotent before the muttering of angry regret that reached his ears.

Clandestine rambles towards the rim of the steppe that lay near the camp became his only distraction from mournful monotony of their colourless life. That vast tome of earth lying open yet unattainable before him held an inconceivable force to attract him. Gazing at the strings of caravans winding over the steppe, at the flocks of birds in flight, at the procession of the storm-winds driving before them walls and pillars of dust, he was filled with undefined longing, the longing for some fresh turn of fortune which should lead him across the trail of new and untasted experience.

When, with the spring, the steppe teemed with the full spell of its hidden strength, he could resist no longer. He went back to the camp in the town and asked to be allotted to farm work. Ignacy, his inseparable pal, went with him. At their request they were sent to the furthest border of the riverside settlements to be disposed of by the district volostny.

When he found himself, after a day's railway journey, on the highway of the steppe, he did not regret the expedition. Upon that broad road the stream of life pulsed free, unchecked, inexhaustible. He did not yield to this victorious metamorphosis at once. "The war . . . the war," he reiterated stubbornly, marching with the measured stride of the soldier. "That's nothing . . . nothing," sang the native carter as his wagon tacked from side to side of the road. "That's nothing," laughed the dust stirred up by flocks of sheep and strings of camels. "They will destroy you, ride over you, raze you to the ground," he persisted, as he passed villages and bazaars. "That's nothing! we shall come through everything!" the waste places of the steppe made answer.

At last they turned off the highway and came by the ruts of a side trail to the volostny who was to solve the question of their further allocation. Overwhelmed with fatigue, and dazed with the flood of impressions, he flung himself for sleep upon a hayrick, and was thankful on the morrow that the question of their assignment dragged itself out till noon.

After dinner he started on the last lap of his journey, his mind empty of all thought, all opposition. The argument of this endless march across the steppe, now almost monotonous in its bareness, utterly overpowered him. And when he reached the farm he was without the strength even to reflect upon the amazing finale of their wanderings—the meeting with that Amazon mistress of the farm.

.   .   .   .   .

It could hardly be shorter. I feel recriminations in the air for not having burrowed into the depths of psychological research, for not illuminating the subtle transformations and

invisible springs, of my hero's soul, for having hewn him in
the rough as if I were portraying an American Indian. Where
is the motherland, where the nationalist drama in the soul
of Tadeusz—where are the yearning for home and family,
the myriad shudders of the wrung heart and mind, where
those mists of ideals that composed the interesting "psyche"
of the pre-war generation? They all had their being, passed
and fell silent before the might of war and the might of man
fighting for his fate.

September 25th.

The day before yesterday we gave an "orgy." It was a
magnificent success, only the other way round. Zosia, who
had been for three days beforehand in a state of high nervous
tension, arranged the salon after her own heart. Vases, flowers, curtains. On the day of the ceremony she asked me at
noon about the menu. And I: "Take away the flowers, take
out all the lumber, and buy a dozen salted cucumbers. Put a
sofa along the wall, and a big bottle of vodka on the table.
We live in an era of thrills." Her curiosity was aroused,
though she shrugged her shoulders. She cleared the salon
almost entirely, and bought the cucumbers and a few other
things besides. But that can't be helped—she always must
cheat me, if it's ever so little. In spite of that our big room
looked quite jolly and was really suitable for a greater
occasion.

All our guests turned up punctually at eleven o'clock with
the people they had brought with them. Klapa, Klaponcia,
the turbid Felix, the exotic padre, a woman engineer, a sculp-

tress, and a few more whom I don't remember. Some of them
greeted us with dignity, others with malignity. Felix kissed
Zosia's hand with ostentatious respect. And after standing
for a quarter of an hour between the sofa and the table, our
guests finally sat down at the table. The woman engineer
drank a glass of vodka—well, why not? They waited till
midnight for somebody to muster up the courage to make a
beast of himself. The chief hopes in this direction were
founded upon me. And I did nothing.

At about one o'clock Klaponcia began to twist restlessly
in her chair, and Klapa went off on the ministerial crisis. I
can't say whether it was she who first began to twist or he to
talk. All the same his "firstly," "secondly," and "thirdly"
is awful. What an idiot! Does he suppose that each one of
us has not his own "firstly," "tenthly," "hundredthly," and
sits quiet for that very reason? Felix spoke after Klapa,
burbling things of incredible highmindedness. I heard him
with a certain emotion, for he reminded me of those youthful
days when we gathered in apostolic catacombs to listen to
lectures about alcohol poisoning the system, or love being a
symbiosis of angels.

No one had the courage to whisper a word after his bal-
samic tirade, still less to reach out for the vodka. The "orgy"
was over, and our guests took leave of us affectionately. Felix
shook me warmly by the hand and looked into my eyes
with sympathy. He must have read something unpleasant in
them, for he was smitten with sudden embarrassment and
sneaked off without even saying good-bye to Zosia.

Apart from that—what a queer handshake is Klaponcia's.
First she gives you her hand without any expression, and

then, just when you expect her to withdraw it, she adds two or three totally unexpected quivers. You can't catch the look in her eyes just then, for they are downcast. A woman out of the ordinary. She impresses me as going through life in a somnambulistic sleep, lulled by the hospital where she works and by Klapa's conversation. She passes for a pedestal of virtue. But what will happen when some one calls her by her name?

I really must note down my conversation with Zosia, which surpassed all my expectations: "Are you satisfied?" I asked her as I closed the door upon the last parting guest. And lo and behold, she wasn't in the least angry, but only looked at me thoughtfully. "Tell me, Stach," she said, "what it is you are really after?"—"I don't know, Zosia. It's just that—I don't know, and I wish I did."—"But it seems to me that you do know, only you won't tell. You're simply making fun of us all."

She wasn't right. I . . . really, I don't yet know what I want and what I am after. That's little enough, it's true, for a man who is a boy no longer and has been through a good deal in his life—but it's always more than that Klapesque "firstly," "secondly."

Zosia had a warm heart for me that night.

September 26th.

I can't come to myself after that unsuccessful orgy. This morning I woke up in a bad temper, and in consequence I upset everybody at breakfast and quarrelled with my chief at the office. In the afternoon I went to my little son's grave at the cemetery. He died before he could say "Daddy."

There won't be another one . . . because . . . well, Zosia
doesn't want to have any more children. My son had clear
eyes with a fearless gaze in them, and I miss them all my
life. My little knight is gone. There will be nobody to say:
" 'Tention! Keep on, old man!" Nothing is left of him but
a mound of earth to which, once a year, I come with clenched
fists.

But it's a great difference when, instead of the eyes of a
child, it is a tomb that reconciles you with life.

Oh, my son!

．　　　．　　　．　　　．　　　．

*Marusia's amazement at the sight of the prisoners brought
upon her a confusion of soul that she could not master.
Speeding on ahead to the farm, she hurriedly prepared
Irenka to meet them and took shelter in her room. And later,
when the travellers arrived at the house, she called in her
brother and Barat and told them to get supper for the strangers and make arrangements for them to sleep in the loft. If
anything was wanting, they must be asked to excuse it. No
warning of their arrival had been sent to the farm. It would
be all right tomorrow. She couldn't see to them herself, the
heat had knocked her out. She didn't feel well—perhaps she
was in for a bout of fever. No, she didn't want any supper
and was going to bed.*

*She did actually feel a painful pressure at her temples, and
her heart fluttered in a restless rhythm. She lay down on the
bed and tried to go to sleep, or at least to calm the inexplicable chaos of her thoughts. Meanwhile the farm rang with
various echoes as never before.*

It was only after supper had been prepared and served in

the adjoining room that silence fell. The soldier still made an effort to talk, but, getting no answers, he too dropped silent. "They must be very tired," she thought, with the picture of them at the moment of meeting in her mind's eye. "Oh, yes, dreadfully tired. And how sort of strange they are! I wish they would go to bed." She moved restlessly on her couch. The presence of strangers, such utter strangers, so close at hand oppressed her unendurably. It had been the same, years before, when her stepmother came into their house. She remembered with alarm that these men would stay a long time—perhaps as long as herself. But this time it was her own fault.

"You're doing a crazy thing, girl!" She remembered the words of the parish priest. "Crazy!"

But whoever could have foreseen that the prisoners were going to turn out like that? There had been so many labourers on the farm. . . .

There were sounds of benches being pushed back from the table in the next room, and the heavy steps of men going out.

"At last!" she sighed with relief. If only nobody came to disturb her!

Nobody came. Her brother called through the door to ask if she needed anything. She did not answer. Let him suppose her asleep.

But people were a long time turning in that evening at the farm. Someone came in several times and climbed the ladder to the loft. The prisoners, no doubt. Somebody went out to the cow-shed. That would be Barat. . . . Next door, the children were talking in whispers. Suddenly the dog barked and ran about the yard. Silence. The pigeons on the roof stirred . . . and a door creaked somewhere. That must be the wind. . . . Silence. . . . Silence. She got off the bed, and went on tiptoe to the window, opened it wide. A broad strip of spring night invaded the room, carrying with it the diamond-studded sky, the smell of the blossoming earth, echoes of far-off sounds.

She sprang back from the window. The impression that someone strange and unexpected was breaking in upon her, to catch her in the very act of loneliness, was again with her. But only for a moment. This time the uninvited guest was known and dear, though perhaps too little valued in the fire of everyday matters. Reassured, she smiled with all her heart. As she leaned again from the window, an irresistible longing surged in her to go out into the open. All the more, that she had neglected, for the first time since her arrival, her evening inspection of the farmstead.

She jumped through the window, so as not to awaken the children sleeping close at hand, and called very softly to Barbos, the fierce mongrel watch-dog. He crept quietly out from behind the corner of the house, slowly wagging his rough tail, rubbed, as was his habit, his broad head against her knees, ran round her once or twice, and then, sniffing at the air, went off to the majdan. The girl ran after him, drawing deep breaths. The fatigue, the unrest, and that unbearable oppression which had been upon her all the evening gradually yielded before the safe and healing calm reigning over the farm.

From the middle of the majdan she glanced over the farmstead. It looked different from usual in the dusk of night,

lighted on one side by the moon's rays. Different—and somehow nearer. If one took in everything, the farm was really
very large.

The house, the barns . . . the granaries and the lumber-
shed . . . the cattle-byres . . . another granary, more byres.
And those huts too. What did it matter that a couple of
strange men had come? There would be room for them. They
simply wouldn't be noticed. One could stroll about here all
day and meet nobody. . . . While as for the steppe!

She gazed at the steppe through the broad chink between
the house and the farmyard wall. It looked like a silver plat-
ter graven by a burin of moonlight into the most intricate pat-
terns. The last streak of evening mist was drifting towards
the river. Far away, the wall of rushes made a line of darkness, beyond which the distance merged into the sky. Two
stacks of last year's hay stood out black at some distance
from the farm. Go over to them, perhaps? Why not? It was
so lovely on the steppe. Lovelier than it had ever been.

Halfway to the ricks she noticed that Barbos had grown
alert and restless. Had the sheep broken out of the fold to
tear at the ricks by night?

"S-s-s! Barbos!" she urged him on. "Fetch him out!
Barbos!"

The dog lifted his nose, sniffed the air, and barking—
softly and not in anger—ran up to one of the ricks.

She redoubled her steps, ran round the rick, but saw nobody. She was looking at Barbos again when suddenly men's
voices floated down to her from above. Startled, she caught at
the dog's collar, pulled him to heel, and instinctively pressed

*against the wall of hay. With bated breath she stood trem-
bling, without even trying to think who could be hiding on
the rick at night.*

*For a moment, hearing nothing, she thought it had been
her fancy. But no! Someone was speaking again. That low
voice . . . a strange voice—no, not strange. It wasn't Barat.
But, of course—she had heard that voice in the road today.
The prisoners! But what were they speaking? . . . Why
. . . why, they were speaking Polish! And so oddly, so
differently—oh! that was how her stepmother spoke!*

*A new wave of alarm, this time deeper and more painful,
mastered her. Rooted to the spot, she did not know whether
to run away, to press still closer against the rick, or to sink
into the earth. Meanwhile from overhead fell, one after another and more and more distinctly, words that seemed foreign and beyond her comprehension, and yet were full of a
painful meaning that wounded her.*

"Yes, Ignacy," rang a low voice, "there's something in it."

"I don't know what you mean."

*"Nor do I. But there is something about this farm! When
I saw those three barring the road, by God, I thought I
was dreaming!"*

"Yes, it was a splendid picture."

*"A picture! Rot! It was a whole fairy story. That old Sart
and that plucky lad. And most of all that beautiful girl.
. . . She didn't look like the people hereabouts. The whole
thing's most unusual! I tell you, it can't be just an ordinary
farm."*

*"Oh, well! you're always on the look-out for something
extraordinary. Lucky chap! How quickly you get over things!*

You were swearing at the whole place and that awful tramp of ours only a minute ago."

"Exactly. And now I'm all right. Did you ever see such stars, Ignacy? Or hear such silence?"

"Rather. You said just the same near Lublin, in the trenches."

"You idiot! Trenches are trenches, and the steppe's the steppe. These stars are finer. And above all—that girl at the farm! She has a sad sort of look in her eyes. I say! I believe there's something moving about under the rick."

"Aha!"

Marusia turned cold. Barbos began to rout in the hay. She tugged at his collar with all her might, desperately. These people must not notice her for anything in the world. Meanwhile the dog set up a mournful howl.

"Why that's our friend Barbos!" called a gay voice from above. "He's up against something, poor chap. What's the matter with him?"—The shadow of a man leaned over Marusia.

"Barbos! What the devil? There's somebody with him. I'm going to get down, Ignacy!"

And someone slid down the rick, dropping on his feet close beside the girl.

"Ah! Pardon!" he sprang back amazed on seeing her face.

"It doesn't matter. . . . I beg your pardon . . ." whispered the girl with quivering lips.

"What did you say?" almost shouted the prisoner.

"I beg your pardon. It's just an accident . . ." she repeated faintly.

"Why! do you speak Polish?"

"Yes. I am Polish."

"Good God!" cried the prisoner, his voice shaking with excitement. "Ignacy! Do you hear?"

"No, no!" she said hurriedly. "Don't! I'm going. It was just by accident! I couldn't know. I'm going . . . good night." She turned hastily away, anxious not to meet the gaze of the other prisoner, now climbing down from the rick.

Quickening her pace almost to a run, she reached her window. Shame, alarm, and some kind of boundless sorrow gripped her by the throat. Pressed into a corner of her room she glanced out, through eyes brimming with tears, to where the steppe lay drunken with the ecstasy of the spring night.

* * * * *

Today I read through my story carefully from the beginning, and it amazed me to see how far I had wandered from the reality. It's more or less true as to the facts. But the character painting of the people? I'm dashing them in as if the roof were burning over them. They haven't exchanged more than a couple of words yet, and something is already afoot. And where is that famous pre-war prattle which used to envelop every spark of inner fire like a cloud of smoke? My God! What a lot I talked to that girl before she ever shed a tear. And it used to drive me wild, for I had to drag every word out of her—she wasn't the talkative kind.

Luckily, abbreviations are the fashion of the day, and the public likes the *meritum* of a thing. For instance, that couple I once overheard in a public garden. "Hela, may I ask you something?" (He was holding her hand, perhaps had his arm round her.)—"No, certainly not!" (I think she squeezed

closer to him here.) —"Because, Hela, I . . ."—"Sh! don't!"
—"Well, what, then?"—"Nothing!" (Here they kissed.) —
"So you won't marry me?"—"Why not?"—And off they
went to the pictures. Not to Wawel,[1] as it used to be *illo
tempore*. Times have changed.

After saying all this, I feel a trifle ashamed to confess what
happened this afternoon. A silly business! Klapa asked me to
call on him to look at some curio he's just bought. I went,
for he is a connoisseur and knows how to pick up a good
thing, though you'd never suspect it. He goes and spends
his last penny on it, and I like him for that. It's the only
thing I do like him for.

So I went and found Klaponcia at home alone. I ought
really to have made my bow and gone away slightly offended.
But our nature is so brutish that when a man finds a woman
alone at home he somehow clings on, though there's no rhyme
or reason in it.

She received me in her husband's study and said he would
be "back directly." As usual, she was dressed in something
dark fastened up to her throat, her hair brushed very
smooth but charmingly done. She kept her arms pressed
against her body—in general, her slender figure looks as if
it were bound with ropes. Her legs, unusually strongly developed, are the only restless part of her silhouette. And
their movements are such that they seem to be endeavouring
to free her from her bonds.

We began to talk about something or other—or, of course,
it was about her hospital. That is, I listened while she drawled
out that measured sweetness which might sicken not only the

[1] Wawel (Vavel) is the hill in Cracow where stand the old Polish royal
palace and the Cathedral in which the kings are buried.

hospital but heaven above. Nevertheless, I listened politely, held by the hidden life of her feet.

Growing impatient at last, I steered the conversation to old times, to our youth, to our school days . . . then to an excursion we all made once together to the Beskidy Mountains. And I remembered an incident that befell me there.

In a clearing of the forest where we bivouacked for some days, we were playing at ball. Klaponcia was then a slender, undeveloped girl, let out of her home for the excursion under the care of the "absolvent" Klapa. We respected him for his learning, and for his use, even then, of "firstly," "secondly," but he was often a laughing-stock for being such a dunderhead. I was the worst of the whole crowd of us, and Klaponcia (or, as she was then called, Lala) often said to me: "You're a wretch! I can't bear you!"

It happened that during the game Lala ran away with the ball and I tried to snatch it from her. She put up such a stubborn defence that I had to catch her by the ankle and throw her, and we both fell down. But she still clung to the ball. I got her by the wrists and pulled her hands apart, crying "Surrender!" And at that moment her resistance completely vanished, the ball dropped from her clenched hand, her pale face burned like fire, and her eyes, filled with an eerie light, stabbed me. "I surrender," she whispered with a strange smile. But I, all out of breath as I was, turned so sheepish that I jumped up and ran off to fetch her some water, and before I got back Klapa, by this time a Professor, had taken her under his wing.

As the devil would have it, I brought that game of ball into our talk *en passant,* and asked her if she remembered our fight in the meadow. She made no answer. I reiterated my question and saw that same glow begin to flood her face. Her downcast eyes lifted and gazed at me in a kind of crazy wonder. This lasted an immeasurable time, and then she got up suddenly and went out of the room. I ran after her, I wanted to apologize, I caught her by the arm ... and together with the arm she leant her whole figure towards me. I saw her half-closed eyes, and parted lips. . . . Oh, the devil! To hell with this exactness of description!—for just then a key grated in the door—Klapa, who, if he were not Klapa, ought to have turned to stone at the sight of us.

We examined the curio—from the front, from the side, from the back, from every angle. I have never been so nice to Klapa before. And he simply thawed. He said that he had had an odd liking for me these many years past. I had to promise him to call on them oftener.

And what am I to do with these people now?

October 1st.

I have sometimes noticed that exceptional events awake unexpected echoes—or perhaps they hunt in couples.

For Felix has just been asking me what I should do if I fell in love, "not without a return of the feeling," with a married woman. Good old burbler! He put this question, no doubt, because when I got home yesterday I found him with Zosia in a state of high-minded excitement. Zosia was also a little flushed, it is true. Well, no matter.

I answered that the thing was impossible. "Why?" he asked with an incredulous smile.—"Because I haven't time."

—Felix was thunderstruck—"What?"—"It's perfectly true. I get up at eight. I'm in the office by nine, and my staff.there consists of old maids—and I come home at three. Dinner and a game with the kid, till four. Then I snooze till five. After that I'm at the publisher's till seven or else have a meeting. At eight I sup and spend half an hour with my wife, and from then on I write for all I'm worth. On Sunday morning, proof-reading; Sunday afternoon, sport or visits. I could, at a pinch, be in love on Mondays and Fridays, between 7 and 8 p. m., because those days I don't have the publishers or meetings. Alas! I fear there is no woman, however wise and noble, who would adjust herself to that."

Poor Felix! I've given him a hard nut to crack! He's sitting at home now and wondering whether I was pulling his leg or whether I really oughtn't to make a change in my time-table.

Poor Felix! If only someone would really look after him, he wouldn't be so unhappy. But I . . . haven't the time. And Zosia! . . . *tant pis!*—he's too late. She's my wife!

.   .   .   .   .

Day was breaking. Buried deep in hay, Tadeusz opened his eyes and, seeing above him a vault of rose-flushed sky, shut them quickly. Then through half-closed lids he made a careful investigation of his surroundings. He noticed a dried grass stem that hung from his forehead. Beside it was another, and another—altogether a whole bundle of hay. But above the stems and mixed up with them was the sky. . . . Pink overhead . . . and gold further down. . . . The east. . . . Now he could see the sun's rim. And to the left, something like a sheet of early mist. And those black specks, trailing aslant above the rick, were birds. Duck—wild duck!

"Oh, how jolly!" he smiled, spreading himself on the rick. *"No barracks,"* he thought with boyish delight—*"no imprisonment, no war, no war! No soldiers, no anybody!"* he asserted joyously, raising his head. *"Damn it, there is somebody!"*—he pished impatiently at the sound of snoring close at hand. He looked round crossly, and burst out laughing.

"Ignacy!"—he shouted into his sleeping comrade's ear. *"Come out of that, you old bull!"*

"What's up?" in consternation.

"Nothing! Rub your eyes and look! Have you ever seen the like of it?"—he waved his arm towards the expanse of steppe before them.

Ignacy dug himself out of the hay, yawned, and looked about him with amazement.

"Why, it's quite pretty here," he said slowly.

"Rubbish! Look over there, at the farm. Doesn't it remind you of anything? Well, manure-heap, cows, goats—aha! and a donkey, too! What a jolly donkey!" he laughed aloud as he saw the donkey, let out of the shed, running in comical zigzags about the farmyard.

But Ignacy was taken up with something else.

"Low-lying land!" he grumbled. *"I told you that they only send prisoners to places like this. Do you see that mist over the river? We'll get malaria here for certain!"*

"Malaria? Well, then, you'll die, you grouser, and I tell you that not a single blade of grass'll grow crooked here on that account. You always must get some fool's notion into your head!" He turned away in disgust, looking for the unruly donkey.

The farmyard, however, had cleared itself as quickly as

it had filled up. But the house-door was wide open, and Marusia was on the terrace with her brother. After speaking to him for a moment she pointed to the rick and vanished into the house.

"They're calling us, Ignacy. We must get down!" Tadeusz made haste to jump down from the rick. He went to meet the boy, brushing bits of hay off his clothes.

"Good morning, sir!" he cried, delighted at being able to startle the lad with a Polish greeting.

The boy stood still and looked cautiously at him.

"What?" he asked.

"Good morning, sir!" repeated Tadeusz, a little less heartily. "You understand Polish, don't you?" he added.

"Yes, I do!" answered the boy reluctantly. "And when did you learn Polish?"

"In my swaddling-clothes, sir! I'm a Pole, as I may say, from birth. But it doesn't seem to interest you."

The lad gave him a sidelong glance.

"Here . . . it's steppe!" he said shortly. "Is the other one up yet?" he pointed to the rick.

"Yes, the other one's up. Oho! he's climbing down. What can we do for you, please?"

"What do you mean?"

"Nothing! I'm awaiting orders."

"No one gives orders here," said the boy slowly. "Here . . . it's steppe. My sister asked me to tell you breakfast is ready."

"At your service!" Tadeusz bowed coldly. "Only please allow us to get a wash first." He beckoned to Ignacy to come down to the river.

"*That's a pretty good lesson!*" he thought, as he doused himself with water. "*That kid's right. It's steppe here, and that's all there is to it. What does it matter that I'm a Pole and he's a Pole? Well, he certainly isn't courteous. Never mind! I shan't have to be courteous either. It's steppe here!— d'you understand, Ignacy?*" he said aloud.

"*Well, and what about it?*"

"*Nothing. Keep your mouth shut. They don't like chatter-boxes here. Are you ready? Come along! That boy's waiting.*"

They found the dining-room empty. On the coloured cloth that covered the table were laid tea cups and bread and butter, and a singing samovar. A bunch of wild flowers stood in a plain earthenware jar in the middle of the table. The sight startled Tadeusz so utterly that he forgot everything else in the twinkling of an eye. There was something so particularly touching in the quiet song chanted in concert by the samovar, the cups, and the petal-dropping flowers. Ignacy was no less abashed. They stood on the threshold, too timid to take their places at that clean table, spellbound by the charm, at once fascinating and strangely sad, that breathed from it.

"*Won't you sit down?*" The lad's voice roused them. He was standing by the table and gazing at them with astonishment. "*Please!*" he said, and smiled. Tadeusz thought him very like his sister at that moment.

"*So it's not steppe here?*" cried Tadeusz, teasing.

"*Why not? It just is that! We're all equal at the farm. Please!*" insisted the lad. "*If there's anything you want, my sister will be here directly,*" he added as he disappeared through the door.

"*What d'you say to that, Ignacy?*" said Tadeusz, sitting down cautiously at the table. "*Didn't I tell you that we must go into the steppe?*"

"*Right you are! Heaven knows when I last saw a table like that. I'd forgotten that I ever was a human being.*"

"*It'll come back to you. Don't touch the bread, damn you! Our . . . hostess is coming.*"

"*But he told us to have our breakfast.*"

"*Well, don't you see that the table is laid for three? Put it down, I tell you!*" he added wrathfully, seeing that Ignacy was still reaching out for the bread. He looked impatiently at the door leading into the next room. Although he was very hungry and not quite certain as to the meaning of that third place, he longed for the girl to come and sit with them at this delightful table. The picture was incomplete without her, and it seemed all wrong for them to go rummaging about here with their big paws. Perhaps they wouldn't even know how to set about it.

But the song of the samovar had long fallen silent when Marusia appeared in the doorway. She came into the room timidly, as if she only wanted to slip through it to the terrace. But when she saw the untouched table she stood still in astonishment.

"*Why aren't you eating anything?*" she asked.

"*We were waiting,*" answered Tadeusz in some confusion. "*Excuse me, but the table is laid for three. We didn't know——*"

"*Well, and your soldier? Isn't he up yet?*"

"*Oh, him!*" ejaculated Tadeusz rashly.

There was a moment of awkward silence. The girl obvi-

ously understood whom they had been expecting, for a slight flush rose to her face. Tadeusz, deeply embarrassed, shifted his weight from one foot to the other, not knowing how to get out of a situation that made him look ridiculous.

Before he could collect his thoughts, he felt Ignacy pulling at his sleeve.

"What is it?" he whispered, furious.

"Introduce me!"

This seemed a good idea. Of course they must introduce themselves. It wouldn't have done to sit down to table without it.

"Please allow me," he said, trying to speak casually, "there's something else—something important, though we are on a farm. We haven't yet introduced ourselves. I am Tadeusz Glina, from Cracow. And this is my friend, Ignacy Michalski——"

"Doctor of philosophy," added Ignacy, hastily coming forward.

A thunderbolt fell upon Tadeusz. For hadn't he and that blockhead agreed to go out to work as simple anonymous people, and not to divulge to a soul what they had once been? He looked on in absolute horror as Ignacy followed up his introduction by bowing to the girl with dignity and, in spite of resistance on her part, kissing her hand.

"What have you done, you idiot?" He turned on his friend when Marusia, wresting her hand from Ignacy, had fled out of doors.

. . . . .

There's something lacking in all this. It simply isn't a novel at all, but a kind of cinema. What heaps of work I shall have to turn it into a decent story. I've never been like this before. I've always written out of hand, in one breath, although the subject was not so near to me, nor so disturbing.

Sometimes I think this diary of mine is to blame. What the devil made me think of keeping a journal just when life has become so monotonous and so—God have pity!—"regulated," that the trifle of energy, the spark of ferment struck out of a man by the common round of daily existence is split up still further, escaping from life in two opposite directions? I mean, backwards and—forwards.

October 3rd.

Eva is ill. Yesterday her head ached, and today she has a temperature. The doctor came this morning and told us not to worry, as all the children in the town have temperatures just now. A pretty consolation! If he had said that all the grown-ups were down with cholera, I should certainly buy the paper to read how many of them turned up their toes a day.

But when children suffer something turns over in me, rebels, and curses. Eva's bright eyes defend the last stronghold of the defeated angels of my soul. When the mist of fever falls upon her eyes, my angels mutter and plot a revolt against God.

October 5th.

Eva is better today. It's quite true, all the children have had temperatures, and no one knows whence or whither. It all ended in the fright, and my shoes must pay the penalty, for instead of getting new ones I bought toys for Eva.

To be quite accurate, not only my shoes. For yesterday I found at the office a letter from Klaponcia, and this note, written in an exquisite even hand, was unexpectedly alluring. I give it here in full, for it's a masterpiece of its kind:—

"Stach!—I really don't know how to make you understand the full horror of what you have done. For you must realize that there was nothing in my behaviour to authorize such conduct on your part. Although I know you will laugh at this, please believe me when I say that I am an honest woman and that I love and esteem my husband. If I had not known you so long and did not like you so much, I should have to tell Adam the whole story, and God only knows what would happen then. Meanwhile I forgive you for the sake of our old friendship, and consider that it was merely a misunderstanding. I should be very pleased to hear from your own lips that such a thing can never happen again. I shall wait for you today at five o'clock at the corner of Zamkowa Street. Please be there, for you have made me very unhappy.

"Helena K."

I didn't go. I keep out of questionable affairs when the child is ill. I know this way of looking at things is not far removed from the mentality of a Bushman, but . . . what can I do? In any case I'm not going to assert that I am prevented by principle or ideals or belief. Prejudice—well, yes, we may as well call it prejudice. If it makes life simpler, there's some good in it.

But what is Helena thinking at this moment? (It goes against my conscience to call her "Klaponcia" now!) That letter, so frank and such a mockery of truth, might be short-

ened to:—"Sir! we collided yesterday upon an even road,
and I don't want to fall. I swear that I don't. I believe you
only made a mistake. I shall wait for you tomorrow on the
edge of the abyss."

And I didnt go! So she is lying above that abyss in floods
of tears. And tomorrow she will have to forgive me again.
But this time it will be for something different.

The devil take Klapa and his curios!

.   .   .   .   .

*The priest found great changes at Marusia's farm during
his next patrol of the parish. He noticed from the steppe
that a much larger area of soil was in cultivation. Waste
land of yesterday was now under cotton and rice, and here
and there a square patch of field stood out, bearing some unknown plant. The orchard by the homestead, too, was flour-
ishing. Under the fruit trees, the soil, that used to be hard
and bare as a threshing-floor, was now covered with rows of
vegetables, and below the windows clumps of flowers nestled
in happy disorder.*

*When he entered the farmhouse, ungreeted and unseen by
anyone, he noticed the homelike order and charm of the place.*

*"Splendid girl!" he thought, looking about the room.
"How well she has managed here. Plucky, plucky child!
What a pity that I've got to pester her again."*

*For the priest had come this time on an important mission.
After corresponding with Marusia's father and talking matters over with her stepmother, he had seen a way of improv-
ing the unendurable state of things in the Radziejowski family. The operating base of the Colonel's station at the
front happened to be one of the larger towns, and the*

*protracted course of the war made it probable that he would
be there for a long time, perhaps till the end of hostilities.
So the priest had proposed that the stepmother should join
her husband with one of the children, while Marusia should
go back to the family home. This plan met with approval,
and Madame Kamila actually wanted to go off at once to
Marusia and dazzle "that stubborn girl" with her own capacity for boundless self-sacrifice. The scared priest had much
difficulty in explaining to her that it was not seemly for her,
the "mother," to make the first step towards the daughter
who had flouted her.*

*The priest had also another object in getting Marusia back
to the town. The girl was now grown up and there was absolutely no need for her to run wild in these steppes; and Judge
Szarota had lately come over from the outlying marshes of
the country to find himself a wife. This quiet, steady man
was much liked by the priest, who had known him in former
days. Their conversation had turned upon Marusia, just by
the way, for the priest disliked all undue haste. But Judge
Szarota had immediately commented upon his loneliness in
his far-off marshes, and had promised to come over when the
priest should write for him.*

*So the priest felt confident, as he drove to the farm, and
full of faith in the efficacy of his plans while he forced his
way across the wilderness of the steppe and visited his neglected parishioners. But the delightful order of things at the
farm disconcerted him.*

*"Who knows how it will turn out?" he drummed with his
fingers abstractedly on the table, waiting for the girl to come
in. New and noticeable details kept coming under his eyes*

as they wandered about the room. A small table in the corner strewn with books and exercise books, a drawing of some sort on the wall, over there a bowl of flowers. Suddenly he was struck by a peculiar object hanging against the wall. He looked at it attentively, and rising from his seat went over to it. It was the cap of an Austrian soldier.

Then he remembered that Marusia was to get some war prisoners for the field work.

"So it's partly their doing," he thought carefully inspecting the cap. "Same as everywhere else!" He came back to the table, telling himself that the whole steppe showed signs of the work of these men.

Nevertheless, that cap disturbed him and gave rise to a kind of unpleasant anticipation. It ought to have been hanging in the entry, not here in the living-room. It had an unusual shape, besides; one might call it over-smart.

"An officer, perhaps?" The reflection made him gloomy for some inexplicable reason. He felt impatient, too, and even angry that so much time passed without anyone putting in an appearance. He went over to the window and saw the girl outside in animated conversation with a strange man.

"Aha! so that's a prisoner!" Suddenly curious, he drew back behind the window-frame, to see without being seen. But he opened the window noisily, ashamed of himself, a moment later.

"Marusia!" he called, "Marusienka!"

"Father!" cried the girl. Then, to her companion, "Didn't I tell you that someone had arrived?" and she ran into the house.

Before the priest had recovered from the shock of hearing

her speak Polish to the prisoner, she was kissing his hand.

"You've taken us by surprise, Father!" she excused herself, looking at him gaily. "Where's your tarantass?"

"It's been driven under the lumber shed," smiled the priest, delighted to see her bright and animated as of old. "Been out in the fields, have you? Heaps of work, eh?"

"Oh, heaps! Haven't you noticed the changes we've made here, Father?"

"Yes, yes," said the priest kindly. "Well? Aren't you tired of it yet?"

"No!"

"Not homesick?"

"No!"

The second "no" rang sharper. The priest made note of this, and understood that his mission would be more difficult than he had thought. The girl's self-assurance bore witness to some inward change which would render harder the struggle—hard enough already—with her opposition. But this time there was no call for haste.

"Can you put me up for tonight?" he asked. "I should like to stay here a day or so."

"How lovely!" Marusia clapped her hands. "We'll show you round the farm. Monsieur Tadeusz——"

"Who's that?"

"Don't you know? Oh, of course not! Well, he's a war prisoner. We've two of them on the farm."

"Labourers?"

"Labourers?" the girl repeated with astonishment. "But I told you—prisoners!" She looked inquiringly at the priest. "Poles," she added.

"Aha! War prisoners!" echoed the priest. "I was wondering, seeing that there are all sorts and conditions among them. But we'll discuss that later"—he looked at the door—"I've a lot to talk over with you this time. But now find me some corner where I can turn in and rest. Now then, don't look dismal again, you troublesome child!"

October 6th.

All is peace and quietness. Nothing is happening. Zosia is taken up with the house, Eva wanders about picking her nose. Peace reigns at the office. Nobody has been to see us. Helena K. is silent. Kunda irons the linen. The clock ticks seconds, quarters, hours, and our life goes on in spite of us.

On such days it seems as if I ought to write more than usual. Whereas it is just the opposite. I am at a deadlock and can't get a move on. I'm not the clock, after all, and can't compete with it. Something must be taking place about me to make me feel that I'm necessary. I and the work I labour upon. And when everything flows so smoothly through me, why should I bother the world's head?

I must sneak out and go off somewhere.

October 7th.

Of course, I went to a café yesterday. I sought out a table of interesting people. A few futurists, an astrologer, the editor of *Movement,* a bolshefying Jew, the inevitable Jewess, and that silent motorist who dreams everlastingly of strings of passing milestones. And *Félix le bohémien,* talkative, quarrelsome, standing neat, sweet, and bitter vodka—a regular cabbies' feast.

They accepted me, as they always do, with reserve. I'm too little of an artist in their eyes. *Pardon!* The motorist likes me, and when he smiles at me I seem to see the kindly sun shining upon him and his hectic races. But the rest, I say, are full of reserve—Felix, because he is writing a play and I've never written one yet; the others because they are thinking about art, whereas I have enough of it by the time I get up from my writing-table. I abhor beyond everything that highbrow mill-wheel which today grinds to powder every grain of creativeness.

I provoked discussion (for its own sake, on any subject that turned up) and brought it to a white heat. The editor got his back up most—he has his own opinion and clings to it convulsively, knowing that if it were wrested from him there'd be nothing left of him. They went for me with the polished shafts of their arguments, and were just going to get me spitted when luckily the jazz-band struck up.

So I grabbed the Jewess by the arm and whirled her away, though the glances she flung at me were fit to poison an adder. As we floated off, I put out my tongue at the "interesting" people and shouted to the angelically smiling motorist:—

"We're off, sir! 160 kilometres an hour!"

He nodded, and fixed his eyes upon the rhythmic procession of couples. I danced till late at night, and when I brought back the Jewess to our table for the last time, she glanced at me humbly and inquiringly. I might even say that it became her. I took leave with extreme amiability and—went home.

A word here about the consequences of that barren occurrence. Felix turned up this afternoon, no doubt spurred on by that restlessness that always awakes in him whenever he tries to oppose me. And I don't know whether he wanted to be agreeable to me or to do Zosia a service; in any case, he spoke at length of our interesting time at the café and of the fun we had had afterwards. I said nothing, since no amount of persuasion will ever convince Zosia that I was in a furious temper from beginning to end; for it was only when I got home and looked at the sleeping faces—so dear to me—of herself and Eva that I shook off my depression.

So I left it to chance; and while Zosia, her usual tact deserting her, poisoned the tea with bitter half-words, I said that she could have a good time, too, whenever she liked. For instance, why not go to the café today with Felix?

At that Felix took fright and grew sheepish, whereas Zosia seemed to liven up and began to behave with that special nonchalance of hers which is so unpleasant and insincere.

Well, they fixed it up for eight o'clock. Up to that hour Zosia and I did not speak to each other. I had a game with Evie at reading the *Courrier*, while Zosia made her toilette very thoroughly and ostentatiously, even changing her chemise.

We exchanged a few words, as usual, before she went out.

"Keep an eye on Eva," she said, "I'm sure to be back late."

"I expect not, Zosia," I answered, "it's awfully boring at that café."

"I don't care if it is. You may be bored there and I not. Only remember," she added significantly, "that it was you who sent me there."

I began to feel sorry for her and for myself.

"I'm not sending you anywhere, Zosia. But if you really want some fun, go and have it alone, or with someone else, but not with me. You know very well that what amuses me makes other people wild."

And on that we separated. If I had said a few words more, she would have stayed at home, no doubt. But it was all the better that I didn't say them. Let her go and find out for herself. She has a fine instinct about people, and the society at the café is sure to disgust her. She'll come home at ten o'clock and we shall make it up for a longer time than would have been possible after those few unsaid words.

Meantime I'm going to take advantage of this rare moment of undisturbed solitude. If my life resembles an errant voyage across stormy seas, there's nothing like dropping one's anchor in a still lagoon known only to oneself. So I will strum on the guitar, gaze at the ceiling, and grow sad, happy that there's nobody to see me at it. But that sheet of paper lying open on the writing-table irks me. An irresistible inner voice cries, "Write! write!" Come along, my still lagoon! I am going back to my memories. That's also a solitude of sorts.

.   .   .   .   .

It was late when the priest woke next morning, and from the silence reigning in the homestead he guessed that the farm dwellers were out at work. Startled and somewhat irritated by the lateness of the hour, he sprang out of bed and went to the window; but the early briskness of the day was dying out of the languid air. His mind refreshed with the view of the distant steppe, he began to look about for the people. The yard was empty except for Barat, who was rubbing down horses by the well. The priest gave way, for no reason, to an impulse to talk with this man.

"Barat!" he leaned out of the window. "Come here, Barat."

"Have you had your sleep out, Khozain?" asked the Sart, coming up.

"I've slept too long. Well, how are you?"

"God is good!" answered the Sart.

The priest was none too pleased when the natives mentioned God's goodness to them, but he swallowed the pill and went on undaunted:—

"Plenty of people at the farm, eh? You never expected that."

"There's room for them all! The house is big, and the steppe bigger. They're welcome."

"Well, to be sure! Are they any use to you as hands?"

"Eh, baryn! There's no hands here. Everyone does his bit."

"And the prisoners too?"

"Too! How could it be any different? They aren't like the folk hereabouts."

"So you don't get much out of them?"

"How do you know that, baryn?"

"Well, you said, 'not like the folk hereabouts.'"

The Sart shot a quick glance at the priest. "They're clever men," he said calmly; "when they don't know, they look in a book and find out. Seen the cotton by the river? That's all out of books."

"Just so," said the priest. "They're praised all over the

steppe. Industrious, peaceable, don't upset anybody," he broke off, looking at the Sart sharply.

"That's it, baryn!" confirmed Barat. *"They don't harm a soul. They're—not like the folk hereabouts,"* he repeated with a hint of irony. *"Did you want anything, Khozain?"* glancing back at the horses by the wall.

"No, you may go!" said the priest more dryly. *"If you see your little mistress anywhere, tell her I'm waiting for her."*

The Sart turned away, but stopped after a couple of steps.

"Isn't the Colonel ever going to come back here?" he asked casually.

"Why do you ask that?"

"Nothing. I only asked if he's coming back."

"I don't know. What does the little mistress say about it?"

"She says: 'He's going to stay in Poland, because it's a beautiful green country.' Do you think they will sell the farm?"

"My good Barat, I don't know. The Colonel hasn't written a word to me about it," said the priest reflectively. *"And the little mistress would be going there too, eh?"*

"Why not? They'll all go there."

"Aha! . . . but that's not good, Barat!" he exclaimed involuntarily.

"You know best!" and the Sart went off to the bottom of the yard.

Abandoning the interview as hopeless, the priest gave one more fleeting glance around the yard and went into the next room to look idly over the books and papers lying on the table. But he found nothing particular among them. The books, of the standard used in preparatory classes in schools, partly Polish and partly Russian, came from the Municipal Committee and even from the parish library; exercise books, scribbled over with unformed handwriting, bore witness to the children's studies. He found no traces of Marusia's hand.

"So the children do lessons," he thought, arranging the litter of papers tidily. "That's a good thing, anyway. She must have got some educated men. Poles, too. But perhaps that's all the worse," he deliberated.

Under the last copybook he came upon a packet of post-cards bearing the Red Cross stamp. The photograph of a woman with a child lay on top. Struck by the unexpected elegance, strange in these surroundings, of the lady in the picture, whom he guessed to be the wife of one of the prisoners, he took up the card, and was looking at it attentively, when he felt that someone had come into the room and was standing behind him.

"Good morning, Father!" The voice was hard and self-assured.

Caught in the act, he glanced quickly round and saw a young man standing in the middle of the room.

"Good morning! good morning!" he answered hastily, and with unusual amiability. "I was just——" he excused himself, handling the photograph awkwardly.

"Oh, please do! That's my wife," smiled the prisoner.

"I guessed it at once. She's very pretty—very pretty!—and looks clever too." He glanced at the card again before

*laying it down. "It must be very sad for you both without
your families, isn't it? These are dreadful times."*

"Well, yes! The war! It can't be helped, Father. Men are
out to kill each other, and God is a long way off. But if one
isn't too exacting, there are worse things than being here on
the farm."

"For sure! for sure! The front, the barracks—I understand. Your lot is not an enviable one" — he floundered
among conventionalities, slightly annoyed at having to be so
amiable to a man who was, after all, only a prisoner. "But
don't you know where Marusia has got to? I mean to say,
Mademoiselle Radziejowska?"

"Exactly. The young lady," he said with a slight smile,
"sent me in to see if you were up yet and to ask if you would
care to have a look round the farm. The horses are waiting."

"Of course, certainly, why not? In a minute"—he hesitated. "Marusia"—he would not correct himself a second
time—"Marusia, you understand—I've known her since
she was a child—has taken to the farm in real earnest."

"I think she has had every reason to do so."

"Well, that depends. Do you know what sphere your
employer—as I may call her—comes from?"

The prisoner glanced sideways at the priest.

"I know"—he answered in a hard voice—"from a very
unfortunate sphere that is off its orbit."

This unexpected answer roused the priest's indignation.

October 8th.

When I sat down to write yesterday, I could have sworn
that my work would go smoothly and that nothing, what-

ever happened, would put me off it.   But I forgot that there is somebody who is privileged to make light of all my creative impulses—Eva! She woke up unexpectedly and, not seeing her mother, tossed on her bed for a long time. I felt that she wasn't asleep, but I wanted to keep her quiet and not give in. Till at last a sigh reached me, then another, followed by a faint little voice:—

"Daddy!"

I don't know how it is, but that word on a child's lips has a particular force. And when it assails me in a moment of solitude, I get the feeling that someone is calling me from another world, someone who has right and power over me. So I put my pen down and went to her. On the way I mustered all my common sense, so that I merely stood in the doorway and looked sternly at her. And she, snuggling into the pillow to show that she really wanted to go to sleep, only somehow couldn't, looked at me with sorrowful eyes and said nothing.

"Why aren't you asleep, child?" I asked, understanding at the same time the futility of the question. That softened me, of course, and I went so far as to lean against the framework of the door. I was being slowly overcome by a wistful fear of the bedroom in which Eva lay, alone and wide-eyed.

"Are you writing, Daddy?" my daughter whispered, realizing that she needn't answer my horrid question.

"Yes, child, I'm writing."

"*Must* you write?"

"I must. What do you want, Evunia?"

"Hasn't Mummy come home yet?" she breathed a moment later.

"No. But she'll be home in a minute."

"In a minute?"

"Perhaps in a minute. You know that Mummy must go into town sometimes."

Eva was silent. The office, the town, visits—these are powers before which her poor head is bowed, in spite of the dumb and resentful opposition in her heart. But sometimes, at a lucky moment, it happens that she defeats the Moloch of real and pretended duties that form the *milieu* in which her angelic childhood blooms. So she tried it on this time.

"Sit down by me, Daddy"—she attacked me suddenly and cuddled still deeper into the pillow.

And I did really sit down. Then my little one, conscious and confident of her gorgeous triumph over my loathsome "writing," fixed me up a nest on the bed, squeezed my neck, kissed me with enormous ardour, and then turned to the wall, drew up her knees so that I could sit deeper, took my hand and put it on her breast. She immediately became good and quiet, and fell asleep at once.

And I, feeling under my fingers the hard little chest and the beating, childish heart—so small a thing, and yet a whole human existence in the palm of one's hand—sat quiet and mused. I wasn't afraid of the night any more, nor did I grieve over the discarded manuscript in the other room. My thoughts were far away, far beyond even the first memories of my childhood, at some bright, sweet-smelling, immortal well of life from which we all came and to which we must return, unless this whole life of ours is a monstrous misunderstanding. And it was both sad and sweet with my soul, both cloudy and sunny.

That was . . . also a certain kind of solitude.

And I fell asleep with my hand captive on Eva's breast, and did not wake until Zosia came in at three in the morning. The picture she found startled her to such an extent that she even forgot the words of justification which, I knew, were on her lips. I naturally had not the least desire to make the situation any easier for her. She got to bed quicker than I have ever known, and only whispered humbly, "Good night, Stach!" I did not answer.

And I haven't even asked her today where she was and what she was up to, though goodness knows what became of her, since the cafés close at one o'clock. But no! . . . what nonsense! She is out of countenance and unsure of herself, and is full, besides, of that soulful activity about the house which she always displays after some more serious violation of the order of our family life. And she pardons everything, understands everything—in a word, a domestic angel. She listens patiently while Kunda, muttering something about "unhappy children," starts clattering her pots and pans at early morn; and she ate without a word of protest a dinner composed of just the very dishes she doesn't like. Let's keep cool. If anything had really happened, she would be bold-fronted and determined, like every woman who has been unfaithful. We'll see what Felix will do. If he has behaved badly, he won't turn up here for ages.

The thing has its good side. I want to write again.

  . . . . .

This unexpected reply aroused the priest's indignation. "What did you say?" he asked in a warning tone.

"*I said what I said. You must know about all that better than anyone.*" *Another unpleasant turn which definitely embroiled their fruitless conversation. It was evident that this man knew a great deal—too much for a labourer taken on for the fields. He ought to have foreseen that, and not have countenanced such plain speaking.*

"*We are talking about unnecessary things*"—*grumbled the priest, rising from his seat.* "*It's time to go and look over the farm. In any case*"—*he paused feeling a desire to give* "*this gentleman*" *a suitable lesson*—"*in any case you are passing judgment in matters which ought to be no concern of yours. You understand, in your position——*"

"*I understand!*" *interrupted the prisoner.* "*In my position one has nothing to lose, Father!*"

The day had started badly and did not mend as it went on. The priest had supposed that the drive round the farm would be taken alone with Marusia, but Jurek and the other prisoner, a certain Ignacy, were of the party. Fortunately, the first prisoner refused to join in the expedition.

And though this Ignacy seemed pleasanter and more polite than the prisoner of the morning, yet he annoyed the priest just as much by his senseless chatter and uninvited eagerness to explain the new order of things on the farm. He did not give Marusia or even Jurek a chance to speak, and behaved as if he were the farm's master and benefactor. The priest's policy of amiability towards Marusia, who listened to Ignacy's explanations with evident attention and pleasure, forced him to a passive condition of silence, though his realization of the extent to which these prisoners already played the master at the farm sometimes aroused his indig-

nation. And his impatience increased at the thought of the task that had brought him to Marusia.

When they reached the confines of the estate, the priest excused himself politely to Ignacy and went off with Marusia towards the bryczka,[1] *telling the others that he had various things to discuss with Mademoiselle Radziejowska—family affairs. Then he told her to drive into the steppe, and plunged into the matter.*

And behold, to his great surprise he met with no resistance, with none of the usual obstinacy. The girl heard him out quietly and without a word of objection. She did not promise, it is true, to return to the town, and she passed over in complete silence the question of Judge Szarota; nevertheless she declared that she quite realized how childish and unreasonable she had been up to now. And that it couldn't go on like that. Monsieur Tadeusz had told her the same thing.

"Monsieur Tadeusz?" inquired the astonished priest. "That's one of these prisoners, isn't it?"

"Yes, it's Jurek's tutor."

"Aha! I know! And this Monsieur Ignacy?"

"He teaches Irenka. The children have made such progress, Father. I wish you could see it."

"And when do they have their lessons?" asked the priest, suddenly kindly disposed towards these men.

"In the afternoon. We all work in the fields in the morning. You don't know, Father, how tremendously hard these men work. Really! Such strange people, not a bit like the folk here"—she turned the warm light of her eyes upon the priest—"I don't know how to thank them enough."

[1] Bryczka (pronounced britchka): a kind of strong four-wheeled cart.

"*Well, that really is nice, very nice of them,*" said the priest. "*And they look like intelligent people. One of them has a very pretty and charming wife,*" he added, casting a sidelong glance at the girl.

"*Oh, hasn't he?*" she cried eagerly, "*and such a lovely little daughter! She was born when he was at the war. He's never even seen her. Oh, what an awful thing this war is!*" she whispered. "*The whole world torn to pieces. Must it be like that, Father?*" she asked timidly.

The priest looked curiously at her. She had grown very sad, and her thoughtful face showed that she was unbosoming herself of griefs that consumed her, and not repeating a lesson learned from others—griefs of which he had never suspected her, and whose existence he had perhaps himself forgotten since fate had driven him into these outer worlds.

"*It is the will of God, my child!*" he sighed. "*The mind of man can do nothing here to help. It is better to think of what it is in our power to do.*"

But between the thing that was "*in our power*" and had brought the priest to the farm, and the anxious soul of the girl, lay such a weary way to cover that it was impossible to link matters up again. So they drove back to the farm in silence. The girl busied herself over the dinner, while the priest took refuge in his room.

The dinner was a quiet social rite that united all the inhabitants of the farm around one table. It was the first time that the priest had had the experience of sitting down to a meal with his own driver. But he appreciated, and even in his secret soul yielded to, the bond created here by the brotherhood of work and misfortune.

He left after dinner, filled with discrepant thoughts and feelings. His mission had been fulfilled more or less, but he realized that Marusia's fate was heading for new ways, unforeseen, incalculable, ways that led to a world far remote from the priest and from these steppes.

At the cross-roads he looked behind him. Marusia's home, barely visible upon the flat steppe, might have been an island floating in an immeasurable ring of seas. The steppe wind was rising along the horizon and striding towards the farm, bearing a mighty wall of black dust.

October 9th.

We're beginning to get to the bottom of the question of Zosia's expedition of the night before last. She was at the café with some interesting people, and afterwards the motorist took them for a run. He drove, as usual, at breakneck speed, something gave way, in the car, and he was tinkering at it till morning. So that I was wrong in saying that we're beginning to get to the bottom of it, for we seem to be quite at the bottom of it. But—it is darker after the clearing up than it was before. They mended a spring, Zosia's virtue is intact, the colds in the head consequent on this nocturnal escapade are getting better—but the motorist called on Zosia today, with Felix, and brought her, for no particular reason, an enormous bunch of roses.

I don't attempt to guess what he meant by it. In any case, Zosia's name-day falls in May, not in October, and the motorist had never been to our house before. Yesterday's "unpleasant adventure"—for thus he justified himself—was really too insignificant an occasion for such a sheaf of flowers. I wanted to tell him that in that case I ought to have been given a greenhouse, but I said nothing. I like the man and could pardon him almost anything. If he has fallen in love with Zosia—for such a lunatic could fall in love in the twinkling of a single kilometre, devil take him!—then let his divine smile protect him. It is only in extremity that a mature woman loses her heart to a man who may break his neck at any moment. If only I don't break my own neck over my stupid aphorisms!

But I have an impression that Felix's idea is to use the other fellow as a lay-figure for himself. When the motorist offered his bouquet to Zosia, with a clumsiness that was engaging in its simplicity, Felix winked at me. This meant: "See him? A victim! Not like us—us, Zosia's owners." The ass! If I were Zosia I would rather have a single motorist than a hundred Felixes.

In any case, a new and noteworthy factor, that may make things a bit brighter for Zosia, has come into our lives. Solitary as she has been up to now, she has gained a valuable ally. It's true I'd have preferred it to be, not a man, only a thing, a thought, or an idea—but if it can't be otherwise. . . . Well, and I? What about myself? I must preserve a magnanimous objectivity in this affair, so long as I can't give Zosia all she needs. And I can't. That would mean giving myself up to her entirely. It would mean sticking fast on the sandbank of a woman's wholly satisfied love. And that, I say, I cannot do, no more than I can demand from Zosia that boundless capability for self-dedication and sacrifice which alone raises a woman's love to the level of great and wonderful phenomena.

It's a vicious circle. If it were not for the fact that Eva turns in it with us, perhaps I should take the simplest way out—divorce.

What a stupid thing to have said!

There, that's enough! Shut up! If one could only say the same to the events of life that go and breed one with another so logically, so stupefyingly, so systematically!

For before Felix and the motorist had taken leave Professor Klapa called with his wife. And this occasioned a classical, charming, social "drawing-room."

The hopeless banality of the combination: Felix, the motorist, my wife and Helena—I and the lamentable Klapa beyond the brackets—put me completely out of humour. I contented myself with a few simian grimaces, a few of the stupidest witticisms I could think of, and made off to the window. From it I can see through a chink in the walls a far-off clump of trees which is perhaps some poor little plantation but which looks like a forest. I always escape to it when anything puts my back up.

And what happened? Helena, who had come all buttoned up, dry and resentful, was put completely out of countenance by my bad temper. After a few minutes she began to turn and twist on her chair and to throw me uneasy glances. Whereby she made me wilder than ever.

Then under some flimsy pretext she rose out of the circle and came over to me. I don't know what it is, but a suffocating heat which makes me powerless flashes out from that woman. She stood above me in silence. I went on looking out of the window. I couldn't see my forest any longer for wondering where that scared bag of bones gets so much determination. Everybody was looking at her, and they must all have seen she was as white as a sheet and had no decent excuse for escaping to the window; and I, I continued to behave like a bear, or rather not to behave at all.

She went back at last, goaded by the other people's curiosity and my indifference. But as she turned away, she got out the awful words:

"Won't you come to us at four o'clock tomorrow?"

I didn't answer. The question was a disagreeable surprise. I hadn't expected such a sudden turn in the situation, and I didn't want it. But it takes a churl to say "no" to such a question. And it takes an unscrupulous cur to say "yes"— for she really doesn't know what she is doing.

The glances she sent me from the table later on, glances full of menace over the unuttered word, glances retracted by the huge blaze of a blush as we separated, were really pitiable.

And now: shall I go or shall I not? I know that Klapa has a meeting of antiquarians at four o'clock tomorrow from which no human power can tear him before night. So that at a little after four Helena is to fall from the pedestal of her hospital virtues into the painful abyss of commonplace sin. She won't fall!—Nothing will happen tomorrow at a little after four. I detest time-tables, and my ship sails only upon open seas.

October 12th.

I've been away in the mountains. At home I said that I was called to the Capital on official business, at the office I applied for leave on private grounds, and I escaped to Dame Nature, to whom I am united in kindly relations entirely free from enthusiasm. If in spite of this I occasionally give way to sentiment with her, that merely proves the rule of "return to one's first love." Yes, I once loved nature above everything. I can't compass such violence of passion nowadays. The reason for this would seem to be her long lack of reciprocity, to the point of utter and shameless indifference, during the worst moments of my life. Yes, yes, madam! I remember exquisite mornings when the pale sun shone upon the monstrous slaughter of war; I remember the gigantic steppe, unwilling to nourish the handful of creatures sown upon it; I remember —oh! I remember many things not worth reminding you of. Even if all that's not quite justified, I'm nevertheless right. I am a man, I feel, I suffer, I err—while you are merely perfect.

I found the mountains gloomy in their grey *demi-saison* habit, their faces thickly veiled. To put it differently, it was just as sad and dark and ugly there as it had been among the people I had escaped from. Just the same, and yet different. Dame Nature is absolutely independent. I go my way, she hers—whereas among people you daren't lift a finger for fear that somewhere somebody is going to suffer for it. So that those two days in which nothing took place about me, those two days passed in aimless wandering, have made it possible for me to take a long view of what is going on. Let's take advantage of it, for in a minute or so something may happen again.

First:—the novel is weaker than I supposed. It hasn't that hidden rhythm that ought to show, through the fabric of words, the beating of the author's heart. Or if it has, it's only in patches. Perhaps the plot is not a great one, though it touches me on the raw. But it must be possible to rise above one's own experience, and even to win through across one's own sins and remorse. If literature were dependent upon authors' confessions, our reading matter would be sorry stuff. Well, perhaps I shall manage to key it higher when the tragic things begin to happen.

Let's go on—Zosia. She still cares for me. Nevertheless, there's a possibility of surprises where Felix and the motorist are concerned. It all depends on me, and the situation would be childishly simple but for one circumstance—that I am not in love with Zosia. Attachment, affection, sympathy, desire to understand her, and readiness to give way—virtues in which I am not lacking—can make up for love with a resigned woman only. And Zosia is not yet resigned.

Idem: Helena. She's in love with me, and I'm not in love with her. There would appear to be nothing to linger over here. But there is. The peculiar passion of that woman has an effect on me. Whence it may come about that she will fall into my arms in the most unexpected manner. A horrid thing it would be, for that affair savours of catastrophe.

Tertio or quarto:—Let's cheer up at last!—Eva loves me and I love her. I foresee no collisions or surprises in that quarter, and we should forgive each other everything whatever happened.

But isn't it tragic and humiliating that, at this rare moment when I'm drawing up a sort of statement of my life's accounts, the balance consists entirely of women? What am I to do? Let's rejoice that we have a quiet stable item of work on the assets side—work, I may say, for an unknown morrow. I work a lot and I work with passion. I go forward and push others before me. I have my office, my committees, my writing. Now and then I give someone a helping hand and don't get wild if he says in return: "Embrace me" ... And I used to shed tears, and grouse because the whole of humanity did not wipe them away for me.

October 13th.

I've been too busy over my life's balance sheet to touch my novel for four days. This diary plays horrible tricks with me. But I get more and more fond of it, though at times it makes me furious and impatient. To be frank, I like it better than the story, and if I could summon up courage to be only a man, and not some sort of an "artist," I should say to myself: —Devil take this novel, Tadeusz and Marusia and all!

.   .   .   .   .

Tadeusz found in the farm a refuge exceeding all his expectations. He had put himself outside the shattering mill of war and imprisonment by a single decisive act. The last re-echo of oppression was gone from the moment he slept off, on the hay-rick that night, his brutal fatigue. The last symbol of violence vanished from his sight with the Russian soldier. And in the strange stern silence of this land forgotten by man and God, he felt the freedom, utter and primitive, that nature gives untouched by human hand.

From the very beginning, as soon as the first surprise had passed, the people at the farm made him uneasy. He was quick to grasp that their presence here was quite as accidental as his own. He scented some drama, some wrong, some vicious circle of human fate, which he didn't want to touch or even to see. Thrown off the rails himself, flung out of the saddle, he needed to lie in the sun and lick his wounds. The consciousness of his impotence against the fate that had hurled him, a full-grown man, to be food for cannon and prison lice, warned him of any desire to take up the sorrows of others. But he was unable to put up a wall between himself and the people with whom he was ordered to live and upon whom he was now dependent. It was then that he took advantage for the first time of the gift the war had brought him —simple comradeship in misfortune. With this silent, unpretending, unexacting comradeship he won over all the people on the farm.

He was helped by that element, the steppe, equal in its monotony to the war, unequal in its benevolence. There, into the desert of untilled soil, into lands wasted by flood, into wild fields of weed and grass, he led the van of the campaign. Not everyone gave back an equal response. But in the end they all gave way to him, and from this arose tangible results of the work, which began to irk him with the question—why? to what end? Willy-nilly he was forced to consider it, all the more that he read it ever oftener in the eyes of those about him.

Feeling that the time had come for enlarging their system of life, he spoke with the girl and asked if she would like him and Ignacy to take up, without interrupting their usual work, the children's education. Marusia replied that it was the only thing wanting to her happiness. He laughed and called her a brother-spirit. Well, since she was so sensible and so very nice about it, why not arrange to prepare the children for schools in their own country, Poland? At the quiet and astonished remark that she saw no way by which the children were to get to Poland, he said that that would come of itself. The thing was to cut one's losses and begin to lead a new life— that is to say, from the time of coming to the steppe. God only knew what the war would leave of the past. So it was useless to think about it.

The girl gave her consent at once, and the field of work was now in part transferred to the house. He chose the boy for himself and entrusted Irenka to Ignacy. The work went ahead with amazing speed. The youthful hunger for understanding that consumed the lad's strong and collected soul awoke in Tadeusz a desire to impart his own store of knowledge and experience. He drew from it freely, not confining himslf to any pedagogic pattern. Over and above "exact" science he put his chief endeavours into the work of preparing the boy for life. And he discovered to his surprise that the material from which he drew most willingly was his war experiences, for in the war all the deadly sins and all the cardinal virtues found their most vivid, most convincing expression. He returned to it with passion, and came to discard all other themes. And for this near past, so accursed up to yesterday, he felt a sudden affection; and everyone at the farm loved the moment when the evening, unofficial part of the lessons began.

Then—he heard a voice calling to him from still further off. The first letter came from his wife, with a photograph of the child born during his absence. It was about this time that Marusia had a letter from her father at the front, and a little *later the priest arrived. The silent but painful disturbance caused at the farm by these events put him off his balance and forced him to profound reflection.*

But he found it hard to arrive at a clear decision. Thinking over his position he came to the conclusion that he had been too quick in disregarding not only the past itself as a factor which had to be reckoned with. For here, beside him, behind his back, had arisen an ardent unseizable stream of inner life so strong, so deep, so widely spread that it almost startled him, though he himself had been largely responsible for releasing it—releasing it and yielding to the illusion that he controlled and directed it. Today he could not even realize where he had drifted. He had an inkling or two, managed to notice and understand some part of it, but the essence of the thing escaped him more and more. Even that "brother-spirit" —that being most dear to him at the farm, and indeed the chief person on it—even the girl concealed ever more closely from him the process of change that was ripening in her soul. It hurt him all the more that his comrade, Ignacy, had begun, rightly or wrongly, to play the part of an initiate. And from this arose the first conflicts at the farm.

. . . . .

But there aren't any conflicts in the diary, and there won't be any. Felix could frighten me only once in his life. I must go to bed, for we've a great ceremony tomorrow at the office.

October 15th.

We have been laying the foundation stone of the new building for our "institute," so there was a great arrival of various bigwigs, and lesser lights were legion.

I wore my frock-coat and took part with the others in putting the thrills of citizenship into the community. It turned out better than I expected. Nothing was overdone, and they played the national anthem only once. No one reminded us that "Poland is a great thing." Thank God! For really she may become so when once we get rid of that slogan.

At the banquet in the evening I got a closer look at our dignitaries. If one may generalize, it's my opinion that we live in an epoch of the hegemony of bulls with short necks, broad backs, and thick bodies. I say nothing about their faces, for I didn't see them. When I went into the hall I was met by a solid wall of backs that made an impenetrable bastion round the buffet, where the bulls were feeding *en masse*.

"That one in the middle, that's the Minister!" whispered our porter, Monsieur Michal, who was fulfilling in the cloak-room the responsibility for the overcoats of our grand guests.

I waited with some curiosity for the Minister to turn round. For during the war the man played a rôle of high dramatic tension. He was one of those who dash at impossible things and win through by accident. But the Minister was one of the last to turn his back upon the *hors d'oeuvre*, and I was obliged in the meantime to cast a final eye over the supper table.

I took stock of him during his speech. His face is out of the ordinary, and you can see that the chisel of fate had hard material to work on before success and prosperity spread a shining surface over it. It reminded me, without rhyme or reason, of that house in the market-place which was once stormed by the Swedes and is now our principal linoleum warehouse. Not a pleasant picture for a fastidious eye—but it isn't the house's fault that the Swedes have vanished behind their thousand mountains.

The Minister spoke badly, though he is reputed to be thunderously eloquent. It was like the buzzing of a xylophone made out of an old weapon. Towards the end, when the moment came for the triumphal chord of prosperity, a philosophic grimace of irony flickered over his face. Well, well! I didn't look for that! The hero, when he started thinking, became a minister—but what will the Minister do if he doesn't leave off thinking?

The sensation of the evening was the Vice-Minister's speech. Quite a different type of man, none of your stony-browed, strong-necked bulls. Let us say, a giraffe, which separates the precious vessel containing its brain from its heart and stomach by means of a long and flexible neck. The idea of citizenship poured from the Vice-Minister's lips, fortifying our hearts with the optimism of a giraffe gnawing salad off the tops of palm-trees.

"Look! there's a statesman for you!" whispered my right-hand neighbour, the wojewodstwo[1] secretary, who is very much in the know.

Willy-nilly, I had to agree. The "Vice" spoke splendidly, and it was difficult to resist the convincing clearness of his observations.

The "Vice" is a new man. What he did before the war, where he disported himself during the war, why he did not display his undeniable talents earlier, why he hasn't yet be-

[1] *Wojewodstwo:* Poland is divided into seventeen wojewodstwa or provinces.

come King of Poland—these are things I couldn't, listening to him, understand.

"Do you know what the Vice-Minister was before he entered the Government?" I asked my left-hand neighbour, a superlatively well-informed editor.

"Nothing!" winked the editor—"he had a nose!"

A pretty vague answer. I couldn't understand whether the Vice-Minister was nothing because he had a nose, or whether he was nothing and had—independently of that—some sort of a nose. God be with him! He became a minister when he left off thinking—and from being a minister he may quite likely become a hero. Unless he breaks his subtle neck—for only those who are always something in life possess a feeling for reality.

So much for our ceremony and our banquet. I will only add that before the end of the junketing a rumour ran round the table that the miners had gone on strike. It made a great sensation and caused a passionate exchange of opinions, until the "Vice" asked where the news came from. It turned out, from nowhere. Somebody or other had started the story and had pulled the leg of the honourable assembly.

"A typical image of the atmosphere of our public life," smiled the Vice-Minister. "Every foolish lie makes us give off a whole volcano of energy, whereas the thing can be solved by a pinch of common sense."

The "Vice" is right in principle—but in spite of that, the miners really have gone on strike. The news came from Monsieur Michal in the cloak-room—and Michal, ho! ho! never passes on unauthenticated news.

·   ·   ·   ·   ·

October 16th.

"Did you want to speak to me?" asked Marusia, coming up to Tadeusz timidly.

.   .   .   .   .

I was interrupted by Klapa, who "dropped in" because he can't understand why we don't go and see them. I squirmed like a snake; nevertheless, he squeezed out of me some sort of a general promise that . . . certainly of course, one of these days. I learned that the Klapas are changing their mode of life. "We must go forth, Stanislaw, upon a wider social arena. Not always those everlasting books of her and the hospital. Firstly, the war is over. Secondly, Helena is bored, Helena is off colour, Helena is pining for something new. Do you know, she made me buy a dozen bottles of good wine and, I'll tell you in confidence, crêpe de chine for her underwear! I was very pleased—the spirit of the age. It's quite pleasant."

It's frightfully funny, but the first and most trusty middle-man of the woman who wants to be unfaithful is—her husband. The "spirit of the age" and the "social arena"—those are her assistants.

Eh! I'd like to spit on all that and go away somewhere alone with Eva.

October 17th.

The devil! The play Felix is writing takes place on the steppe and his heroine is "partly" (his own expression) Marusia! I don't want to be prejudiced, but the very idea of it puts me in a passion. That ape must have got to know that I'm writing a novel about those times, and his imitative mania has done its work. I can just imagine the remarkable play, which appears to be almost finished.

There is to be a ceremonious "reading" of it at Felix's the day after tomorrow.

October 18th.

My publisher has written to ask if I've nothing ready in my portfolio, and when may they count on something? Reflections and hesitations. Shall I tell him about the Radzie-jowska novel or not? The thing is hardly begun; it's really only sketched out, and I don't yet see the ending. Then— shall I publish it, even if I do manage to find some successful winding-up? Shall I—damn it!—put Marusia behind shop-windows?

I keep asking myself all these questions, and I know that tomorrow, or perhaps at once, I shall write to the man and tell him that I've a novel going and that it will be ready by the spring. Meanwhile I shall ask him for an advance—that advance which is, was, and ever shall be the most powerful motor of artistic "creation."

     .   .   .   .   .

"Did you want to speak to me?" asked Marusia, coming shyly up to Tadeusz, who was busy reading his newly arrived mail. "Perhaps later on, when you've finished your let-ters——" she glanced at the table.

"I've finished," answered Tadeusz briskly. "I've practically finished. There's nothing new." He put the letters down. "They're well, and getting along somehow. Just fancy, my

wife is worrying over my having been sent into the steppe! And of course she asks who is this Radziejowska lady."

"You wrote to her about me?"

"Why not? I had to explain my new address——" he broke off, observing a cloud on Marusia's brow. "Are you angry?"

"No!" Marusia tried to smile. "But I like it so much better when nobody knows about me . . . thinks about me . . ." She grew embarrassed under Tadeusz's attentive gaze. "We had something to discuss. . . ." She sat down on the edge of a chair.

"There you go—discuss!" interrupted Tadeusz lightly. "I wanted to have a talk with you, and ask your advice, just as usual—as between pals."

"But Monsieur Ignacy——"

"Oh, Ignacy! Ignacy is always mysterious—rather—well, shall we call him?—a dark horse. Anyway, what has Ignacy to do with this? You were not to speak of that to anyone."

"Well, but Monsieur Ignacy——"

"Hang Ignacy!" he waved his hand, discontented. "Well?" looking kindly at her, "have you written that letter?"

Marusia gave a sigh of relief, as if she had been waiting for the question. Cautiously fumbling at her neck, she drew a neatly folded sheet of paper from under her blouse.

"Here it is," she whispered, handing it to Tadeusz.

"Why give it to me?" He was surprised. "Am I to read it?" He looked inquiringly at her. "Are you going to entrust your heart's history to me?" He broke off, noticing her suddenly overcast face. "But, Mademoiselle Marusia"—he took her hand—"don't be sad. I haven't the least intention of reading your letter. Just tell me in a few words what you've written."

"I don't know how to say it," she answered. *"Please read it, because I don't know if it will do. Monsieur Ignacy advised——"*

"Ignacy?" He drew away his hand and took the paper off the table. *"All right, I'll read it, but I won't say a single word!"* He unfolded the paper and took it over to the window, anxious to spare the girl embarrassment.

And this is what he read:—

"Dear Reverend Father:

"Both your letters have reached the farm and I have read them very carefully. I consent to come to town and make Judge Szarota's acquaintance. Please write to him to come, and then what must happen will happen. If he likes me, I shall make it a condition that the children go to him with me; and their tutors too, Monsieur Tadeusz and Monsieur Ignacy. And one thing more; he must not expect anything from my father, as I have renounced all my rights in favour of Jurek and Irenka, so that they can afford to go to Poland and finish their education.

   "I kiss your hand and await your reply.
                                          "Marusia."

Tadeusz ran his eyes two or three times over the letter after reading it through. There was something in its severe simplicity that at once amazed and touched him.

"But, Mademoiselle Marusia!" he turned round, forgetting that he had not been going to say a word about the letter. *"How can you write to people so frankly? And you mean to send it?"*

"Yes," Marusia said in astonishment, "unless there are any mistakes in it. You are laughing at me," offended.

"God forbid!" he contradicted eagerly. "Unfortunately, I must tell you that your conditions—anyway one—are unacceptable. You can't write such things."

"You mean about the children?" she asked.

"No, not about the children! about me, about Ignacy! There isn't a man on earth who would consent to such a thing; don't you feel that?"

The girl looked at the ground, and was silent and thoughtful for a long while. Then she suddenly got up and reached out for the letter.

"So you say I mustn't write like that?" she asked in a hard voice.

"No, you mustn't," he said decidedly. "You can't make such a condition."

"Very well, then. . . . I won't send this letter."

"And what are you going to write to the priest?"

"That I'm staying on at the farm!" she broke off, looking round for the door.

With a gesture Tadeusz begged her to remain in the room. It was he who had inspired the letter, and he felt it was up to him to find some way out of the situation created by its unexpected contents. His sensations were strange as he looked at the girl's face, clouded and resentful and yet humble as it was, and breathing some deep sorrow.

"Poor thing," he thought—"strong, tender, obstinate, naïve somehow, and at the same time aware—well, and pretty too," he could not take his eyes off her. "But I must advise *something——*" *he shook himself and fixed his eyes on the window.*

"*I must think it over, Mademoiselle Marusia!*" *he excused himself, racking his brains for a practical decision.*

But his mind, as if to spite him, turned only about two poles of possibility. Either to tell her that this whole notion about a Judge Szarota fallen from the sky was a piece of foolishness which ought to be ended once and for all, or to explain to her frankly that . . . that their further existence upon the farm might lead to a thousand dangers, that . . . Ignacy's romantic moods were nothing but the trifling of a silly fop, that . . . that he also, Tadeusz, sometimes fell under the charm of her personality, that finally they were here, alone on this desert of a steppe, and God alone knew what might happen.

"*Judge Szarota—or us,*" *he repeated in thought, realizing that he couldn't say it to the girl.* "*Judge Szarota, or one of us. Yes, but which?*" *he floundered on, more and more uneasy and embarrassed.*

And then the sound of paper being torn reached him. He looked round. The letter to the priest, in ribbons, was dropping from Marusia's fingers.

"*What are you doing?*" *he caught her hands instinctively.*

Caught her hands and forgot the letter, forgot Szarota, forgot his unendurable thoughts, everything. He was fanned suddenly by the breath of warm feeling that was reflected from her clear eyes, that poured into his hands from the light pressure of hers.

"*Really and truly, Mademoiselle Marusia,*" *he explained gently,* "*you mustn't do things right off like that. You must*

think over it again. For we"—he held her hands tighter—
"*for I . . . we . . . we are just come-by-chance people. You
mustn't take us into account or become attached to us. The
time will come*——" *he broke off, seeing the glow that
flooded her neck and ears and face.*

*With an abrupt movement he wrested his hands free, and
to spare her confusion went over to the window. His mind
began to work at fever speed.*

*"Do you know what?" he turned round, his face lighting
up*—"*Write and ask the priest to bring Judge Szarota here.
We'll have a look at him and talk it over and everything may
be settled. Really, do write."*

"For him to come here?" the girl asked reflectively.

"Of course! could anything be better and simpler?"

*"Very well!" she answered, and, glancing at the strips of
the letter on the floor, she went away.*

*Tadeusz accompanied her to the door and stood leaning
against the wall as she crossed the yard, his eyes following
her slender charming silhouette. The rapid beating of his
heart proclaimed the storm raging within. He neither heard
its voice nor wanted to hear it, gazing at the girl as at the
rising sun.*

"How lovely she is!" he whispered, smiling.

*But she disappeared behind the wall of the barn. And just
then Ignacy ran up from the other end of the farmyard and
went quickly after her.*

*Tadeusz drew back into the room and slammed the door
behind him. His heart grew quiet, but a sudden cloud of grief
descended upon him.*

·　　·　　·　　·　　·

October 19th.

Idiot! clown! How dared he write such nonsense, such absolute piffle, about that girl! What has he made of her? A sort of Princess Hiszu-haszu, in love with Ignacy the troubadour. And I am, of course, the unscrupulous churl that rapes the Princess at the very moment when the troubadour is pining, under a maple-tree, for his distant motherland. A divine piece of work! And then this temperately impassioned knight, this troubadour Ignacy, unable to endure contumely, flings his lute at the Princess's feet, shatters with bitter words the cloddish seducer whom he had once loved "with the brother-love of youth," and goes off to an unknown fate, without even any bread and butter. Unavailing are the tears of the Princess, who only now realizes what the ideal Ignacy was for her. . . . Too late! . . . too late!

There you have the play of that idiot. I don't mind his having made a clown of himself and a beast of me; I don't mind his having written a thing without a particle of talent—but he ought to have a lesson for painting Marusia in false colours and insulting her by his beggarly fantasy.

The wretch had an inkling of what was up when he was reading the second extract, the part where the Princess throws herself at Ignacy, and Ignacy, though deeply in love with her, defends himself with the shield of the ideal. His voice quivered like Eva's fret-saw, and his eyes flew to me from his manuscript—he even forgot all about Zosia, though he had spread his drama under her feet like a Bokhara carpet at the beginning.

When he had finished the last scene he got up, came over

to me, and begged me "very sincerely" to tell him without
beating about the bush what I thought of his play.

I replied that I hadn't expected anything so rotten, even
from him.

Need I say that the whole séance, arranged with such
emotion and ardour by Felix, was shattered by this word?
Half the people were confused, half of them offended . . .
and a few grew sad. Helena went so far as to efface herself
in a corner, gazing at me with terrified eyes.

And I came home. Zosia stayed on, and hasn't turned
up yet.

October 20th.

The idea of inviting Judge Szarota to the farm——

.   .   .   .

No! . . . I can't! I'm off my novel today! And off my
diary too! What I did yesterday simply isn't done. A silly
childish revenge . . . and today I'm as much ashamed of
myself as though that unlucky play about Marusia were my
own production. And the worst of it is that by going on like
this I'm pushing Zosia into that blighter's arms. Sometimes
I think I'm losing my inner balance. I must take myself in
hand.

We have a general strike from today, so I'm going out
to see what's happening.

October 21st.

Despairing misery, I greet you!
It was enough for us to hear your mighty roar, to look

once into your ill-boding eyes—and our souls are at peace.
The town throbs with the crowd that is getting ready somewhere underground for the fray. How good it is that close
by, beside us, about us, before us, slumbers a force so for-
midable that it can sweep us off the face of the earth and turn
the world of our splendid endeavours to powder.

Despairing misery, I greet you!

With one blow of your powerful arm you have flung off
the stone of oblivion under which I had crushed you; you
have seized me by the scruff of my neck and shaken me with
a mighty hand. And though I know that your sword is blind
and disaster tracks you like a shadow, though I know that
you will yourself put on tomorrow the fetters you cast off
today, yet the thought that your name is million, while I am
but one, stirs me to the depths.

We stay at home feeling small and kind and humble. I
don't go to the office. The headquarters of the Central Strike
Committee are next door to it . . . and the entrance-key has
gone so far astray that even Michal himself can't find it.

We stay at home. Felix and his play, Helena, business
affairs, duties, books and publishers—all this on indefinite
leave. We have nothing to occupy us but the four walls of
the room and the crowd looking in at our windows from the
street.

Zosia gives lessons to Eva and marvels at the changes in the
child's mind. Kunda is having a great tidying up in the
kitchen. Horror possesses her, no doubt, at the layers of dust
and rubbish that have mysteriously accumulated in corners
and on shelves. I hammer more firmly into the wall nails that
have begun to totter, dust the ancestors' portraits, and turn

over the archives in my desk. And I read my pre-war verses, those despised and worthless scribblings forgotten years ago. Or I glance over letters from people who used to be fond of me, knowing that I should come to nothing, and who turned their backs on me when I made something of myself after all.

At home, of course, we talk only about the simplest things, about our having meat for dinner, which our neighbours haven't. Our motorist brought it from a friendly butcher who lives thirty kilometres out on the southern road. We are to get white bread too, for he has gone off on the western road after it.

From the window I watched his powerful machine sailing off to the middle of the town among the waves of people. Nobody raised a hand against him, and nobody put a rod between his spokes.

True, my friend's car is grey and modest and rather knocked about, while he himself looks like a workman in his dusty coat. The crowd, itself an element, feels in him the servant of an element, which accounts for this strange peace and harmony between them.

But look you! Before the market-place, where the crowd is a little thinner, the motorist gives a signal from his horn, and vanishes down a side street on his second speed. The idyll is ended. He is pursued by a hail of stones and a hundred hostile looks.

There's nothing for it, gentlemen! the elements are not always at peace among themselves.

· · · · · ·

The idea that Judge Szarota had been invited for inspection caused great unrest at the farm. Judge Szarota, though he wrote back at once his intention of coming at the first opportunity, shortly afterwards sent word that he was very busy and would not be able to make the visit for some days. A little later he again begged Marusia to wait, as he was obliged to communicate with his father and pay a visit to his mother. He next asked if the roads on the steppe were safe, as there were rumours in the town of trouble among the natives. At last he wrote requesting that the documents of the district might be examined to find out in whose name the farm and all its appurtenances were inscribed.

Marusia brought every one of these letters to Tadeusz, and each of them put a fresh seal upon his lips. He took the first communication seriously, advised this and that; the next he met with artificial gaiety; and later said nothing, handing the letters back to the girl with a heavy heart. In his mind's eye he saw this arid Judge Szarota scrupulously weighing the business side of a marriage with Marusia. But he kept his own counsel, stifling the bitter words that rose to his lips. For it seemed to him that every letter shown him by Marusia contained a mute and pitiful question directed to himself—a question for which he had no answer.

And a twilight fell between him and the girl and made a widening breach between them. They saw less of each other and had less to say every time. This discordant mood took possession in some mysterious way of the whole farm, disturbing the existing order of things. Work was at a standstill, meals were no longer taken in common, and even the children's lessons and the evening talks that followed them took place only when some accident brought them all together for a while. Everyone developed a strong desire for aimless rambling, and there were times when nobody knew what had become of the others or what they were doing.

Then one day a messenger brought a telegram. Tadeusz took it in and went off with it at once to the undergrowth by the river where the girl used to roam.

He knew well that wild thicket, with its marshes and hiding-places, its tunnels trodden out by the foot of some mysterious unknown beast; nevertheless, he wandered about for a long time before Marusia's voice answered him from a hidden lair. Impatient, he thrust his way in that direction through the wall of reeds, and came suddenly out upon the very brink of the river, in a corner grown over on all sides with dense bushes that met overhead. In one of its turnings sat the girl, leaning over the river.

"Marusia!" he cried, waving the telegram—"a wire! It's probably from Judge Szarota to say he's on the way. Marusia!" he repeated, seeing that she did not turn her head.

He went nearer and stood above her, wondering if she wished to be undisturbed in her solitude or whether she was too deep in thought to have heard him. The still silence of her retreat abashed him and put upon him its intoxicating spell. He stood motionless, listening to the splashing of the river and hearing another voice—very quiet—mixed up with it; the voice of human tears and stifled sobs.

And then, for the first time in years, painful and impotent grief gnawed at his heart. The telegram he had brought, all his daily affairs, the pains he had taken to come to terms with his fantastic life—all these things seemed to him unimportant, unnecessary, pointless, futile.

He sat down beside the girl, shoulder to shoulder. His gaze

*fell on the ripples lapping against the steep bank, lingered
upon the pool whirling at their feet, floated down the river
to the hazy far-off cross-roads on the steppe.*

*"Marusia!" he whispered her name and put his arm lightly
round her.*

.   .   .   .   .

*They did not open the telegram till they got back to the
farm. It said: "Coming tomorrow with Madame Radziejowska. Szarota."*

October 23rd.

> My daughter, my little one. My mote
> driven on a sunbeam. Come to me,
> bring your doll and your jumping jack—
> all you care for. Oh, and a shoe,
> Mummy's torn shoe . . .
> . . . That lovely shoe! . . .
> Sit on the floor, and Daddy will too,
> though he has no doll, no jumping jack,
> and calls the shoe horrid.
> Let's play at something! Dolly and Jack
> can get arm and arm into the shoe.
> And you? oh, you too!
> It'll be a ship, Daddy . . .
> No! Daddy'll be the sailor
> and tow the ship on a string.
> . . . Jumping Jack is drowned! But wait,
> we'll bring him round, and put his head
> on Dolly's knees, and Dolly
> shall hold him round the neck.

What will they play at now? At love!
Don't you know what love is?
Love is everything. Except
the chimney-sweep, and the man upstairs
who wouldn't give you his dog.
The black cat? that's not love either,
no, nor the house. Properly speaking
love's only you and Dolly and Jack
and this old shoe—and Daddy. . . .

Daddy's writing verses again after all these years.

October 24th.

They've been making their way since early morning—in
fours, in columns and singly—towards the middle of the
town for the great strike meeting. Their eyes shine and the
storms of revolt are knotted in their brows.

They feel that they are a power, an invincible army—they,
poor wretches of yesterday, despised by the whole world.
How ardently their bloodless hearts beat, how their tired
brains are working! A hymn of hope is rent from their
bosoms and soars above their drab heads. Disciplined they
go, quiet, self-absorbed, all given up to the one thought.
There is nothing they would not sacrifice for it just now.

The strike slogans no longer suffice them, increase of
wages no longer enthrals them—they want to overthrow the
world of yesterday and bring about a new order.

I know very well what is going on in their minds. And
my heart aches for them.

On they go. There's no end to these crowds.

"Where are they going?" asks Eva—one can't get her away from the window today.

"To the town, to the market-place. They have a meeting there, child."

"They're every one of them going to the town?"

"Every one."

"And aren't you going?"

"No!"

I turn away from the window. I don't want to hear the question Eva has on the tip of her tongue, for I won't tell her, not for anything will I tell her what I saw, what I heard, what I gazed at in alarm when that army of salvation took the trenches of the old world. For I too once walked on such another march and the first that consumed my breast was sacred.

October 25th.

So we have riots, shooting—street fighting. A shameful battle of secret slaughter, of all forms of combat the most abject. Treachery is a condition of victory, and the shot most applauded is the bullet in the back. Men lie in pools of blood on the streets, and the wounded are finished off three times. Hail, dawn of freedom!

The citizens and comrades who have not gone forth to slay take counsel together. Their wordy skirmishes are every bit as rancorous and unscrupulous, every bit as hopeless, as the battle raging in the street. Right and left, classes and masses, Government and community, bourgeoisie and proletariat—these are arguments that whistle like bullets and are out, like bullets, to wound and to kill.

One of my colleagues from the office, an uncommonly decent fellow, honest and even kind-hearted, has just been in to see me. He came to ask me to join the ranks of an armed force that is to fight the revolt. At some length and quite convincingly he explained that "there are moments" when nobody has a right to be neutral. I refused. He thereupon asked me, in a higher tone, to tell the truth—on which side were my sympathies.

We separated coldly, though I like the man and value him, and he has often shown me sincere regard. He thinks me a coward or a traitor, for I told him that I'm on the side that doesn't exist.

And now I'm sorry I spoke so shortly. I ought to have told him I've seen too much of blood and hate and violence, and that I want to see no more; that, in spite of all the great reasons of State and society, somebody somewhere must be the first to say to himself:—this shall not be! Though it may be against reasons of State, against the interests of the classes, things shall not be that make the soul of man recoil.

We will not hear the whistle of bullets!

We have had enough of the clanking fetters!

The muzzles of cannon gleaming in extinct citadels are as abhorrent to us as knives sharpened in underground cellars.

Hands off our homes, you tracking murderers! Hands off our brains and hearts!

Accursed be every threshold whereon lies the corpse of a man.

. . . . .

It has been quiet in the town since noon.

October 26th.

There's peace today too, or properly speaking a general retreat. It is said that the strikers have won, but I read a different tale in their faces—quenched, tired, aged as if they had lived a score of years during these few days. The strike demands were fully victorious, but that demand which fired their hearts a day or two ago lies underfoot, trodden and shamed . . . by their own doing too. They see it and feel it, but they won't admit it, and they flee cursing whence they came. Tomorrow the quarrelling as to who was to blame will begin.

Felix—he has appeared on the horizon again, taking advantage of the disturbances—is of another opinion. He says that this is only a truce, and that it will start all over again tomorrow. And he smiles darkly and hints at great events in store for us. He cannot say what the resultant changes in himself will be. A revolution, he says, is too great a phenomenon for him—a writer, a poet—to be able to pass over as if it were nothing. He goes about humming the opening bars of the "Marseillaise."

Really, the unlucky man disgusts me more and more. I'd like to take that writer and poet by the collar and rub his inspired face in the pools of blood that are still lying about the streets.

And they say that the harvest is monstrous.

October 28th.

1) Thou shalt not shoot in the back;
2) thou shalt not kill off the wounded;

3) thou shalt not punish without trial;

4) thou shalt not dishonour the dead;

5) thou shalt honour heroes;

6) thou shalt spare the innocent;

7) thou shalt respect the man in the enemy;

8) thou shalt protect women and children;

9) —and for the rest, do as you like, devil take you! It's not for me to write a new decalogue.

All the more, that peace really is concluded. It's the end. We are returning to our usual occupations and trying to live as we did before, as if this mountain of corpses torn from among us had not grown up between today and yesterday.

And I too have been to the office. I bowed to my chief, he to me, as though each of us would have said: "You're alive— so am I—delighted, I'm sure! Better not think about the rest."

It went harder with Michal, who raised loud lamentations on the subject of "some people" not being right in the head. And how he defended the office against invasion and trembled for the State moneys! But in spite of his obvious wish Michal talked more about the crazy world than about the State moneys, and you could see he was greatly astounded at the indecisive issue of the fray.

No less puzzled is my office colleague, the one who came to see me the other day. We soon made it up, and he asked me to explain what I really meant by "the side that doesn't exist." I promised to clear it up—another time.

For the rest, there is general consternation at the bloody harvest, and no power on earth could summon anybody to a renewal of hostilities.

These are strange times, when every struggle ends in a defeat for everybody. When everything is tottering and nothing can be overthrown. When every work of our hands is estranged from us before it leaves them. We are going forward into a chaos of events that are none of our making, and mounds of buried experiences grow up in our souls, cutting off all return.

.　　.　　.　　.　　.

He cracked his whip three times before the homestead, drove into the majdan at full speed, and pulled the horses up short. "Ignacy!" he shouted to his friend, who was peering out from behind the corner of a barn, startled and curious. "Hold the horses. Let me help you down"—he gallantly took Madame Kamila's perfumed hand. "Mademoiselle Marusia —I should say Mademoiselle Radziejowska—ah, here she is!" he broke off on seeing the girl, advancing with a stiff but decided step to meet her visitors.

.　　.　　.　　.　　.

No! this won't do. I keep repeating myself in the form and the action. Somebody is always arriving at the farm and going away without accomplishing anything. And it's supposed to be a novel!

Of course there are exonerating circumstances. The real action is played out in the deep places of hearts triple-locked and barred, so that a certain monotony of exterior phenomena may be permissible. But does one feel it strongly enough, this tension that must give way some fine morning and blow up the dreaming farm? I don't know. And it's a bad sign that I don't know. Up to now I have always known what was wrong and where and why.

Perhaps I'd better change the way I'm writing it, and push on to the end in rapid bounds. And go back and build it up afterwards? ... We'll see. One way or another I must get off the farm as quickly as may be.

Oh, I'm just worked up, that's all. The strike had a tremendous effect on me, though, damn it, I've had plenty of practice in bearing that sort of thing. The sound of firing goes on in my head, and I'm still devoured by the memory of that horrible struggle which has left the difficult question: Why?—or, more exactly, why in that way?

And then those two funerals today. Two processions of terribly gloomy people dragging after them such a pestilence of grief that birds might die of it and leaves drop off the trees even if it were not autumn.

I can't breathe! Our history, after all, cannot be one everlasting chain of unsuccessful drama.

November 2nd.

Tadeusz left the horses to Ignacy, for he did not want to witness the greetings; turning on his heel, he escaped into the out-buildings to take up the first piece of work that came to hand. In the woodshed he came unexpectedly upon the boy, who was sitting idle on a log.

"Good morning! are you taking a day off?" he cried with the remnant of his morning gaiety, which had unaccountably changed, at sight of the girl, into a feeling of irritation. "You might go to the visitors," he added; "your sister is sure to need you."

"Have they turned up?" asked the lad without stirring.

"See for yourself."

The boy got up carelessly, went over to the door, and looked out at the farmhouse.

"Goodness! what a height!" he muttered. *"That'll be Judge Szarota. I don't think he'll suit Marusia a scrap."* He turned round. *"Aren't you going over?"* sitting down on the log again.

"I?" said Tadeusz in wonder. *"I may go, if it's necessary. But what are you thinking about?"* he looked at the boy attentively. This lad, apparently so quiet and so indifferent to everything that did not concern the innermost sphere of his passions and duties, often startled him by some remark that showed secret, independent reflection. These remarks were always naïve, but always firmly expressed and put forward with a kind of ruthless obstinacy. And they were always very near the truth.

Once when Ignacy made various comments about their all going to Poland after the Colonel's return, the boy declared that they would have to go alone, seeing that his father had gone to the front to escape from their stepmother and would never come back. Another time he called his sister's renunciation of all rights to the farm a piece of folly. And again he grumbled to Marusia that Irenka sat too long before her looking-glass and would grow into their stepmother over again if they didn't look after her.

When his sister scolded him, or Tadeusz told him he was too young to pass such judgments, he seemed to give way; but it was difficult to convince him, and he went on obstinately in the line of thought he had chosen. These thought processes formed an interesting problem for Tadeusz; and apart from that they often shed a flood of light on the canvas of the farm happenings, growing daily more entangled. So now, noticing that the boy was in the throes of some new decision, he turned to him, more curious than he had ever been.

"I asked you what you were thinking about," he repeated impatiently.

"Nothing special"—the boy put him off. "I was only thinking that nothing'll come out of this Judge Szarota's visit."

"Don't you like him?" smiled Tadeusz.

"It doesn't matter whether I like him or not. But Marusia isn't for him. Because if she was going to get married she— she——" he broke off with a frown.

"Well?"

"She'd marry you!" he got out, "and you're married already and there we are. Are you angry?" His face changed, and he looked at Tadeusz with that child-like air that sometimes made him so like his sister. "Let's go to them, shall we?" he fidgeted about the shed, avoiding Tadeusz's eyes. "I expect dinner's ready. Marusia'll be in a wax. There, they're looking for us." He pointed to Ignacy, who was going round the yard from one out-house to another.

Startled by the boy's admission, for which he had no answer, Tadeusz jumped at the opportunity to interrupt their conversation, and called to his friend from the door of the shed. Ignacy came up, unusually quick and alert.

"What's up?" asked Tadeusz. "Dinner?"

"Dinner," replied Ignacy. "But it's just about the dinner that . . . I must speak to you—alone——" he looked at the boy.

"What's the mystery? Go ahead!"

"You see, I want to tell you that I'm offended."

"With me?"

"Lord, no! with that Szarota man. Just think, he told Marusia that it was the first time in his life he'd seen a table laid for the servants and masters together."

"And Marusia?"

"Well, of course, Marusia said that there were no servants here, and that we always had our meals together and should now. And that if the visitors didn't like it she could lay a separate table for them."

"Oh, she said that, did she?"

"Yes, and then she went to look for you, but she couldn't find you. So she asked me. Well, what are you going to do about it?"

"I? Go to dinner, old chap," said Tadeusz, vexed. "D'you suppose I care for Judge Szarota?"

"I shan't go," sulked Ignacy. "I can't submit to insult, you know. I, a doctor of philosophy——"

"You're a fool!" said Tadeusz, suddenly angry. "I'm going whether you like it or not! Well?"

"I can't submit——"

"Oh!" Tadeusz shrugged his shoulders, took the boy's arm, and went with him towards the house.

November 3rd.

It appears that they got in a shot somewhere at the motorist. A bullet through the neck, in some roundabout way between the spinal column, the wind-pipe and the arteries. So the lad's lying up in hospital and smiling at Helena, who has been transferred to the wounded from the children's hospital. He's no grouse against anyone, doesn't curse a soul—"Some poor devil," he says, "fired at me, that's all. He'd a good eye, the beggar! Got me right in the neck." I'm sure that if the motorist hadn't crumpled up from that shot he'd have taken on the "poor devil" for his chauffeur. You need men with a steady eye for driving a car.

Zosia and I went to the hospital this afternoon. She brought flowers for the motorist, and I a bottle of "Hungarian." But Helena would not let us take them in to the patient. She is more valiant in her hospital pinafore than in life, though she has none of that charity in her which makes the motorist think of his unsuccessful murderer today as a candidate for a chauffeur's job with him. Some inner impulse binds her like the hospital pinafore in which she wanders among the beds, beautiful as a picture and just as lifeless.

The greatness and sorrow of recent events, and our meeting thus "at the post of duty," served to bring about a reconciliation between us. When Zosia, who suddenly remembered an urgent commission in the town (I sometimes think that Zosia wants to facilitate—for reasons I know not—certain situations for me), left the motorist's beside, I went to see Helena in the nurses' room. As she was just coming off duty I decided to wait and take her home or for a walk. She excused herself for a moment and disappeared behind a screen to change her dress.

And there I distinctly heard her taking off with the utmost speed her apron, her dress, and I think something else too. No doubt she was just in her underclothes—aha! those crêpe-de-chine undies! And then ensued a long pause for which I could find no simple and straightforward reason. I only heard her sit down on a chair. And I could have sworn that she had put her head on her slim bare arm and was dreaming—dreaming of shameless things that defied the hospital habit lying at her feet.

I won't pretend that I endured that pause with complete stoicism. If I did not stir from my seat it was chiefly because of the innate pusillanimity of the male in regard to love-making; whereas the fact that I followed up this misbehaviour by whistling through my teeth may be put down to the shamelessness of the male in such situations.

An assistant, who came in to tell the nurse that someone in the ward had died, put an end to this billing and cooing. We went out into the street and separated at the gates of the hospital.

Now for a slight digression. What could one call my "relations" with Helena? Our forbears would have said simply *une cochonnerie,* and we ourselves used to say a flirtation, an expression which has endured beyond its time here and there right up to today. Whereas a modern flirtation isn't a flirtation by any means. For you hardly converse with the woman at all, and speech and *double entente* are going more and more out of use. This abbreviated and practical intersexual behaviour excludes all manner of flirtation.

A truce to terminology, seeing that the old meanings have lived themselves out and the new are not yet created. There would still remain the moral scruple. Does it exist or not?

A truce to morals! If I were to say they exist, I should have to blush—and if I were to say that they don't, I ought to go and look for a rope.

My digressions don't seem to get me anywhere.

November 4th.

The world—our own real actual world—has its ghosts, spooks, and spectres. This afternoon, just as I was going out, I had a visit from my old schoolfellow, Szmid. That is to say, from Szmid's ghost, for how to describe otherwise the frightful skeleton which is all that remains of the jolly fellow, brisk and happy, of years ago?

Szmid is a war-disabled, and a second-rate one at that from the point of view of society, for he lost his leg as a soldier in the Austrian army, somewhere in Montenegro or Albania. A splinter of shrapnel struck him on the head, besides, injuring the optic nerve. He can hardly see at all, and conceals his blindness behind enormous black spectacles that emphasize the terrifying aspect of his face.

Szmid is a poverty-stricken creature, living on the charity of his old schoolfellows. He has no relatives, and the country he fought for has fallen into little pieces, to the triumph of historical justice and the satisfaction of the citizens of the republics that have arisen out of the ashes. Szmid knows this, and hides himself in mouse-holes with the memories of his unhonoured wounds, oppressed by shame and alarm before a world he has in nothing served. His old schoolfellows are the only people in whom he has any confidence. He evidently sees that the last sense and meaning of his life was on the schoolroom benches. After that everything was misunderstanding and error.

I knew all this about Szmid, more or less, but the sight of him was a tremendous surprise. What is Szmid for me today? A beggar or a colleague? An intruder, a nuisance—or a guest that I haven't seen for ages?

We stood in the hall for a minute without exchanging a word, and then I asked him into my study.

He had a moment's hesitation on the edge of the mat, afraid to step on to the parquet in his muddy boots. The black spectacles that conceal his eyes give one the impression that he sees everything without needing to look at anything.

"Stach!" he said at last. "So you're back again, Stach! I've been meaning to come and see you for ever so long. Well, old man, you've been through an awful lot!" he added, shaking his head.

I answered that it was all over now and that it hadn't been so awfully awful. But he smiled indulgently.

"I know, Stach! One doesn't speak about it. A man can stand a great deal. I, for instance . . ." he became motionless and concentrated. I felt his regard piercing me with all the despairing effort of the blind—"I, for instance, I'm not doing over and above well, but I can't say that I don't manage. My wants are few and rather Spartan, you understand"—he straightened up his meagre chest manfully and immediately shrank again, not sure if I believed him.

I can't describe our conversation; I only know that it was simply torture for me. I learned that Szmid has no settled lodging, for he's used to freedom; that he does not eat, for people guzzle in the most unnecessary way; that he loathes smartness, and so wears no collar; that he doesn't believe in overcoats. Only boots—he likes to have good boots, and he has them, for he has borrowed a pair from our old school-fellow, Moritz. That funny Jew-boy on the third bench.

At sun-down Szmid proposed our having a walk. I agreed, feeling from his voice that he particularly desired it. And by weird little by-ways far from the main streets we came to that park on the outskirts of the town where we used to spend half our time as boys. There Szmid, now very cheerful, planted me on a rotting bench at the corner of the football ground.

"Stach!" he shifted cautiously to my side—"do you remember?"

Yes! I remembered, though the night was so black about us that every outline melted into the dusk. It was as if Szmid's enormous spectacles hung before my eyes and opened a vista upon the bright world of my childhood. It was late before we separated. Szmid stayed on in the park, for he appears to be sleeping there "for the moment" in an old gardening shed—the shed we used to hide in from the park guardian when we were boys.

I asked him to come to me whenever he was in need of anything, and, for that matter, whenever he liked. It was only when we were shaking hands that he told me he had a great request to make. He has heard that I write books—if I could possibly manage to give one of them to an old schoolfellow—because, when the sun shines in the park, he . . . he can still just see letters.

. . . . . .

At his first glance round the dining-room Tadeusz noticed

a heavy atmosphere of ill-will that boded no good. Marusia, very pale, was sitting in her usual place at the head of the table, with Judge Szarota, stiff and stark as a scarecrow, on her left side. Madame Kamila, looking very bored, was strolling about the room arm in arm with Irenka.

"Good morning!" *he said loudly, going straight to his accustomed seat at table.* "I beg your pardon for being late" —*turning to the girl*—"but I thought you might have things to talk over."

"Dinner's at one o'clock!" *and Marusia smiled reproachfully.* "Don't you know what's become of Jurek and Monsieur Ignacy?"

"Jurek was just behind me, he ought to be here in a minute. And Ignacy"—*he glanced with sidelong irony at Judge Szarota*—"felt so shy of the visitors that he's going to dine with Barat. I think there's no use waiting. Ignacy's fairly obstinate."

"Did you speak to him?"

"Well, yes—more or less."

"Because, you see, Judge Szarota was surprised at our eating at the same table," *she said calmly.*

"Just so. I heard about it."

"And now he's convinced it can't be any different—aren't you?" *she turned to her guest.*

"By no means," *answered Szarota, with deliberate emphasis.* "It ought to be different. That Monsieur Ignacy, as you call him, seems to understand. Well, the lady of the house has the first word, of course. We're only visitors here, we came and we shall go, and we don't want to upset your* *arrangements"*— *with a wry face*—*"but Colonel Radzie-jowski would be much surprised, I've no doubt,"* he added with evident satisfaction.

"My dear sir!" Tadeusz interrupted carelessly—"why drag in Colonel Radziejowski, who has never even seen us?"

"Well, there you are!" Judge Szarota shook his head. "Colonel Radziejowski is at the front. And perhaps he is just now fighting against your own brother. And here are you prisoners living in clover"—he broke off, catching a movement of impatience from the girl.

Tadeusz had a sharp answer at the tip of his tongue, but he realized how unprofitable a battle of words would be, and how unpleasant for all concerned. He therefore controlled himself and determined to take no further share in the conversation.

Dinner was eaten in silence, under a crossfire of surreptitious glances of mutual investigation. From his place opposite Madame Kamila, Tadeusz was able to study her closely. She was young—very young to be Marusia's "mamma." One had only to look at her fine, well-cared-for complexion, the curves of her figure, and a certain grace of shallow coquetry in the whimsical face and gestures, to guess what it was that had drawn the Colonel into his second marriage. After catching a few of her veiled glances, Tadeusz could not throw off the impression that the Colonel's lady was observing him attentively and perhaps—perhaps even rather flirtatiously. The moment he caught the quiver of a smile at the corner of her mouth he met her unrestrained glances more boldly.

But Marusia's uneasy gaze admonished him. He forgot

"mamma" in a second and sent the girl a cordial smile. Her face grew brighter, while Judge Szarota became stiffer than ever.

Towards the end of dinner, over the cups of tea, Judge Szarota asked Marusia when he might speak with her in private on a certain matter known to herself. She replied shortly that she was at his disposition at any moment, and best of all now.

"Excuse me," drawled Szarota, "I'd rather not, before people. However you look at it, we are concerned with questions of a confidential nature."

"We are among ourselves," Marusia answered.

"Not quite!" objected Szarota, with a vexed glance at Tadeusz. "Would you come for a walk with me? Or perhaps we might stay here with your mamma, and Monsieur Tadeusz could take the children out. Well, sir?" he twisted his features to an amiable grimace.

"At your service!" Tadeusz got up, bowed to everyone, and went out into the yard. He sent the children off to Barat, and then took a deep breath. Szarota's caustic temper annoyed him horribly, and he wanted to do all in his power to bring the courtship at which he had so incautiously assisted to any kind of a conclusion.

In his soul he foresaw the failure of the whole business, and was at once glad and sorry. A few glances of Marusia's, caught that day, and her unusually submissive behaviour towards himself had greatly disturbed him. He could not get rid of the idea that the result of this visit would be entirely different from what he had expected. All the more because he had felt the charm of the girl today as never be-

fore. The prospect of her marriage to Szarota, which had seemed so simple and comprehensible up to his arrival, roused in him a stormy protest now that he had seen the suitor. If you looked truth straight in the eyes, who had a greater right than he to that "confidential" talk with the girl? And suppose he were really to stake everything upon that one card?

Assailed by a swarm of wasp-like thoughts, he wandered about the farmyard seeking some lonely spot where he could be secure from people's eyes. But before he had made a choice he heard the patter of hurrying feet behind him. He looked round. Madame Kamila was running after him.

"Can I do anything for you?" he stood still, concealing with difficulty his dissatisfaction.

"Yes! I wanted to ask you to take me for a walk. That Judge Szarota is too boring for anything!" she pouted capriciously.

"Boring? How funny! I thought you were on such good terms with him."

"The idea!" she shrugged her shoulders. "You see"—she smiled confidentially—"I'm obliged to act the mamma. He wrote and told me he was engaged to Marusia and said I must accompany him, for the sake of propriety, on his first visit to her. So I came, and now I'm sorry for it. How frightfully boring the whole thing is! Do take me somewhere, won't you?" she glanced round the enclosure.

He accepted her company, willy-nilly, and they took the first footpath into the fields. Somewhat startled by Madame Kamila's free and easy manners, and irritated at this invasion of his solitude, he strode swiftly ahead in ostentatious unconcern, whistling some tune or other between his teeth.

But Madame Kamila did not seem to notice his ill-humour.

"Does all that belong to the farm?" she asked, pointing to the far edge of the fields with her parasol.

"All that and more too."

"And you ploughed it over yourselves?"

A murmur of assent.

"Well, really! And Marusia gives the orders?"

"That is so."

"Excuse me," asked Madame Kamila with some impatience, "what are you really?"

"A prisoner of war," he answered balefully.

"Of course! You're all prisoners of war. But I mean, what were you before the war?"

"A married man and the father of one child."

"Oh!"

"You see!" Tadeusz could not resist saying.

.   .   .   .   .

What the deuce! Why it's four in the morning. I've been sitting at this a perfectly impossible time. I shall be as flabby as a pickled herring tomorrow and fall asleep at the office, however exciting the reports may be.

But apart from that, *à la bonne heure!* A few hundred lines of my novel and ... about as much of my diary. It's all Szmid's fault. He's lying in his shed now, curled up in his ball of poverty. And dreaming, no doubt, of his bench at school.

November 5th.

I went to the park today with books for Szmid and couldn't find him anywhere. I was just thinking of coming home when I was arrested by the silhouette of the park guardian, who had been keeping me under his eye for some time. His figure seemed familiar. I looked hard at him and remembered. Why, it was that unforgettable, historic Mikolaj,[1] who used to chase us with a stick when we stole roses for our lady-loves. However many years ago? Never mind! But I at once understood that there must be some essential link between this man and Szmid. I went up to him and asked if he happened to know a lame man with black spectacles who——

"Antos?" he asked without waiting for the end of my sentence.

I had cast my mind backwards. Yes! Szmid's Christian name was Antoni. That name, applied to Szmid today, rang strange and pathetic in my ears.

"Do you know him?" I asked, suddenly drawn to the old man, while he looked at me as sharply as if I were hiding a stolen rose under my cape.

"Who doesn't know him? Have you got some business with him?"

Something undefinable kept me from admitting what was my business with Szmid.

"Oh, nothing particular. I just wanted to see him. You see, he's an old schoolfellow of mine."

"Aha!"—the old man bucked up—"I guessed that at once. In that case you'd better wait a bit, for Antos is mighty fond of his old schoolfellows. He ought to be here directly"—he glanced at the park gates.

"Why? Does he come regularly?"

[1] The Polish form of Nicholas—pronounced Mikolai.

"Lord, no, sir! Sometimes he ain't here for weeks together. But you see, sir, we've a reading at my place today."

"A what?"

"A reading. We read books, sir." He drew himself up with obvious pride.

"Meaning, who?"

"Us! Antos, I, and my daughter, here in my house. My daughter does the reading, Antos being so blind. But Antos explains what she reads. You ought to hear him one day, you schoolfellows of his. It seems to me that Antos, though he's so disabled, yet he's got a great spirit in him, sir!" he looked stern and drew down his bushy eyebrows. "It's easy enough to shoot people to bits."

I didn't wait for Szmid, nor did I leave him my books. I escaped, hiding them under my coat from the angry eyes of the old gaffer just as I had hidden those stolen roses in our school-days.

Only the roses were exquisite, innocent, and sweet-scented.

November 6th.

That last dialogue with mamma Kamila is rotten. It doesn't hold together—quasi-banter, quasi-flirtation. Whatever induced me to get that woman out to the farm? Just to show that she exists? Or because I may be needing her yet? Poor reason. I really must stick to the principle of writing only the indispensable things most closely bound up with my subject. Better cut our losses and take out that bit about her at the farm.

Or no—we'll leave her there, once she's arrived. After all,

one can give her some more essential role, and then her presence will explain itself. It might, for instance, be like this—Madame Kamila smells a rat and starts intriguing against Tadeusz. That would be in accordance with her character, as well as with her aim at the moment—her intention to get rid of Marusia by marrying her to Szarota. One could even take it further. Supposing Madame Kamila, seeing that the Szarota combination will lead to nothing, were to push Marusia into Tadeusz's arms and then fling her, humiliated to the dust, out of her path?

Man! recollect yourself! you're writing about real events and living people. You've got to stick to truth here, since every lie you write will strike somebody.

So . . . we'll break off here with the stepmother and leave that bit till later, when the further action will show if it's needed or not. Let's concern ourselves with Judge Szarota, who is leaving the farm with a long nose and a resentful face. He has been refused.

     ·   ·   ·   ·   ·

When Tadeusz was on his way back to the farm with Madame Kamila, he saw from a distance the tarantass harnessed for the journey.

     ·   ·   ·   ·

That's not the way to write! Monotony, incompetence, a sort of creeping verbal paralysis! Let's get off the farm. Its climate has a dreadful effect on the story.

     ·   ·   ·   ·

Tadeusz was prepared for anything after the unsuccessful suitor had departed, but he never imagined that within a fortnight of that visit he would find himself back at the prison camp in the town. The change came suddenly and inexorably, like everything that had happened to him since the start of the war.

For one morning two soldiers arrived at the farm with strict orders to bring Tadeusz—prisoner of war from such and such a regiment, without delay ("without losing a moment") back to camp. They carried out the order with precision and with a certain precipitation that showed they had received urgent oral instructions as well as "papers."

They took him off so quickly that he had hardly time to pack up his few poor belongings and send Jurek off with the news to Marusia, who was out somewhere. They were three versts from the farm when he heard the beat of horses' hoofs behind him and saw the girl riding like the wind, with her brother following her, and Ignacy running after them on foot.

They were alongside in a moment and forced the soldiers to halt by barring the way. Marusia's face was stormy, her eyes filled with anger and excitement.

"What's all this? What's happening?" she panted.

"Can't you see?" replied one of the soldiers churlishly. "We're taking this young fellow back to camp."

"But how? What right have you to do it?"

"By what's written down here," answered the soldier, handing her the paper with the order.

She snatched it, glanced over it quickly, and, turning frightfully pale, read it over again, slowly, with an effort, as if she wanted to learn it by heart. Then she got off her horse and went straight up to Tadeusz.

"*So it's true. They're taking you away?*" she asked, white-lipped.

"*Yes . . . you've read it yourself——*"

"*And isn't there anything to be done? Can't you get out of it?*"

"*I'm afraid we can't do anything. Anyway, not just now?*"

"*We can't? So they're taking you away!*" she passed her hand over her forehead as if to chase away a thought she could not grasp. Her breast shook with a spasm of weeping, though she strove with all her might for self-control.

"*So it's no use! My God! my God!*" she whispered with helpless sorrow. "*No use!*" and desperately she fought back the tears that shone like stars at the corners of her eyes. "*Don't obey them!*" she cried with sudden determination.

"*Eh, little mistress!*"—one of the soldiers came between her and Tadeusz—"*Don't keep him any longer, or there may be trouble. Come along, sir!*" he caught the prisoner by the arm. "*It's no good gaping at her—we must be off.*"

"*Leave me alone!*" Tadeusz wrenched himself free. "*I'll go willingly, but you'll wait a minute. Hands off, I tell you!*" he looked compellingly at the man. "*Marusia*"—he came up to the girl and took both her hands in his. "*Don't cry! please pull yourself together—you mustn't cry! I'm going away for a time, but I'll come back, I'll come back as sure as God's in heaven. And now*"—he made to bend over to kiss her hands—"*my Marusia, my poor girl . . .*"

And then it was that the unexpected happened and startled him like a thunderbolt from a clear sky. The girl kept his hands in a strong grip, pressed them to her, and with a sud-

den pliant movement leant towards him. Her face, wet with
tears, was against his. At the corner of his mouth he felt
her moist lips begging for a kiss, and he fastened upon them
frantically, with all his heart, careless of the stupid faces and
gestures of the soldiers, careless of Ignacy, who had caught
up with them and stood still, changed into a pillar of amazement.

A short handshake with the boy, and he was off. And he
did not once look back.

That farewell kiss burned him and filled him with unrest.
He strode along without looking at anything, without speaking to anyone, as if he feared to scare away the memory of
the girl's mouth, that seemed still to cling to his own. He
felt its pressure, the moisture of her warm salt tears, the heat
of her full lips.

He passed indifferent through the network of formalities
that restored him to his prison life. Like a stranger he greeted
his companions of former years and turned a deaf ear to
the buzz of barrack-room news. Only the huge package of
letters from home startled and somehow alarmed him. He
gave them a cursory glance, postponing the reading of them
till later. And he would not take up his abode with the others
in the really very comfortable barracks—or, as it was called,
the officers' hotel—but chose to occupy a lonely decrepit hut
at the far end of the camp, although it was said that three
of its inhabitants had already gone west. He hadn't the least
desire to be the fourth, but he needed solitude, and his yearning for the girl was stronger than camp superstition.

So he settled down in the hovel alone and at once wrote
a long letter to Marusia, explaining at length and with pas-

sion why he had not been able to confess his love for her before.

Then with furious determination he threw himself into the work of finding out who was responsible for his recall from the farm.

. . . . .

Short and concise. I have opened a vein that was strung unbearably tight, and the relief has been immediate. But now I must go carefully, for we are getting down to the serious part of the story.

November 9th.

Today Zosia asked me whether I loved her. I can't remember what started the conversation that led up to this strange question, but I think it was the key of the attic. That, however, is neither here nor there. It might just as well have been a lamp or a potato or Mickiewicz or the depreciation of the currency. A woman has only one thing in her mind, and if she talks about anything else it is obviously from necessity or diplomacy. Well, she asked me if I loved her. She spoke as if she were cool and indifferent about it, but I felt in her voice the fear of one who gazes into the jaws of an abyss.

I answered stupidly: "Well, what do you think, Zosienka?"

But she was not to be put off.

"I'm not asking you what I think. That's my business. Tell me, do you love me?"

I answered: "Yes."

"Say: 'I love you!' "

I said: "I love you."

Then Zosia sat down on my knee, put her arms round my neck, and burst into tears.

November 10th.

Where do these extraordinary moments come from—when people, grown tired and indifferent, with nothing to say to one another, become suddenly reconciled and fall into each other's arms? How has it happened that since yesterday peace reigns between Zosia and me—peace and harmony and actually understanding . . . and . . . love, in one of those numerous modifications of it that we can rise to at our time of life? Perhaps the secret lies in the fact that, whatever happens, marriage is not a romance, though it may be a cycle of romances. Only one must be for ever seeking new forms of mutual understanding, be able to make fresh attempts, and not forget that the times change and that we *mutamur in illis*. We and other people as well. If you bring goodwill to it you can have a period of honeymoon tenderness even after fifty years of married life—only there must be no onlookers, or you run the risk of being dubbed an old fool.

So it was a good thing nobody saw us either last night or up to the present moment today. My God! If only one could love like that all one's life without getting too brainless to do anything else besides. That would be in itself a certain sort of ideal.

But why bring in ideals when I feel happy and am anxious for this fresh episode with Zosia to last a long time and not be the final one? Our present life, relying as it does on incessant diplomacy, and based upon the problem as to who shall outwit whom and get the upper hand, wearies me: worse, it hollows out an empty place in my heart which the acrid fumes of reason invade. Sterile criticism of myself and others is becoming a habit with me. It crowds out all enthusiasm and robs me of that capacity for emotion which is the greatest treasure of the human soul. Oh, help! It's not quite so bad as that yet.

And the desire we both feel to take up some good work, over and above our sentiment for each other, proves that this renaissance of my marriage has a deeper source and is not merely limited to the trial of some new way of our life together. Our eye has fallen upon Szmid. Zosia made a big sacrifice here, for she doesn't like Szmid and is rather afraid of him. She defines him tersely as a beggar or a degenerate, and it was only yesterday that I was able to make her understand that he is an unfortunate man who must be helped, and that it's useless to expect any violent change in his relations with people and with the world. I don't know, of course, what she'll think about him tomorrow, for I've never yet come across a woman who was really convinced by so-called arguments; but for the moment she is full of pious desires and is conscientiously shaking out enough of my old garments to clothe several Szmids.

And I—I am thinking over a lodging for that poor unfortunate. Zosia suggested some widow-woman on one of the other floors here, but the plan fell through, and may God deliver me from all ties with this house! But where can I put him? We've no room, and that man can't live with ordinary people. Aha! I have it. The motorist.

November 11th.

He agreed. It appears he knows Szmid from having just missed running him down several times.

"It's better to have him under my roof," he said, "and then he won't keep getting under my wheels on the roads."

He's giving him a quite separate room near his garage, with a bed and heating and light. If I were small-minded I should say he had done it at Zosia's request, but I don't want to be small-minded. I affirm therefore that the motorist is what you call a crank of noble cut who always gives as much as is required of him.

We are going to drive to the park for Szmid this afternoon.

November 12th.

Szmid is by now residing at the motorist's. Yes, residing, though such a thing hasn't happened to him since time immemorial. I must describe how we got him there.

We went for him in the car, Zosia, I, and the motorist. The car stopped at a side entrance to the park, and I went in alone to reconnoitre.

I found Szmid quicker than I expected, in the wood-shed (he seems, by the way, to be ill) and, without saying a word about our plans, started talking of one thing and another, cautiously steering by roundabout ways to the subject of a lodging. Here I encountered my first difficulty, for Szmid was loud in praise of his shake-down in the park.

"You may not believe it, Stach, but it's like living in Paradise. Nobody interferes with me, I do whatever I like, and they can't chuck me out. If I cared about it, I'd even put in a stove. But I don't like stoves, they smoke so."

I clutched at that stove like a life-belt, and started to convince Szmid that there were nevertheless better dwellings than his.

"Oh, there are!" he agreed after some thought. "D'you know, when I was at school, my father took me to Vienna, and we went to Laksenburg, where the Emperor Franz Joseph lived. Have you ever seen it, Stach? Have you? Well, you'll agree with me that he had a splendid dwelling there."

He got away from me like this two or three times, and I don't know till now if he was making a fool of me or whether he was afraid of being made a fool of. I got impatient at last and put my cards on the table, asking him straight out if he wouldn't like to live in the house of a friend of mine who has a room to spare. And—would you believe it?— Szmid, instead of pouring out his gratitude as anyone might expect, merely asked in what quarter it was and on what floor, and who was the owner—just like any normal rent-paying citizen.

I described the *locum* in great detail, and defined the motorist as a man almost non-existent. I had to hear Szmid out—he doesn't approve of motoring and has no praise for people who spend their lives outside their homes—but at last I got him to come with me.

A curious thing happened at the park gate. Szmid, scenting a motor and strange people, stopped and asked me who was there. I told him, my wife and the gentleman who was going to put him up. He asked me if we would wait a moment and went off into the garden at a great pace. The "moment" lengthened out beyond a quarter of an hour, and I was just beginning to think that the whole thing had gone to the devil when Szmid came back, out of breath, carrying several beautiful chrysanthemums.

"Lucky, isn't it,"—he whispered gaily in my ear—"that Mikolaj had a few plants left? You understand, Stach, that I—this bouquet. . . . One must always be chivalrous to women."

I understood, as I had understood a good many things that day, though the understanding makes me doubt if our venture with Szmid will be a success. For we forgot, as I am sure we shall always forget, that Szmid's disability doesn't lie only in his having those blood-shot, clouded eyes; Szmid has his whims, his habits, his ideas, his philosophy, and his whole outlook on the world, all different from ours. If one wants to get him to do anything, one is simply obliged to enter into his thoughts and feelings.

But the world that surrounds me, the world nearest to me, Zosia, Klapa and his wife, Felix, and everybody else—isn't it a gallery of just such Szmids?

There is uninterrupted harmony between Zosia and me, and we are on affectionate and delightful terms—sometimes even ardent terms—with each other. But my story suffers by it. I haven't been able to write a single word for two days.

November 15th.

I'm afraid I've been a fool. I've read my novel, as far as I've got, to Zosia. I acted on the hypothesis that she had seen it already, or anyway most of it, so that there was no sense in keeping it dark. The hypothesis was fundamentally faulty, for if she had read it, why upset her over again? But I'm subject now and then to attacks of "high-minded" frankness, which, while they dazzle me at the first blush, generally turn out in the long run to have been nothing but unnecessary chatter.

Zosia bore up under it valiantly; she evidently wants to maintain this unexpected high temperature between us. And her comments on the tale were very much to the point. She described it as splendid in some places, but pointed out weak spots here and there, and she was right as usual.

At last she sighed and kissed me, rather apathetically, but sincerely. And she called me her "poor great man." A very pretty conjunction, that winks at my self-conceit.

And it might all have passed over and left no traces, no results (although wounds to a woman's self-love are said to be of the incurable kind), if it had not been for Felix, who came in with the news that his play has been accepted at the theatre and will be put on in a month or two. Of course he was in an angelic temper. He thanked me for having given him, in time, a "severe but just" criticism, which had helped him to make several changes in the play.

But here Zosia flew at him unexpectedly and with violence. She said the most spiteful things about his play, and when, somewhat stunned, he reminded her that she had liked the thing only the other day, she hissed contemptuously that one's bound to be pleasant to old friends now and then.

In a word, she poured out upon Felix all the rancour that had been accumulating in her while she listened to my story. I beg your pardon, not all. When our friend went off in dudgeon—and convinced, of course, that it was I who had turned Zozia against his work—she asked me what brings Felix here so often and what can be the tie between me and him, calling him a man without character and a writer without talent. "Unless," she added with a gleam in her eyes, "you need Felix as a kind of experimental rabbit for your observations from life. Or as a puppet in your marionette show."

"I don't know what I need Felix for"—I pretended not to see the thrust—"I've never had time to consider it. And I daresay I never shall consider it, since the question also comes in of what Felix needs me for. Or needs you for."

"Me? I don't come in here at all!"

"I dare say you come in a good deal. But, Zosia"—I made an effort and took her hands in mine—"don't let's talk about it. Do you regret that spell of fine weather we've been having?"

She was silent. But I felt a lurking bitterness in her heart that may break out at any moment.

November 16th.

No! Marriage is not a cycle of romances. Everything in it depends on the amount of goodwill one brings to bear. But if there isn't any? If our nerves, those intolerable nerves of ours, refuse to obey? Then we fall back on the trenches of common sense.

My novel is a blessing at such times; it has a queer way of disconnecting me from life. But Zosia? What does Zosia escape to during our long spells of trench warfare?

That thought is for ever haunting me.

    .   .   .   .   .

He had not the slightest doubt that his recall was closely bound up with Judge Szarota and that stepmother. The priest, too, might have pulled some strings in the background; he had a lot of influence with the authorities. And though Tadeusz understood that the clearing up of this question would do nothing towards changing his situation, yet the desire to fight the intrigue and his lust for a personal reckoning gave him no peace. He had rested at the farm, his strength had come back, and after all this time he felt new zest for the battle of life. His furious, ceaseless longing for the girl, made stronger perhaps by the thought of Ignacy staying on at the farm, was a powerful goad.

Meanwhile the question was solved quite easily and entirely as one might have expected. The posts of camp secretaries were now filled by war prisoners, and from these he learned without any difficulty that his recall had been by order of the military commander. He next nosed about in the "war chancellery," where prisoner comrades were also installed by now. And he was told that the matter had been instigated by the priest and by a certain Judge Szarota, a near relative of the "Staff." He asked nothing further. As he might have known, he was up against a conspiracy of powerful people—all-powerful, in view of his own abject situation. The discovery would not have upset and disheartened him if it had not been for the great change in his relations with the girl. He had won a moral safe-conduct for dealing with the people about him, if only on the principle of reprisals for the wrongs he had suffered; but he felt restrained by scruples that bit the deeper into his soul the more he rushed towards life.

The pile of letters found on his return from the steppe were like a deliberate reminder of his difficult position. Things were going badly with his wife. Her hard struggle for existence was visible between the lines of every page. Reading her letters, he could not shake off the thought that he might have acted more like other men in captivity—here accepted his officer's pay and even have earned something over, as so many did, and have sent his wife a little money for a rainy day.

Then the child. It had been through a severe illness and had been saved "by a miracle." He had never seen it and could not picture it, and yet he read every allusion to it eagerly and with deep feeling. He realized that beyond the sphere of formal obligations there were duties of kinship which played a strong mysterious role in life and would have much to say in the time now ahead of him.

After thinking it all over—quickly, feverishly, with a passion dictated by his heart's awakened rhythm—he decided to fold his arms for the time being and wait. He had a strong ally in the rushing torrent of life, which had so often brought him an unexpected unravelling of the most complicated situations.

November 18th.

I must find some way of protecting Szmid from my friends' philanthropy, for the affair has been bruited about, and people have gone dotty over it. Klapa rushed in with a plan for calling a consultation of doctors to examine his eyesight; and Felix is organizing a benefit performance, with recitations from his own works, for Szmid. Charitable people have taken to Szmid's room as a goal for their pilgrimages. Luckily, he's never at home, for he only turns up there for the night, and then at all hours.

So I mitigate and pacify and soothe, and when that doesn't act I take refuge in rudeness. And I explain to everyone that, even if it were possible to turn Szmid into a normal being, we must first consider whether he wouldn't greatly lose by it. The chief principle should be—not my way, but Szmid's way. This unthinking endeavour to make other people happy after one's own fashion is a positive curse to the world.

Zosia was the first to back out of the general chorus of pity that has broken loose over Szmid. Somehow, and through some agency known to women alone, she discovered that Szmid sold the clothes he had been given and bought cakes with the money. These he carried off and ate somewhere out of his home.

This opens up the possibility that he may carry off and sell something belonging to the motorist. And how shall we look then?

I listen to all this and to much else of the same kind and am dumb. Since Felix's visit and our unfinished talk Zosia has been possessed by a perfect ecstasy of criticism which embraces simply everything. Today, for instance, she grumbled at the tram for making a noise in front of our house, though we've been living here for two years and the tram has never bothered us. Tomorrow she will be angry with the sun for rising at 7.30 and not at 7.35. The day after she will have a down on strawberries for ripening in June instead of November.

Joking apart, even if a woman simply can't reconcile herself to the fact that two and two make four and there's no help for it, one can't draw any conclusions from that. She must be loved, loved, and loved, and then she'll forget about trams, astronomy, and mathematics. After all, she only takes up these things through or for somebody else.

．　　．　　．　　．　　．

The long days of waiting for the girl's answer were made still longer by his unrest and by a strange feeling of impatience which hampered him in spite of his increased strength. All his calculations were upset by his getting no reply from her. He wrote again, and this time his letter was longer, and, as if in defiance of his doubts, warmer. He was just starting a third letter full of bitter reproaches when the idea came over him that his correspondence was possibly subject to the same machinations that had torn him from the farm.

This time he followed the beaten track of inquiry to the post censorship, and there he found out that the commander himself took away his letters for inspection.

He entered into no further details and went, very embittered, to call on the parish priest at the presbytery.

But it was some time before he confronted that pious countenance. The priest was engaged, and as soon as he had finished saying Vespers he was summoned to the prison camp hospital. Anyway that was what the sexton said, looking with suspicion upon Tadeusz as he walked up and down the audience room, as impatient as a caged wolf. It transpired that the priest had driven straight from the hospital to some of

*his parishioners, but Tadeusz never thought of giving in,
though night was drawing on and together with it the hour
at which he ought to be in camp.*

*Late in the evening he heard heavy steps in the corridor.
He ran impatiently to the door and collided with the powerful figure of the priest.*

*"Good evening, Father!" He made way politely, his one
desire being to get the priest inside the room. "May Jesus
Christ be praised!"[1] he added, with a touch of irony.*

*"For ever and ever!" responded the priest. "Who is it?"
peering at him.*

*"Don't you remember, Father? We met at the Radzie-
jowska's farm."*

*"Ah-h!" cried the priest, with a sigh of such deep affliction
that Tadeusz had no more doubts that he had come to the
right place.*

*"Won't you sit down, Father?" He suddenly felt sure of
himself and dropped into the first chair to hand. "As you
recognized me so easily, perhaps you'll guess why I have
come."*

*"Directly, directly," returned the priest automatically.
"But"—he looked at his watch—"you ought to be in camp at
this hour."*

*"If it comes to that," Tadeusz cut in malignantly, "I
ought rather to be on the Radziejowska's farm at this very
moment. But I realize that it's the same there as here, one
omnipotent word from you——" he broke off, arrested by
signs of dissent.*

[1] A greeting formerly in universal use, now employed only by the country
clergy and by peasants.

"Not so fast!" panted the priest. "You're overhasty. Who can say what's for the best? Well, well, let's talk it over." He spread himself out in his chair and folded his hands on his stomach.

"Of course you've come about Marusia," he began after a moment. "You're much upset, no doubt," he added, looking attentively at Tadeusz with a calmer expression.

"My being upset doesn't matter——" responded Tadeusz in a hard voice. "We are not children, Father. This is a case of facts."

"Just so! It's your recall from the farm, no doubt."

"Oh, that too, though it's a bit late in the day for that question. Just now I am more concerned with Marusia's letters. Don't you know, Father, who it is that steals them?" He used this harsh expression deliberately, for the priest's imperturbability irritated him.

But the priest was not to be put off.

"There, didn't I say that you were upset?" and he twisted in his chair. "You've no reason to be. For though, mind you"—he wiped his forehead—"the letters are actually here in my house—two; one came yesterday—they've not been opened by anyone. The person who brought them——"

"Judge Szarota!"

"And if it was! Anyway, he had no intention of opening them. I don't mind telling you for a fact that I was going to take them back to Marusia. And now you know all there is to it. All the better. All the better." His eyes wandered about the room, but he kept glancing attentively at Tadeusz. "Wouldn't you like to speak with me quite frankly?" he asked unexpectedly.

"*Certainly!*" *Tadeusz consented none too willingly. Something urged him towards that conversation and something held him back from it, for, judging by the priest's manner, it aimed further than the mere question of the letters. He was unprepared for it, and this very fact made him curious as to how far their talk would go.*

"*Well, now*"—*the priest went straight to the point*—"*please tell me what are your intentions in regard to Marusia.*"

Tadeusz was disagreeably startled. This somewhat churlish question, designed to unravel the problem at the very outset of the conversation, was like a flung stone. He had no mind to unbosom himself so quickly.

"*First of all*," *he answered after a moment's silence*, "*I should like to get Marusia out of that place. To take her away to Poland, to Europe, you understand—to the sphere she belongs to.*"

"*Excuse me! You want to take her away—and in what capacity?*"

"*Well, not as luggage, anyway!*" *exclaimed Tadeusz.*

"*You don't try to understand me, and you said we were going to speak quite frankly*," *grieved the priest.* "*Perhaps you would rather not go on with this?*"

"*No, on the contrary. Only be a little patient, Father, and explain exactly what you mean*," *he prevaricated, anxious to gain time for reflection.*

"*Oh, I'll explain, though it seems to me simple enough, Heaven knows. You say you want to take Marusia away. Well, so I ask 'in what capacity?' For she can't go alone, ignorant of the world as she is; and who knows if her father would allow it?"*

"Well, but she is of age——"

"Pooh! of age! Something more than that comes in here. Even, mind you—well, even if you had the very best intentions, we must think of the girl's good name. In these out-of-the-world places"—he grew animated—"we attach great weight to these things. And it can't be otherwise. We are among foreigners. Here, either a man holds firmly to his God or else he simply goes to pieces and becomes the scorn of his own compatriots and of other people. If you had lived half a century here, as I have! You new arrivals get angry with us and find us old-fashioned or even perhaps half-crazy," he went on with increasing fire, "but we were very different when we came out here from what we are today. Half of us are exiles, men for whom even your wise enlightened world was too far from perfection. You probably think nothing of Judge Szarota. I admit he's a dried-up, caustic sort of man. And yet he was sent here for revolutionary conspiracy."

"Szarota?" Tadeusz was amazed.

"Yes! My dear sir, he rotted in prison for two years and then had five years of deportation. But I'm getting off the point. Well, so we people here are used to simple and established relations between people. And where a woman is concerned—a young lady—an orphan——"

Tadeusz listened to the priest, deeply interested. The indignation, mistrust, and eagerness to pick a quarrel with which he had come to the presbytery gave way before the reflection that he ought to arrive at an understanding with this upright man.

"*You would like to know, Father*"—he made up his mind to probe the raw spot at once—"*what is my attitude towards Marusia?*"

"*Not necessarily—but if you will be so good——*"

"*Well, I'm in love with her.*"

"*Aha!—and what more?*"

"*Wait a bit, Father. I've the impression, we may say the certainty, that Marusia is in love with me too. It can't be helped, Father*"—he smiled, seeing the priest wave his hand as if to ward off the words—"*you must reconcile yourself to this state of things, just as I and Marusia have had to do. It's simply happened, without anybody wanting it. If you know Marusia, Father, you must realize that it's no trifling matter. And when I think about the consequences——*"

"*That's just what I wanted to ask you——*"

"*Well, to tell you the truth, I don't yet know what I'm going to do. It's a difficult situation, and it's bound to mean serious trouble. The first thing I must do is to regulate my position in regard to my wife. There will have to be a divorce, no doubt.*" He was amazed at the facility with which he was arriving at conclusions which had seemed so far off yesterday.

"*You will abandon your wife—over there?*" said the priest shocked.

"*God forbid! I couldn't do that, if only from principles of the simplest honesty—which are not unknown to us either, Father, I assure you. In reality, I ought to go back to Poland and put the matter through there. But to escape is unfortunately a difficult and dangerous business—and then on the other hand I'm afraid to leave Marusia alone. You know, Father, that the times are becoming awfully unsafe.*"

"*Oh, yes! one hears the strangest things.*"

"*Taking all these considerations into account, it's clear that I've a difficult job before me, and,*" he concluded with emphasis, "*I'd rather nobody interfered with me over it. Otherwise something may happen against my will—and against yours too, no doubt.*"

They fell silent. Grief and worry had knotted the priest's brow, making its bumps and wrinkles more numerous than before.

"*It's a bad business!*" he said at last, partly to himself. "*A very bad business! Worse than I thought. And wouldn't it be better*"—he looked at Tadeusz inquiringly—"*for you to try going right away somewhere, to some distant part of Siberia? I'd arrange it for you and pick you out some nice healthy spot. I might even be able to get you freed from all supervision. Hang it all, we'd even give you the documents of a citizen of this country. For it's simply a terrible misfortune, my dear sir!*"

"*Of course it is! But what about Marusia?*"

"*What? Oh, she'll maybe forget——*"

"*D'you think so, Father?*"

"*She'll worry through it.*"

"*Oh, but why? Is she to blame? Do you think it's fair that she should be a victim all her life? Isn't it enough, what she's been through up to now?*"

The priest's brain grew more and more puzzled under his clouded forehead. Time after time his broad hand passed over the knots on his brow and fell back helplessly on the arm of his chair.

"Are you quite sure that she cares for you?" he muttered in indecision.

"As God's in heaven!" Tadeusz burst into rapturous laughter. Into the dim light of this difficult conversation, which was like an unknown forest where he wandered wearily in torment and alarm, fell that one truth, clear and infallible, a ray of sunshine. He suddenly felt sure of himself, and going over to the worried priest, smiled at him consolingly.

"There's no help for it, Father. It's a very hard nut to crack. But these are such beastly times that nothing can happen in the usual way. Well—are you going to give me those letters?"

"I could, certainly—but what will happen next?"

"Time will show."

"What do you mean, time? Well, yes, it is all in the hands of God. But perhaps you will promise me something."

"You want to lay down conditions? I'm listening."

"Oh, not conditions. I appeal to your goodwill. You won't do her any wrong, my dear fellow?"

"Wrong?" whispered Tadeusz. *"Who ever could have the heart to do her wrong?"*

As he said this his soul was flooded by some bitter sorrow and foreboding of disaster. Something like shame forced him to seek comfort in the priest's eyes. But the priest, depressed and resigned, was looking at the ground.

A moment later he got up heavily from his chair, opened a secret recess, and handed Tadeusz two letters.

They separated without another word.

I think there's a good deal of expression and what people call "truth" in this unexpected ending. That piece of dialogue hangs together, too, and might figure in any decent novel. It comes out a bit long, I admit, for the terse repressed style I've been using up to now. But it doesn't matter. Perhaps when I'm making the fair copy I shall alter some of the other parts.

It has come into my mind that if the priest were young and in love with Marusia the book would gain in expression and the plot be stronger. But then that world of upright people really did exist, and such a short time ago; and it must have its testimonial, in spite of the axiom that in literature, as in Heaven, there is more joy over one sinner than over a hundred of the just.

November 24th.

It's snowing. It began in the night. When I opened my eyes, I saw through the window falling rime-stars, and roofs covered smooth and white with snow. I think one's soul responds to the first snow-fall more than to anything else in the whole year. Where the idea came from of four seasons I don't know. It must either have arisen in the cells of wise men, or else in southern countries where snow never falls. We know only two seasons here. One has a triple name—spring, summer, and autumn; and the other is called winter. That fantastic term, so unlike anything else, "the first snow-fall," marks a boundary no less expressive and inexorable than death itself.

But it's very weird that Szmid should have chosen today

of all days for taking up his goods and chattels and leaving the motorist's house. No one knows where he's moved to.

November 25th.

Oh, damn! I'm not myself today. It keeps on snowing, and the white shroud over the town is getting deeper and deeper. It's foggy too—you can hardly see the houses opposite. The people mooning about the streets look tired and gloomy and half-asleep. For some reason or other everybody has too much time on his hands. Work is at a standstill in offices, trams run late, cabs stand empty before public-houses. Even the street lamps were lighted later than usual, though it's so dark that they really ought to have been burning all day.

I hate these pauses in life's tempo. The only salvation for our generation, which has nothing to think about, nothing to say, and nothing to digest, is to go ahead and live and whirr, whirr, whirr like a machine run mad, without a stop, without reflection, in mortal terror of the problems we haven't the courage to face. On and on, in the feverish hope that something will come of it, something live after us to redeem us, something by which others will live!

But we ourselves—will anyone reward our labours? Will anyone lighten the darkness of the world in process of transformation?

November 26th.

Someone has turned up to lighten it—Felix! At this moment of horrible blues he has sent us a written invitation to a rehearsal of his play. Go up top, Felix! There is something about his modest, infallible ordinariness that you can always rely on, and that has even a style of its own. I am gradually beginning to understand why I need Felix in my life, and where our friendship comes from.

The idea of the rehearsal put me and Zosia in a good temper at once. We went an hour too early, as if we anticipated an unusually delightful evening.

The theatre was nearly full. Felix had asked everyone he knows, and that means everyone we know too. I repeat, the place was nearly full. Bowing right and left (Zosia knows how to do this with the expression of a well-known author's wife), I took my place in a box just as a monkey squats down on the top of a palm-tree, among a crowd of other howling apes. There's nothing like being surrounded by your own kind.

The play itself affected me quite differently this time. Not as a play, for it's very weak, although Felix really has re-written it and changed it into a kind of knightly tourney between himself, me, and Marusia. Without rhyme or reason, they all love each other, make sacrifices for each other, and go off at last on their several ways, with much inward satisfaction, to the four corners of the earth. The steppe remains after them, abloom with flowers.

Taking it all round, it is really worse than his first idea.

And yet—and yet, when the curtain went up on the steppe with the farm slumbering beside it, for a moment I could not breathe. A fragment of life rose up before me, tragically incomplete, wrapped about with the sweet spell of those early days when things might still have been different. I forgot everything for a while. My thoughts flew backwards and I plunged with all my soul into the past. Oh, my God! There was a moment when I felt with the strength of my heart of years ago—so many years ago.

"My" people recalled me to myself.

"What's the matter with you?" It was Helena taking my hand.

"Memories!" answered Zosia, sarcastically. "Everything that has any connexion with his prison life upsets Stach dreadfully. And the steppe!" she smiled wanly.

The heroine who played Marusia did the rest. In the first place she wasn't in costume; secondly, she was absolutely unlike Marusia; thirdly, she brought an atmosphere on to the stage that was something between a dance-hall and a basement dwelling.

So I came to myself. But it left a dead weight in my heart which I simply had to drown in drink.

It was lucky that everybody else developed a need to get tight at that weird rehearsal.

Ergo, a small group of us went to a restaurant for supper, and after supper to the Klapas for coffee. We rather overdid the drinking. Then we danced, Zosia with Felix (the motorist doesn't dance) and I with Helena. Some demon possessed me, and I held her so close that where our bodies touched it seemed as if we had nothing on. I bent her over backwards, clasped her, and loosed her again in time to the music, with embraces that would have been quite inadmissible even with an experienced dance-hall "vamp"—not to speak of that fragile creature.

And yet the fragile creature displayed more endurance than myself, and actually the longer we danced and the greater the liberties I took with her, the bolder and freer became her movements . . . and the happier and more drunken her eyes. At last I held in my arms an element of burning passion, uncannily alluring.

She tired me out in the end, and she must have been tired too. For in the last dance, somewhere towards morning, her body grew limp and her eyes clouded. But she still kept them fixed upon my lips as if waiting for the decisive word which really ought to have come as a winding up if we had been healthy people.

But I kept my teeth clenched.

"You are lost!" I whispered at last, looking into her sleep-walking eyes.

"I don't care! . . . Destroy me! I love you, love you," she answered, wrapping me about with the magic of the dance.

Fie! What a witches' sabbath!

For the first time Klapa said good-bye to me dejectedly.

November 27th.

And today I'm a bear with a sore head. That frenzied *saltomortale* which we modern people take from one vital situation to another, from one state of mind to another, needs the constitution of a horse and the nerves of a bull. A crazy, bewitched kaleidoscope! After all, when you've only one life you can't live a hundred times over and differently every time.

All the same, I've noticed that women come through such things far more easily than men. Zosia has been singing all day like a lark; and when we met Helena in the street this afternoon she was radiating spring, as if she'd been on a May outing. According to them, we had a "frightfully jolly" time last night.

The world is upside down and humanity is drawing to its end. For if the women are all going to turn into harlots, the world will go to the devil, for the simple reason that it'll be beyond us men to satisfy them.

November 30th.

Marusia's first letter:—

"Dear Tadeusz:

"I really don't know what to write in answer to your letter. The change has been so sudden that I simply can't think or talk, and I just live from day to day as if I were under a spell. I'm so afraid of what will happen now. But no! nothing will happen. It can't. And I'm sad again, because it can't.

"When you had gone I was dreadfully ashamed of—you know! I couldn't look at anybody, and I minded Monsieur Ignacy most of all. It's better now, since your letter came. But is it true that you don't think badly of me? For it was all my fault, only mine.

"You ask me what I have in my heart for you. And I beg you not to ask. Don't be angry, my dear Tadeusz.

"But please write again. I read your letter all in a breath. I wear it on my heart, I won't be separated from it till—but I can't write.

*   "Marusia."*

Marusia's second letter:—

"*My dear Tadeusz:*

"*Another letter from you, and I see you never got my answer. I'm so very sorry, for I put everything I could into it, and I shouldn't be able to write it over again. Perhaps it is just as well you didn't get it.*

"*It's horrid at the farm. We wander about like lost sheep and everything goes anyhow. Monsieur Ignacy has changed in such a funny way. Sometimes he's cross, and then again he's quite jolly. I can't understand him, he's somehow different from us all.*

"*And we miss you. If you could only see Jurek. He's as sullen as a wolf, and goes about with clenched fists. We simply daren't speak to him. But he's never been so kind to me before. The other day when I ran off to the river—to that place, you remember—he came after me and told me not to be sad, because he was going to make everything come right. Funny boy! I'm grateful to him for his good heart, but I don't see any way out.*

"*And please don't try to find one, Tadeusz. Because I—I never—not for anything, against your wife.*

"*Only I don't want to part with you in such a way as we were parted.*

"*That wild rose bush you brought in from the steppe all dried up, but I planted it in the garden and it has blossomed so beautifully. I stroke its leaves . . . and somehow I understand you quite differently now.*

"Marusia."

.   .   .   .   .

I read this over and I wonder—is it possible that only a few years ago someone spoke to me in such a way, that there were people near and dear to me? . . . No, my friend, don't be so upset. For really in essence there's no difference between those letters and Helena's "Destroy me, I love you!"

But there is a difference, for I loved Marusia and I don't love Helena. . . . Full stop.

As to the letters themselves, I think they're not bad, though one instead of two might be more effective. But I've still got to tell how and when and where they were written. Unluckily prose has rules that are often horribly burdensome.

December 1st.

Six months went by, and Tadeusz was still in camp, living in his solitary hut. The loneliness that he found so hateful at the outset had flung its great wings about him and borne him away from the field where fate played havoc with humanity. He understood the blessing of the closed camp fences and of his own four closed walls.

No one interfered with him. Judge Szarota had gone back to his distant steppe, no better off than when he came; the priest, whom Tadeusz saw at the presbytery every Sunday, had nothing to say to him and, greeting him with a kindly smile, seemed to express a quiet satisfaction in him. Now and then his companions dragged him to a noisy meeting of the emigrant colony. Here he met Madame Kamila and took the opportunity of finding out whether she had any new plans in regard to Marusia. She told him that she had given up "all that," having more important matters in hand. The part

*which she played in the little world of emigrants' committees,
and the evident pleasure it gave her, made him feel sure there
was nothing brewing from that quarter. And he stopped
going to the meetings, put off by the futility of these exiles
and all their works.*

*Regularly once a week he sent a letter to Marusia, telling
her all he thought and felt in his solitude, hiding nothing
and passing nothing over, laying bare his soul. And though
every word of these long letters, written through whole days
and nights, signified "I love you," nevertheless the words ran
into thousands and every word had its own weight, its own
meaning.*

*With equal regularity came the girl's replies, only her
letters were short and almost ordinary. Once she asked him
to forgive her if she left off writing about things "that make
one's heart ache"; and after that she only described the daily
happenings at the farm. But she always ended by saying
"Please don't forget to write."*

*So that their correspondence became like a conversation
between two people of whom one opens his heart while the
other says "I'm listening." Tadeusz suffered a good deal
before he got used to this state of things. He tried to break
down the girl's obstinate silence, and in one letter reproached
her bitterly. Her sad and despairing answer pulled him together. He realized that it could not be otherwise, and submitted, yielding utterly, as time went on, to the powerful
spell of their conversation.*

*And he found more and more to say, though nothing was
asked, nothing demanded. The mass of undigested observations and experiences that had been gathering in his mind*

*during the past few years—years in which he had forbidden
himself to think or feel—now found outlet in words, and
through his letters the whole world spoke to the girl. And
although he was seized at times by a doubt as to whether he
was not blinding her to the more essential aspects of her situation by flooding her with his mature and tempting thoughts,
yet her every fresh—and, as he felt instinctively, more eager
—"I am listening" spurred him to further, deeper, and still
more unfettered confessions.*

*With time this grew to be the only thing he lived for. And
the pile of unread letters from home grew higher on his table,
while beyond the camp walls a fresh storm was gathering to
change the history of the world.*

December 2nd.

Klapa called on me today at the office, and suggested our
going out "for a snack." "Why not?"—he rubbed his bony
hands, acting the blood, in the come-along-old-chap-let's-
have-a-drink style. His joints cracked, his eyes twinkled, he
made the weirdest faces. Poor Klapa! Something had gone
wrong with him, and all his stops had struck work. He even
forgot about his "firstly" . . . "secondly."

We went to a well-known bar where at all hours you can
see distinguished citizens practising the national rite of
drowning their errant wits. A fabulous place, stiff with tra-
dition. Who hasn't been drunk there, my God! They say
that all the ghosts from the tombs of the deserving assemble
there o' nights.

Klapa, acting on the advice of the bar attendant, ordered

two vodkas of the larger and stronger kind. We drank them, and he choked horribly, for he can't stand alcohol. Under the inquiring glances directed at him by the dignitaries bivouacking in the place, the poor devil fled in confusion to a table in the corner, but he ordered another round of drinks. We drank them. He ordered a third and something from the buffet.

I made up my mind to put an end to this, for the Professor's courage in the drink line savoured of a sad ending. And there was another thing. I hadn't the least intention of letting him touch upon his hopeless reasons for dragging me out to this place. Before he had managed to force down his third glassful I caught hold of his arm.

"Professor!" I said, "have you ever gone home drunk?"

It acted. He dropped his arm, pushed the liqueur-glass slowly away, and looked at me with amazement.

"No, never!" he replied.

"Well, then, don't drink any more."

He wasn't far gone, for he obeyed me at once.

"You're right!" he said more cheerfully, and the eyes he fixed on mine grew brighter. "For that matter, I know you wish me well. There are very few people like you. But that's just——"

At that "just" I went off to pay the bill, and we left the place arm in arm. I wanted to say good-bye at the first corner, but he expressed a desire to see me back to my office. On the way he spoke with animation about a new scientific work he was writing, and pressed his thin arm in a friendly way against me. Then he grew pensive. His arm relaxed and hung helplessly on mine.

In the doorway he looked at me from under his brows.
"I know," he repeated half to himself, "that you're not like
other men. But that's just——" he brandished his arm and
went off stooping down the street.

He made me both sorry and angry. What did he want?
What can I do to help or advise him?

Oh, Professor! You have had, firstly, science; secondly,
the God-fearing Helena; thirdly, curios; fourthly, a good
digestion; and fifty other "—— lies!"—and when just one
of them is lacking, you come unwound like a watch without
a cogwheel. But one "firstly" must be able to get along with
a broken cogwheel. The chief thing, Professor, is the spring!

December 3rd.

Anybody reading that last bit of my diary would call me
a cynic. I should be much more readily forgiven if I had got
the Professor tight, drunk *Bruderschaft* with him, gone
home with him to Helena, and seized some opportunity to
pinch her in the calf of her leg. Then they would call me a
gay dog.

The world is coming to an end! I've begun to analyse my
own diary.

December 4th.

No! one can't behave like that with people. I've made a
sort of pawn of Klapa and pushed him on to the chess-board
—whereas he's a man, who thinks and feels and suffers. It's
just the same with Helena and Felix and—to some extent—
Zosia. Sometimes I'm terrified when I look at my life and
consider my relations to people. I get to know them better

and better, and they come to like me and even grow quite fond of me, but I only become more lonely. There's something in me that attracts them and something that keeps them off.

What will happen when I've estranged everybody in turn and find myself quite alone in the world?

.   .   .   .   .

One week no letter came from Marusia. Tadeusz felt it terribly and became very uneasy. Of course it might be caused by innumerable reasons which had nothing to do with the girl; but there had lately been a note of hidden suffering in Marusia's letters. And that last postscript—"I have had distressing news, and I don't quite know what to do next"!

Tormented by uncertainty, he wrote a doubly long and ardent letter. And had no answer to it. He tried again, and when his letter brought no echo from the steppe, he sent a telegram. A few days later came the answer:—

"Forgive me—Monsieur Ignacy will explain."

Ignacy turned up at the camp soon after the telegram. His scared face and the ceremonious way in which he greeted Tadeusz showed that his mission was a depressing one. And you could see he was in no hurry to come to it. He lengthened out the formalities of camp registration beyond all custom and need, and then rushed to the barracks under the pretence of shaking hands with his friends. At last, Tadeusz, in a furious temper, got him by the arm, and dragged him almost by main force to his hut.

"Tell me what's happened at the farm!" he attacked him, without any introduction.

"Nothing special! You needn't get the wind up!" Ignacy

twisted about on the edge of the plank-bed. "We really ought to discuss the thing thoroughly——"

"Oh, I think we can come down to it right off. If only you'd speak to the point——"

Ignacy glanced at his friend with pity that concealed misgiving, and settled himself more comfortably on the bed.

"You want to know about those letters, I suppose," *he drawled lazily.*

"You've guessed it, old man. I want to know about those letters. I want to awfully. All the more, because——" *he looked on the table and took up the telegram, with the idea of reading it to Ignacy and clearing up the situation. But when he glanced from* "Monsieur Ignacy will explain" *to the kindly irony on his friend's face, he folded the paper up and slipped it into his pocket. The knowledge that Ignacy might have come to him with some secret message from Marusia stung him horribly.*

"What's that—a telegram?" *cried Ignacy.* "So you have had news of some sort?"

"Yes. Marusia sent word that you were coming."

"Oh, she sent word, did she?" *For some unknown reason Ignacy seemed pleased.* "Didn't she say anything else?" *He looked hard at the rim of paper sticking out of Tadeusz's pocket.*

"No!" *broke in Tadeusz.* "If she had, I shouldn't be asking you. Tell me about the letters, man!" *he demanded impatiently.* "Don't you know about it? Listen—Marusia has left off writing to me—she used to write every week regularly. I've had no news for a month, and . . . of course, I want to know why."

"*Yes, yes, all right. If that's all you want to know, I can tell you everything. Look here*"—he paused for a moment, smiling with the indulgent grimace of a man who knows through and through the helplessness of his neighbour's position—"*Marusia had a very unpleasant letter about a couple of months ago.*"

"*Who from?*"

"*From her father, my dear chap. Colonel Radziejowski*"—he pronounced the name and title with particular respect, even bowing his head—"*who had received very exact information about us two, and especially about you, categorically forbade Marusia to have anything whatever to do with us. That is, partly with us and—if I'm to be frank—chiefly with you.*"

"*What have I done to merit such a distinction?*" asked Tadeusz, incredulous.

"*Well, really, I couldn't understand either at first. But I've found out that it's because you're married—only I'm not quite sure if I'm right—*" he added quickly, noticing the violent change that came over Tadeusz's face. "*I didn't read the letter—well, you know what I'm like about that sort of thing. Only Marusia dropped a word here and there. She was awfully upset over it——*"

"*Was she? Then she spoke to you about it?*"

"*I give you my word of honour!*"—Ignacy turned unexpectedly crusty—"*Marusia has shown me a great deal of confidence lately, though I haven't been forcing myself on her at all. You know yourself it's not in my nature to do it.*"

"*Of course I know, and I shouldn't dream of doubting it,*" said Tadeusz, "*but we can talk about that later.*" He *ran over in his mind all the possibilities that Ignacy's story suggested. "So the reason she stopped writing was her father's letter! It's not true!" he declared. "There must have been something else. Don't you know anything more?" he looked at his friend sharply.*

"Perhaps I do!" mumbled Ignacy, who seemed offended. "If only you'd let me speak——"

"Oh, go on! I'm listening."

"All right. But I warn you, her father's letter had something to do with it."

"I agree. What next?"

"Next came another letter."

"From her father?"

"No! from somebody else."

"Who?"

"Well—if you will have it! But it's beastly for you——"

"Never mind me, I'm pretty tough."

"Well, then, it was from your wife."

"What?" shouted Tadeusz.

"Your wife—Wanda. Of course I haven't read the letter and I didn't even know about it for some time—but it's enough in itself"—here he choked, disturbed by a violent movement from Tadeusz, who turned away to the window, very pale, with a cloud in his eyes.

"If you only knew how I tried to explain it to her—what a lot of influence I used——"

"That's enough!" Tadeusz interrupted.

"And how she——"

"Shut up! I know."

.   .   .   .   .

I think I shall have to make the first serious deviation from the truth here. That letter was a clever forgery made by mamma Kamila. Zosia, although she knew a little about Marusia at the time, never mentioned the matter to me, and never wrote to Marusia at all. It's always been one of Zosia's unwavering characteristics to avoid anything underhand in her relations with me and with people in general.

But about the story. Magicians of the pen have often built up a novel round the intrigues of shallow women; and if I were actually to exploit the various doings of Madame Kamila I could make a wonderful book. But the drama between Zosia and Marusia is simpler and stronger, and I like it better. What is a novel if it isn't a simplification of life?

December 7th.

Felix's play, *People of Yesterday,* as he has called it, was put on today for the first time. I went to it in a state of inward resignation, listened to it without aversion, and came away without any grouse against Felix. It was bound to be like that. Anticipation and recollection are the worst plagues of humanity. Reality is never so awful or so splendid as we imagine it to be.

The play is middling, or perhaps less than middling, and, judging by certain signs in the audience, it won't have a long run. One of the most grateful spectators was myself. I applauded, and exchanged friendly glances with Felix now and then. Nobody else could have understood the meaning of that white kerchief the heroine had on, in the scene where they are all having supper together at the farm. Marusia always wore one when we gathered round the table after our day's work, and, simple as it was, it made a lovely frame for her girlish face. And then that way she had of always carrying her head a little bent, as if weighed down by thought. Altogether, Felix had managed to copy her outward appearance with extraordinary accuracy of detail, and if the actress had only kept her mouth shut, I should really have had Marusia before me to the life. So that at times the barrier between me and the stage simply vanished, and I found it hard to understand why I, one of the chief actors in the play, couldn't go on to the farm-yard there and direct the action better than it went on the stage—and better than it went in life.

A cloud of acquaintances descended upon us after the performance. A lot of them—perhaps all of them, who knows? —are initiated into the truth of the play, or have at least nosed out a good deal. But the spying glances and questions and half-words that they flung at me like baited hooks fell into a void. I was too deeply moved to let myself be moved. I refused to join the supper party, pretexting urgent work, and handed Zosia over to Felix's care. I'm fed up with that drinking racket which we use to stifle the poverty of our doings.

The winter night was black and cold and damp. As I came along the streets I seemed to be alone with my memories; and I and my memories—that's pretty well I and Marusia. But besides us two there was my native town. There were empty streets and leafless avenues, and alleys and walls with the night murk above them. How alien it all seemed to me! I didn't recognize anything, nor want to admit anything—I was simply surrounded by meaningless, accidental, and importunate things that thrust themselves between me and the girl, just as once before everything had combined to tear her from me.

My stroll soon became an impatient walk. I don't know where or how I found my way to the bridge. I hurried on, for the river drew me. They say it acts on a tormented mind like the sky, or the calm of a forest, or the wide spaces of the sea. And though it is less sublime than they, yet its very unrest drives one to clear and concrete decisions. Everyone knows that it is easier to drown yourself in a canal than to jump into the ocean or to leap into a precipice from mountain tops whose majesty robs even death of its meaning.

That remark, by the way, is purely philosophic. Suicide was not in my mind. I was merely trying to catch the gleam of some happy thought wherewith to blunt the edge of memory.

But there was a man who disturbed me. No, the shadow of a man; a spot or rag of darkness crouched upon a stone seat. I went past, irritated as I always am when anyone invades my solitude. Then I turned back—as I always do. Whatever may be in our minds about the sublime power of the elements, whatever the forces to which we are entrusting our griefs, we turn back from Heaven itself for one word from a fellow-creature.

The solitary shadow on the bench was Szmid, and I felt no surprise at the meeting. He greeted me as calmly as if he'd been waiting for me on the bridge for some time.

"I'm glad to see you, Stach!" he said, with his way of

going straight at a thing. "You've come just when I wanted you. I'm thinking and thinking, and I've nobody to speak to."

"What are you thinking about?"

"Don't laugh. About this stone——" and he struck the bench.

I felt a real link between Szmid's thoughts and my own night wanderings.

"That stone? Do tell me, old man! I'm frightfully curious!"

"Well, how they gouged it alive out of the rock some-where, and rolled it downhill, and beat it with hammers—how they brought it from God knows where and measured it and ground it flat and built it into this bridge. And it makes no protest—just serves . . . it doesn't so much as quiver—serves me—me, you know, a beggar! Such a big strong stone." He nodded his head in amazement.

"All right! but what are you getting at?"

"Well—this whole world—but don't laugh, Stach!—you know, this whole world of ours, living and lifeless, must resign itself to fate, must help itself, must give in. And all that, you see, with humility, in wonder and terror, as I may say, before such forces——"

"Well?"

"As could grind us to dust."

Thus spoke Szmid who is the dust of a man.

December 8th.

It's a pity I can't see Szmid today; I could add a lot to our last night's talk. And I left him without saying a word.

What a pity! I should have hundreds of answers for him today. In the first place:—those forces not only can grind us to dust, but make a rule of doing it. The fact, gloomy enough in itself, is put into the shade by the question when and how we let ourselves be ground. Besides, we ourselves are part of those forces, and the weight and worth of our life depends on how much of them we can take in and multiply and cast away. One man toils all his days over a grain of sand, another throws down and transforms a whole mountain. Woe to him that lets go! The tragedy of existence is a synonym for impotence, my poor Szmid!

That's what I think today, or perhaps only at this early hour before the spell has evaporated that flows into my soul through the windows of my new-awakened eyes. It's the most beautiful moment of the day, in my opinion. What can be lovelier than to alight on earth at the top of one's form in body, brain, and senses? Only it's a pity that we're obliged, during the first few seconds of our morning thoughts, to live through the experiences, regrets, and disappointments of all the years behind us.

I shan't write any more. I can see the dark wings of worries flying at me from every side. They smell fresh meat. This evening I'll write down how much of my liver they've devoured.

Now I'm going to put on my best clothes, as befits this Sunday morning, and take Eva to Church. She's been bothering me to show her God for ever so long.

. . . . .

Since his recall from the farm Tadeusz had been turning slowly in his safe and secret ring of dreams, but now his brain urged him to a rapid decision. While he was talking to Ignacy he had understood in a flash that he must find a way to see the girl in spite of everything. Next day, after the torments of a sleepless night, he made up his mind to go to her at once. He believed the story of his wife's letter—what else could have kept Marusia from writing to him? But the letter was merely a bare hard fact, while the consequences it had brought about in the girl's heart might be manifold. There were no two ways to it—he must go to Marusia, and must go with some clear and simple conclusion and a definite plan of action.

Divorce! In spite of all his inward fear, in spite of the prospect of bitter regrets opened up before him by the thought of abandoning his wife and child, he saw no other way out.

With a heavy heart he read now at last all his wife's neglected letters. Their hard tone, and the bitterness that breathed here and there through the ones last written, confirmd his opinion that she really did know about Marusia.

"All the better!" he thought, going over in his mind all his wife must have felt when she sent those cramped and conscientious epistles.

He came across something like a flash of despair on a card with the child's photograph on it.

"You haven't written us a word for six months, though I know you are alive and doing fairly well. Whatever you may have in your mind, Tadeusz, remember our child, growing up in such poverty and distress. I've always cheered her up with the thought of your return. I don't know what I'm to do now, but I go on hoping that you won't desert us, Tadek."

*He looked hard at the child's likeness. "How she's grown!"
he whispered, astonished to see such a big girl. "Of course,
she's going on to three now. So she really may know something or other about her daddy. Pretty, too!" He went over
all the details of her face and figure.*

*And he was obliged to admit regretfully that the child
looked wan, that her legs were thin, her eyes underlined with
dark circles, and her neck puny, though the full-gathered
dress concealed—perhaps on purpose—the frailness of her
figure. If it hadn't been for the expression of her eyes, which
were bright and alert, and held the gleam of adventurous
dreams, she would have looked quite pitiful. But those eyes!*

*Paternal vanity made him reach out for his mirror. He
looked at himself, but put the glass down with distaste when
he saw the reflection of his own healthy, sunburnt face, which
seemed to have gained in manliness.*

He nailed his daughter's picture above his bed.

.   .   .   .   .

This novel goes from bad to worse in the matter of form
and order. It's extraordinary! I'm getting towards the climax,
and up to now I've always written my climaxes as if they
were a torrent let loose; whereas the tempo of this tale gets
slower and slower. The rhythm is lost, the situations are stiff.
—I still get the dialogue pretty good here and there.

I'm stuck! I swear I'm stuck. Can I be really worked out
as an author?

It can't be helped. The subject wasn't well chosen. This
everlasting collision with one's conscience and the desperate
cautiousness I have to use in the middle of these problems

so near to reality and as yet unsolved by life act like a brake to check and hamper and stifle me.

All the same, I ought to finish it. Mayn't I be allowed to write a bad novel for once?

December 9th.

I didn't find time yesterday to note down a discovery I made in Church. I noticed that Eva is devout. Her rapt face, her eyes fixed upon the altar, her little hands clasped for prayer, all witnessed to something more than may be ascribed to the external impression of the service. I've been struck for a long time by the absorption with which she says her evening prayers. Oh, yes! My small daughter is devout from the bottom of her heart.

But although, as I said, I've felt it for some time, it was only yesterday that I confirmed the fact—and it startled me. The thing would seem to be quite in order. In this epoch of liberal tolerance, when the rule of the day is to understand and consent to everything, can there be anything very astonishing in such a trivial circumstance as my daughter's devoutness? But that's just it:—tolerance goes hand in hand with scepticism, and this scepticism won't let me get reconciled to the idea that a generation, believing with the strength and simplicity of our forefathers, can grow out of us and our ruined foundations of belief.

Perhaps my daughter is an exception? Tolerance says: be it so! and scepticism declares that exceptions do happen. But I, Eva's father, blood of her blood and bone of her bone, feel tormented, for I don't know what to do with the child

now. I can't develop her piety, for where could I find in myself the conviction for it? And if I opposed it, it would mean
loving her with the love of a gorilla. The hopeless idea comes
into my head that I've no other course but to keep up appearances. But no—a thousand times no! I'd rather resign
the role of "bringer-up" entirely, and live at Eva's side without the least pretension to guide her life. And because she's
small, only a tot, not made for life, a fragile scrap of a thing,
I shall help her with a father's arm—no! not a father's! with
my own arm, such as it is. And may she, God, and the world
work out the rest among them.

December 12th.

Klapa is a learned booby, Helena has a screw loose, Felix
is a cipher, Zosia might be something if she had time for it,
Szmid is a mixture of Diogenes and Job, and the motorist—
what's the motorist? I can't classify that man, for all my
trying. I suspect him of being either quite stupid and empty,
or else uncommonly wise and full of inner worth. Don't let
anyone suppose that's a paradox! The soul of the classical
type of blockhead is just as mysterious and undecipherable
and full of incalculable possibilities as the soul of a genius
of wisdom.

But there *is* a paradox in the fact that the motorist is
neither an out-and-out donkey nor a sage, but simply a man
you can't put into any category. I haven't the slightest influence over him, though he's driven into my life in his
hundred-horse-power car and . . . is rather in my way.

I wonder how many magnificent surprises he has in store

for me, that man who brings such heavenly charm to everything he does.

I saw him lately drinking vodka in some low-class pub with his chauffeur, and he really looked like a cherub carrying out some heavenly ambrosial rite. The other day he spilled into the ditch, with the smile of a child, a cart that was on the wrong side. He flirts with my wife in such a nice, enchanting, distinguished manner, so natural and modest and engaging, that I really can't reproach him. Damn it! I'm even on his side, seeing Zosia's caprices and Felix's sullen phiz.

I made the first serious step today up the ladder to the cuckold's (what a horrible word!) pedestal, for I grumbled to Zosia about her unkindness towards the motorist. But I caught myself up quickly and saved the situation. Our conversation is worth putting down, for it may come in handy as material for analysing what happens tomorrow. "Well," I said to her, after one of their usual runs in the motor, when my lady paid for the petrol and smiles and flowers of the motorist by an acid "Thank you": "You really might be a little nicer to him."

The storm that flickered across Zosia's face at this died down immediately.

"You think it would be more proper?"—she flung the word at me with baleful nonchalance.

"Of course!" I answered. "I've always been of the opinion that if one accepts services from anybody—and such a lot of them and such a first-rate sort—one's obliged to make some return."

This remark, which I may call, without self-flattery, an

extremely happy one, would in the normal way have ended our conversation at one blow. But Zosia has lately been displaying a tendency towards serious discussion. She came in with an argument of big calibre:—

"Do you realize what a woman's 'return' generally means?"

"Of course. You can buy him a pair of sleeve-links."

"Don't try to be funny! You know what I mean."

"I know. And"—(a splendid idea came into my head)— "I'll tell you everything I have foreseen about this."

Who could describe the astonishment I saw in Zosia's eyes?

"What?"

"Yes! I've been thinking about you two for a long time, and I more or less realize what's going to happen to you"— I was lying like hell. "I'll tell you if you like."

"Go on, I'm listening," Zosia whispered, somewhat incredulously.

I collected my thoughts and made a highly detailed sketch of Zosia's relations with the motorist. The first part was given up to an analysis of their characters. Zosia listened with bated breath. Then I came to the conflict between me, her, and the child. Zosia turned as white as a sheet. Unluckily, in this place, where, if I had left off on a question mark, I might have won an unheard-of victory such as there's never been yet in the annals of our marriage—in this decisive place I got carried away by literary imagination.

I forgot Zosia, myself, Eva, and the motorist, and produced a fantastic romance full of unexpected turnings—and really not bad at all. I got worked up; I was quite intoxicated.

I was just reaching the climax when Zosia's hearty laughter rang out.

"Why do you interrupt me?" I asked indignantly, not quite sobered.

Zosia went on laughing. Her voice resounded with that jolly deep chest note that always delights me in Eva. I understood what she was after and—laughed too.

"Oh, you old duffer!" Zosia came over and put her arms around my neck. A moment later she was sighing: "But tell me, tell me yourself, how is anyone to live with you?"

December 13th.

The prison camp boiled with excitement. A thousand rumours ran through it from end to end, up and down and round about, day and night. And this was not one of those paroxysms of feverish gossip that broke out from time to time in the camp like a malaria epidemic, and died down suddenly after inflaming it to white heat, leaving a deeper depression than ever. This was news that knocked at doors and windows, sure of itself, arrogant, importunate.

There was no doubt about it. Away beyond the camp walls, beyond the town, beyond the confines of the steppe— far off where the powers of the world were gathered together —something was happening. The home mail, which came quicker and more regularly than usual, spoke of it, was full of mysterious hints and unfinished phrases about great and imminent changes. The newspapers, dull, colourless, but with quivering unrest eloquent between their lines, testified to it. The town, with its manifestation of long suppressed amuse-

ments and its roaring trade, bore witness to it; while the slackening rigour of camp rules brought conviction, for the commanders were absent and the soldiers on guard gave up their supervision of the prisoners and got drunk singly and in companies on the principle, now clear enough, that "something's going to happen."

Yes! . . . something was happening over there, and the camp stirred out of its long sleep and seethed with all the raging hunger of hearts and minds starved upon the barren desert of captivity. The more impatient among the prisoners prophesied a violent revolution, swift and inexorable as a thunderclap, tomorrow, today, at once. Others foretold fundamental changes, incalculable as yet. And even the most cautious, the sceptics of the camp, admitted that things could not go on as they were.

Not one of them could put into words everything that swarmed in his mind, for all their talk. The flash of freedom that ran through the camp in the track of the news passing from lip to lip went to their heads in an indescribable way. But they never lost their burning thirst for vengeance, and all their dreams of liberation started with the defeat and annihilation of the enemy. For some of them Russia was not the enemy they had in mind, for this camp, outwardly composed of so many different elements and cold at heart with hatred, had as many enemies in the world as there were nations at grip in mortal combat.

And so this body of men, long buried in a fetid prison cage, again groped their way towards freedom, caring little if on the threshold of their new life they left the mouldering corpse of the whole world.

The pathos of the language in that bit isn't out of place here. Only I don't like the expression "and so," though it certainly has something final about it, as who should gather the folds of his pilgrim's cloak about his shoulders after reciting a poem and reciting it none too badly. I think it's better to avoid such gesticulations. Let's try and go on. It's not so very late, and I must get ahead with it. I don't want to work, but that's neither here nor there. I've got to want to do it. I must say to myself: "In the morning I go to the office, and in the evening I write my novel. That's my trade."

Let's have a cigarette.

.   .   .   .   .

Tadeusz was the last to creep out of his hole, dragged from it by the force of events on that memorable day when the rumours and prophecies and babbling gossip of the camp encountered a great reality.

This was the manifesto issued by the new revolutionary Government in Petersburg, announcing that the Tsar and his old regime had been dethroned and that the people, in the persons of their "provisional" representatives, had taken over the ruling power. The camp commander himself proclaimed the news to the prisoners at a solemn meeting convoked for the purpose.

Tadeusz had never seen such an unsuccessful ceremony. The captain's voice stumbled helplessly among the break-neck heights of the manifesto, and he was unable to strike a single spark of enthusiasm out of himself or an echo of sympathy from his hearers.

Not for a moment was lessened the gulf between the grey crowd of prisoners scattered about the yard and that camp satrap, the captain, who, soulless and passive though he was, was no worse and no better than many others. The trumpet-calls of liberty, equality, and fraternity resounded over heads bowed by years of slavery, recoiling from the stench of misery, humiliation, disease, and hunger, evoking nothing but ironic laughter and spiteful whispers.

There was a horrible moment after the reading of the manifesto. Thousands of eyes were fixed on the commander to stab him with the question: What now?

The commander hesitated. "Citizens!" he began loftily— and then, glancing round the crowd, fell silent. Suddenly he shouted passionately:—

"Dismiss!"

A double ration of sugar was issued to the prisoners that afternoon.

Tadeusz slipped away at once to the town. He had been perhaps the only one among the exiles whose heart was wrung by the manifesto. Not by its high-flown language, but by its naïve faith in speedy and beneficent changes. He was terribly anxious, for he saw the storm of events on the track of the pale breath of this guiltless and bloodless revolution. He ran through the length and breadth of the town, observing and listening.

At the Soborny Place he came upon a great meeting of citizens. The Governor of the country was reading out the same manifesto that had just been proclaimed in the camp, and his voice and manner reminded Tadeusz of the camp commander.

But the attitude of the crowd of citizens was very different from that of the prisoners. These well-fed people, safe and bursting with jollity in the far rear of the war, greeted the manifesto with contemptuous indifference. A couple of witticisms, a few coarse dialogues, and the crowd moved on in an untidy procession to the Pushkin monument, where some braggart discoursed on the subject of the war, connecting it perfidiously with the dawn of liberty, equality, and fraternity.

But knives were being sharpened in working-class districts and soldiers' barracks. The deeper Tadeusz penetrated into them, the greater the dark revengefulness he read in their eyes and faces. Liberty, equality, and fraternity were met here by the biting derision of men athirst for the uttermost reckoning.

By the time he returned to camp he had decided to take immediate action. He considered for a while the tragic role of that provisional Government on the banks of the distant Neva, with its manifestoes dispersing like smoke over the heads of the citizens.

But he did not dwell upon the thought for long. He was burning to act, to act quickly, to act before others should do it.

Next day he applied at the camp headquarters for a few days' leave on personal business, and gave his word of honour as a guarantee of his return.

To his rage and amazement, however, the leave was refused, and he was sentenced to fourteen days' incarceration in the camp jail.

. . . . .

December 15th.

Zosia and I have been quarrelling ever since dinner. The subject: woman; woman as wife, woman as mother, woman as member of the community.

It came about through a visit from my cousin Alfred and his wife, who are breaking their journey here on their way to Zakopane. Strictly speaking it is only she that is going there to stay—Cousin Alfred is merely taking her up for the Christmas holiday (he has a cheap ticket) and is returning to his job at once, to put in extra work at nights and make up the advance he took for his wife's requirements.

I shouldn't mention this couple if they were not so typical of the times we live in. She in silks and furs, with roses and jewellery—he in a threadbare overcoat, a slovenly jacket, and dirty socks that ruck down into his shoes. She fresh, highly-coloured, with the bloom of an apricot—he as yellow and wrinkled as a lemon. She full of high-flown ideas and artistic aspirations (she asked me what I was writing)—he weighed down by earthly cares (he asked me how much money I made). She the flower—he the stalk: she *le chic*— he stinking poverty; she the butterfly—he the beast of burden.

But out of the two nothings I prefer Alfred, though I'd like to give him a thrashing. For there's something remarkable about the utter resignation with which that idiot sacrifices himself for the monstrous ballast Fate has given him in the shape of Alfredowa.[1]

And she? A more shameless creature I never saw in my

---

[1] "Alfredowa" (pron. "-ova"), as we say "Mrs. Alfred."

life! She considers herself a model wife, but she's just as strong in her belief that she could be a first-class harlot; she "adores" her children—and she curses the moment in which they were born; she thinks she has a right to everything, a voice in everything—but she doesn't know the value of things and can't do anything.

In a word, she's simply nothing as a wife, and one can't imagine her in any other capacity, though her whole personality quivers with the longing to play some part in a larger repertory.

And this was just where I found an analogy between Alfredowa and nearly all the other ladies of the intelligentsia. I don't know when or where or how arose the myth about the "Polish mother" and the "Polish wife." If she ever existed, it was in the past. The type of woman that has arisen in her place can do everything and can't do anything—her pretensions are enormous and her possibilities nil; she wants to use life without creating it. In her own estimation wronged and unappreciated, she flings the responsibility for her incompetence upon the first creature to hand, who is generally her husband; and then her unscrupulousness knows no limit. She is in every sense of the word unproductive—even in her love affairs she exchanges the bed for the dancing-hall.

I got worked up and told my thoughts to Zosia. She retorted fiercely, with just those feminine arguments that give you nothing to take hold of and of which the essence lies in their million-fold contradictions. First she said I had no business to meddle between Alfred and his wife. Then she called Alfred a duffer and a good-for-nothing, and declared that if he has made some sort of a career it is entirely

owing to the efforts and skill of Alfredowa, and that something is due to her, too, for it. (I wonder what is due to
Alfred.) Of course she couldn't go to bars or to his whist
with him. (So Alfred does get his due.)

And she advised me to keep my hands off the Polish
mother and Polish wife, for we owe our national existence
to them. And I had better keep quiet about our modern
woman, because she's the only thing in our country worth
talking about. (Well done, Zosia! You got in a good argument that time!)

And anyway, a man has the wife he deserves.

But I caught Zosia out here.

"In a word," I said, "you renounce equal rights."

"How?"

"By putting the responsibility on to us. Did you ever hear
of a man being worth as much as his wife?"

"It does happen."

"Yes! It does happen. But you admit yourself that those
are painful exceptions. Generally a man is still able to answer
for himself."

"What has that got to do with equal rights?"

"Oh, heaps. You can't take advantage of the privileges
of the female while you're reaching out for the rights of the
male."

Zosia, reflected, a smile of mischievous irony on her lips.

"You can!" she said at last with conviction.

It's no good talking to her. She doesn't want the goat to
be eaten and would like the wolf to live by the Holy Ghost.

.   .   .   .   .

December 16th.

He stood at the farm gates, looking about the empty yard where a frosty wind was dancing. Only a short distance separated him now from the tight-shut door of the house. But he was in no hurry, though his frozen limbs longed for warmth and his body, worn out by a fortnight's march, for rest. Behind those closed doors a broad bench and a warm fire awaited him, and something else as well—the kindly care of people very dear to him, and the warm heart of a girl. He only had to stretch his hand out. But he was in no hurry.

Here, at the goal of his pilgrimage, he felt abashed and anxious. He had been another man when he broke out of jail, evaded the sentry, and made his way across the frozen wilderness among a thousand difficulties and dangers. There was only one more step to take, and he could not take it. The frost pierced him through and through, he was terribly hungry, his heart quivered at the hope of seeing the girl—but all these things made no difference. He stood at the gate motionless, timid, full of fear. His eyes ran over the yard a hundred times seeking something to encourage him and draw him on, to remind him of his old rights here.

But the wind howled across the yard and desolation gazed at him from every side with fierce eyes to repulse him. He did not seem to recognize the farm, though everything was in its place, memorable, unaltered from the day he went away. The well, the barns, the reed-stack—nothing was changed about them, and even the tree-stump for chopping wood was not more splintered than before. The scene was absolutely the same as the picture he had kept in his mind and called

*up in the long days of separation. But the mind-picture was
alive, and the farm seemed stony and dead.*

It was so quiet in the yard, and the closed house had become so much one with the earth, that he began to wonder
if the people had not died or departed into the steppe.
Perhaps it was no use to go over and knock at the door.
Better get back to the camp, perhaps, however awful the
way might be.

But a light column of smoke was rising from the chim-
ney. They were there. If he could only look through the
window.

He lifted feet heavy as lead and went towards the house
with stealthy steps. "Just to have a look—" he said to the
fear within him that prompted flight—flight unforeseen and
sudden, straight before him, in any direction.

The garden. A few neglected beds, evidently not dug over
this year. He had planted that one himself. Over there, a
bed he didn't recognize with a bush swathed in straw in
the middle of it. He didn't remember it. Wait a minute!—
He knew something about it.

"That bush you brought in from the steppe"—the words
came into his head as he looked at the fantastic straw figure.
"That wild rose bush"—he suddenly felt glad and began to
shiver—"has blossomed so beautifully. I stroke its leaves,"
he quoted the letter. "Yes, I shall swathe it up for the winter,
I shall wrap it up carefully and look at it every day." He
glanced over the ground for traces of the girl's footsteps.

And though he could see nothing on the garden path,
frozen as hard as a stone, he suddenly found the thread that
had brought him all the way to the threshold of the farm-

house. He went quickly up to the door, and stood there a moment, waiting to control the storm in his heart.

He knocked energetically, loudly, ceremoniously.

His eager ear caught the sound of something being pushed aside, as if someone were getting up from a chair.

Without waiting for an answer, he lifted the latch and went slowly in. He was over the threshold. He fixed his glowing eyes upon the girl, who was standing in the middle of the room, facing the door, beside an overturned chair.

Jurek and Irenka got up from behind the table.

He was so strongly moved that the words of greeting were stifled on his lips.

.　　.　　.　　.　　.

Some situations are so unendurable and so full of tension that there's no way of dealing with them. One has no words for them, no turns of phrase—it's really that one simply hasn't breath enough. In real life such matters end with a sudden snapping of the tension. But not always. It sometimes happens that we live for whole hours, whole days, under the high pressure of powerful experiences.

But a novel won't stand that. You exhaust your means of making a crescendo of words and style and rhythm quicker than the action can catch up. And you have to break off before everything is said, for otherwise the tight drawn lute-string starts squeaking like a flageolet out of tune. If the indignant reader could see the exhausted heart and brain and face of the author at such a time, he would forgive him everything.

December 17th.

Yesterday I wrote a lot of futile things in my novel and also in my diary. Never mind about the novel—it's a failure, anyway; but the diary ought to be above reproach. I was quite wrong in my judgment of that arrival at the farm, as I always am when I try to value my work at night. Only the morning hours are any good for criticism.

But still, how could I overlook the fact that there are too many reminiscences of my former prose in that bit? Or that this unexpected atmosphere of sentiment is out of tune with the events that come before it? I don't know why I've become so sentimental, unless it's that I've been thinking too much about Marusia lately.

The whole thing's very extraordinary. When I started to write this novel I thought I should say in it everything that I've been obliged to suffer in silence all my life. Whereas it's turning out quite differently, and the places where I give way to my feelings, and imagine I'm expressing myself, are the weakest. It's extraordinary what a big part is played in literature by the discipline used in expressing oneself in writing. This business of "putting it down in black and white" has forced people to be careful, and even obliged them to tell lies, ever since the world began, and it muzzles our tongues when we're writing a simple letter. And you have much less room in literature than in life. You can't yearn without a reason, or get sentimental at the wrong moment—you can't even allow yourself a piece of folly or a bout of frenzy. "There's no sense in his writing!" the reader cries at once, though his own life is often a loose tangle of absurdities.

I think the artist differs from the ordinary mortal in being able to bridle his fantasy.

Evening.

Felix's play is rather a success. It was put on today for the tenth time, and they say that the house is always full. I shouldn't have believed it if I hadn't seen with my own eyes the crowd coming out of the theatre this evening.

I can't understand it. The subject's out of date, it's treated in an absolutely pre-war manner, the style of writing is below the average—so how comes the theatre to be so crowded, and at a time when the public taste is so critical and definite that it would rather digest interesting wickedness than noble-minded banality?

I fire off my aphorisms, and life and people go their own way. Look out, my friend! Diogenes was very witty, but I'd rather live in one room with a kitchen than in a tub.

But it's a fact that Felix has cut the ground from under my feet with his play. The novel about Marusia must be much better, crushingly better, to get over the prejudice against a subject that's been used before. And I'm not doing it well. Besides, the very circumstance of competing with Felix . . .

Perhaps I undervalue the man. I once wrote that he's always a day late behind me, and yet he has outstripped me, or rather forestalled me. At the first night of his play I'd have sworn it would be a failure—and the play's run-

ning. Well, and his relations with Zosia? Hasn't he thrown
her off her balance once or twice already? Even if he is a
cipher, who knows what he may do if he grows desperate?
A coward may accomplish marvellous feats of heroism when
pushed to extremes.

However that may be, for the first time in many years a
feeling of uncertainty about him has come over me. And
that's not all. My position is shaken in regard to other
people:—Zosia, the motorist, Klapa, Szmid, Helena.... And
Eva. . . .

Oh, Eva's a certainty! Nothing can cloud the splendid
sureness with which we rely on each other.

December 19th.

I've been buying Eva a heap of ornaments for the Christmas tree. We spent the whole evening shopping, with such
a funny ragamuffin from the market-place to carry the basket. We all had our share in the buying:—first Eva's eyes
lit up, then the ragamuffin whistled through his teeth like
a connoisseur, next the shop-woman had her say—and last
of all I pulled out and emptied my purse. And somehow we
always arrived at an understanding. It was a fine evening,
the shops sparkled like the treasures of Sesame, and the
snow powdered everything. I was quite cleared out. Away
went the last advance on my salary and even part of the
advance from my publisher. It's a good thing he didn't give
me all the money at once, or I shouldn't have had a farthing
by Christmas. What a jolly publisher! If only the poor
devil knew what I'm getting ready for him.

It's true they didn't greet us at home with quite that angelic light-heartedness we brought back with us, together
with our pack of wonders and the impudent face of the
ragamuffin.

Zosia hardly glanced at our treasures. Kunda shrugged
her shoulders, muttered: "Just like the master," and vented
her wrath on the ragamuffin in the kitchen, though she gave
him a cutlet from yesterday's dinner. That didn't mean that
I'd won her favour, alas! She thinks, just as Zosia does,
that I've been spending money unnecessarily, frivolously,
and wronging someone by it. Heavens! It always seems to
me that I cheer up the whole world when I make the child
happy.

The unwrapping of the parcels wasn't the success I'd
hoped for. Eva kept looking at her mother. Time after time
she showed her the tinsel toys and, put off with faint praise,
came back to me increasingly thoughtful. At last she glanced
at me suspiciously and asked with a sigh:—

"Daddy, what are you going to buy for Mummy?"

"A very pretty present!" I replied without hesitation.

"You will? you really will?" inquired my little tormentor
obstinately.

"Of course I shall! Did you ever know Daddy to break
his word?"

That quieted her. But something went running on in her
head, for she left the toys and went slowly over to Zosia.

"You see!" she said to her mother reproachfully. And
when Zosia took her on her knee, she added with a deep
sigh:—"Oh, Mummy, Mummy!"

Splendid kid! I've had the feeling for a long time that

in, so to speak, fundamental matters she's always on my side. But I'm sorry for Zosia. She has brought up Eva with wonderful self-denial, and sacrificed her best years, the only years of a woman's life, to her.—How she must suffer on that account sometimes.

.   .   .   .   .

~~In spite of his determination to spend only one day at the~~ farm . . .

Tadeusz's firm resolve ~~to come~~ to the farm only for a decisive talk . . .

~~If Tadeusz let himself be carried away by his feelings~~ . . .

Days and weeks passed by, and Tadeusz was still at the farm, although the aim of this dangerous visit was to have been just one serious talk with the girl, after which he was to return to camp without delay. But this talk did not take place either on the day he arrived, when fatigue and the shock of the meeting kept him from uttering a word, nor on the following morning, when he was sunk in the depression he always felt before an important decision.

And later on . . . he was disarmed by the girl, who never asked by word or glance or gesture why he had come back to the farm. More, she seemed to evade the conversation. Every time he mustered his strength to come by roundabout ways to the matter, she sealed his lips with a look that said: "You must not!" Whenever he attempted to spring it upon her and himself by a resolute word, she put him off with a smile that said: "Very well, but not today!" It was as if the conversation had no interest for her, as if she knew its contents in advance and did not ascribe the least importance to it in face of the thousand other matters for concern that were bound up with his person.

He was looking ill, and he must be fed up; he had been overdoing himself, been thinking too much—he must rest and not think about anything; he had some great decision before him—he must get up his strength.

She surrounded him with an ocean of kindness, divined all his needs with an unfailing foresight that was never importunate, forestalled his desires, cured his ailments. When he revolted and resisted, she begged him not to rob her of her happiness. Didn't he see how happy she was to be able to show him her love?

Yes! She admitted it openly, with all her soul, with the voluptuous submission of one completely conquered and so having nothing to lose. Assailed with a look, she did not turn her shining eyes away; caught by the hand, she gave back the warm clasp; and though her face flamed at his touch, she did not shrink from it. Only her lips were silent; tight-shut, they begged his silence too.

He became strangely used to this condition of things. He was saturated with it and responded to it. It was well with him. He understood the luxury of that passive determination which awaits events with bowed head, and smiles to the happiness of the moment. And there seemed less and less need for a hasty decision in view of the uncertainty of the morrow.

December 20th.

Christmas is upon us! I must get ahead and write something as fast as I can, because we shall be in the thick of extraordinary happenings before we can turn round. First we shall bring home a fir tree cut down from a plantation and arrange a forest somewhere in the corner of the room between the grand piano and the dresser. Then we shall hang on it gleaming balls and toys made of tinsel and paper and glass, and persuade ourselves that they are fabulous treasures.

One night, when we come home from workshop and street, when the world's tumult grows quiet and the machines that serve us slacken their tempo, we shall stand at the window and look for the sky among the roofs of houses, and for a star through the fog and smoke in the sky. Then we shall count ourselves to see if we are an even number. Some member of the family will be arriving by the last express at a minute or so after five. At a given moment we shall humbug the children with the angel, our neighbours with the wafer, and the whole world with the peace of God. And we shall make a ring round the tree singing songs about the Holy Child and the cattle and the Wise Men.

Next day we shall get up with the appetites of cannibals and welcome all comers, whoever they may be, with traditional Polish hospitality, return their visits, overeat and overdrink ourselves, and fall into one another's arms.

And if a feeling of doubt comes over us, or the voice of criticism stings us, or we are pierced with regrets for something that is ending and will leave nothing new behind it— then we shall give ourselves up to the festival with all the greater determination.

Christmas! Who has ever been able to resist it? The voice of a thousand generations, right back to the cave-man, reaches us and reminds us of the childish, simple, holy first fathers of mankind.

And we surrender to it, in fear and humility—as Szmid puts it, helpless before the forces that could grind us to dust.

.   .   .   .   .   .

"Can I come in?" someone knocked at Tadeusz's door.

"Come in!" cried Tadeusz, half undressed. He had recognized the boy's voice. Surprised at this late visit, he looked hard at his guest standing motionless in the doorway.

"Come nearer!" he said encouragingly. "Sit down on the bench."

"No, thanks, I'll stand," the boy replied in a strange voice. His face was clouded and reserved, and he kept his eyes on the floor. He stood very straight and soldierly, and the tension visible in his whole figure showed that he had come about something that moved him deeply.

The pleasure that Tadeusz had felt on hearing his pupil's voice vanished. It was true that the boy always spoke roughly, and never took a step towards friendliness without holding himself ready for a backward spring; but Tadeusz had never seen him so icy as this. He might not have minded it but for the boy's extraordinary behaviour during the past few days. He hadn't spoken to a soul, had left the farm every morning and not come back till night, looked daggers at everybody, tormented his younger sister, and kept out of Marusia's sight.

His sudden appearance so late at night augured something out of the common in importance. That "something" worried Tadeusz, who had already made several unsuccessful attempts at reconciliation.

"*Come nearer!*" he said again, anxious to keep up a friendly attitude, for he really liked the boy. "*Don't look so gloomy!*" he added jokingly. "*You don't want to frighten me, do you?*"

"*I don't want to frighten anybody!*" said the boy obstinately. "*If anyone's afraid, that's his own look-out.*"

"*Not so high-falutin', old chap!*" Tadeusz cut in impatiently—"*I'm not used to such expressions, mind you! If you've got something to say, say it! And keep your remarks to yourself.*"

The boy, out of countenance, gave Tadeusz a stealthy glance. His eyes were so clouded with trouble that Tadeusz mastered his anger.

"*Well, never mind!*" he said in a conciliatory tone. "*Say what you like. I've been wanting to have a talk with you for ages.*"

"*But I—I haven't anything to say. Only one question. Will you answer it?*"

"*Of course!*"

"*And you won't tell me a lie?*"

"*I don't need to lie to you, my boy.*"

"*Well, then, tell me why you came back to the farm!*" he said, hacking the words out one by one.

The question acted on Tadeusz like an affront. Such a wave of anger came over him that he forgot the promise he had just given and sprang to his feet.

"*What right have you to speak to me like that?*" he shouted, going up to the boy.

But Jurek stood the attack calmly. He stiffened himself

still further, cold and proud; but his face whitened and he bit his quivering lips.

"I'm Marusia's brother!" he replied quietly, but with a strength and self-assurance that forced Tadeusz to listen.

The words, "You puppy!" which were on the tip of Tadeusz's tongue, died away at the reflection that he must talk calmly with Jurek as with an equal. Luckily an argument came forward of itself.

"Are you speaking in Marusia's name?" he asked, looking at the boy through narrowed eyes.

"I'm speaking for myself. But it's the same thing."

"Are you sure of that?"

Jurek hesitated, with deep and sudden anguish in his face. "No! . . . I'm not! Why do you ask in such an underhand way?" he burst out again. "Why don't you answer my question? I won't go away until you do."

He was so excited that the last words rang out in a high half-childish treble. But there was no yielding in his eyes and he stood there manly and resolute.

Tadeusz shrugged his shoulders.

"You may be sure," he replied emphatically, "that in that case I shan't answer. If you take that tone we shall never get anywhere, for I can be obstinate too. If you intend to stay where you are, please do; there's room for us both." He went over to the bed and lay down in his clothes. "If you want to lie down, there's the bench!" he added with irony.

"Thank you! I'll stand!" answered the boy. And he really did go on standing, leaning against the edge of the

*table in the middle of the room between the bed and the
door, with his back to Tadeusz. It flashed across Tadeusz
that his slender silhouette and regular profile had something
noble and knightly about them.*

*"What a pity," he thought, slyly observing the intruder,
"that I can't come to terms with this youngster! Devil knows
what he's after!" But he lied to himself, for he knew quite
well why the boy had come. About Marusia, it was perfectly
clear! About their sudden intimacy. The ass! nothing had
happened and nothing would happen . . . could happen . . .
ought to happen.*

December 21st.

The Christmas paroxysm has begun. Housecleaning. My
corner is always the first to be attacked, for Zosia swears
it's always the most cluttered up. When I came home today
I found my writing-desk in the hall, my inkstand on the
stove, and my manuscript on the cupboard. (Why does
"tidying up" always begin with such frightful untidiness?)
So I'm writing on the pedestal cupboard in the bedroom,
with all the windows open, for they're going to tidy up here
in a minute. I tried to settle down in Eva's nursery, but Eva
is tidying up too, and everything is upside-down there.

Altogether it's awful. Two frantic women (Zosia and
Kunda) and that mite of an Eva sweep about the house,
chasing me from corner to corner with all the pretentious-
ness of women's work that mustn't be disturbed. Looking at
their cloudy malignant faces, I get the impression that they
consider themselves victims, the victims of Christmas, of

family and social customs, of hearth and home. They haven't a scrap of conviction or a spark of the philosophic calm which resigns one to one's lot. Dusters and brooms scorch our ladies' hands as the prayer-book scorches the devil. You can take it further and say that they hate their other home duties just as much, except perhaps dressing and kissing their children.

I must get out of this! I can't endure the sight of people doing things because they must. So I shall shut up shop and go, as they say, "into town." I shall learn something *de publicis,* for all good citizens, driven from their firesides, meet in the cafés today.

December 23rd.

A few words on the corner of the chest of drawers—I have it! I have a splendid pendant to yesterday's observations. I went round all the bars, from the highest to the lowest (there's not much difference: to put it roughly, the food and drink are equally good everywhere, and the places and plates equally dirty), listening to everybody's conversations with everybody else. They didn't talk at all about the Christmas Eve fish, or the tree, or their private annals, or any of the various practical questions that concern us, but only about the Government, the State, and the community. That's nothing new. The ideas of our citizens about the problems of the day would make a leading article. But the rest—the facts and information—is simply chaos; inexact, unconfirmed, and grouped anyhow.

I learned that : (1) the land-owners are furious, (2) the

peasants are resolved on everything, (3) the Government officials are embittered in the highest degree, (4) the intelligentsia is at its last extremity, (5) trade and industry are on the verge of collapse, (6) the proletariat is dangerously exasperated—even the firemen are boiling with wrath, the war-disabled threaten war, and the veterans revolution.

A charming prospect, isn't it? My good colleague from the office, whom I met at one of the shrines where you flood your liver and pour out your gall, said to me, deeply worried:

"Do you see what is happening? Have you heard what they're saying and how they say it? What will come of it, my dear sir?"

"Nothing!" I said to console him. "A State in which every single class of society has a grievance may look to the future calmly."

"You're joking——"

"Not a bit of it. The more the citizens grumble, the more they feel the need for some support. The Government and the State—in a smaller sphere the family and the hearth —will long continue to be the fence for drunkards to lean against."

January 1st.

I had a New Year's dream. I dreamt I belonged to a country where every citizen did what he had to do. The generals studied strategy and the higher arts of war, the ministers governed, the Diet passed laws, cobblers made boots, poets wrote verses, priests said mass, the peasants ploughed, the workman stayed in his workshop, and the thief

sat in prison. Walking about the streets was not the highest
act of patriotism, and the nation and State and Government
were not blamed if the meat was overdone.

Women bore children without any pretensions to heroism
or a historical mission, so there were fewer idiots and ne'er-
do-wells.

As a happy citizen of this dream-country, I hardly knew
it existed. Once a year I paid taxes which were justly imposed; once in three years I voted for the best man to look
after my interests in the Diet.

I wrote a lot of good books. And I spent my leisure reading the works of men wiser than myself, or looking at beautiful things; and in my thoughts I sought to approach immortal problems which would outlive me, my circle, the Government, the State, and the motherland.

January 4th.

Devil take it! I reckoned that the holiday might rob me
of three or four working days, but it's over two weeks since
I wrote a word of my novel. The diary has been laid aside
too.

And I could have written. Zosia went away four days
ago to the mountains with a school friend. Felix and the
motorist have gone there too. Eva and I and Kunde are
at home, in complete harmony. If you want to live at peace
with others, you must be sufficient unto yourself. All the
same, the way that mite, Eva, suffices unto herself is perfectly amazing.

So why don't I write and why do I spend whole days in

unparalleled laziness? Am I bothering about Zosia?
A little! I saw that school friend of hers once and
remember her as a shallow sly creature with a highly developed "art of life." She is kept by some kind of an uncle—
the brother of an unknown father, or the friend of an unknown husband, or something. I think she always keeps
somebody too. They say she pays her husband alimony. She's
a very original woman and in quite good society. Zosia met
her at one of the Christmas parties (you come to us and
we'll come to you). She criticized her very much. Couldn't
understand her at all. Went to the theatre with her. And
then went away with her for "a few days." I was to have
gone too, but my work—or rather its unlucky mirage—
kept me.

(It's a damned trade! for you know not the day nor the
hour when you may be taken with a writing fit.)

As soon as Felix heard about Zosia's trip, he flew off after
her, leaving no tracks. The motorist went this morning and
did not forget to call here and propose my going too, to
visit my wife. He's a classical type! Only I can't understand
. . . is he making a fool of me, or does he want to teach
me, in a delicate way, how I ought to behave with my own
wife?

But what about Zosia? It's such a stupid idea, and yet
it's an understandable one, that there, somewhere in the
mountains, something may happen—that, to say it right out,
someone may . . . behind my back—damn it! it's horrid!
The very possibility of such an idea makes me furious. I,
her husband—I, a man! And I don't even know what I
should do if I learned that she . . . Like every other hus-

band I have thought out the whole *modus procedendi* in such a case.

No scenes. A quiet talk, a packing up of belongings, the furthest possible concessions in material questions.

There you go! You may be all your life getting ready to be struck on the head with a club, you may even take part in doing it—but when you get it, you'll see all the stars in heaven, just the same.

January 8th.

Yesterday, late in the evening, the motorist brought Zosia home.

"I couldn't bear to see you in that crowd!" he justified himself, kissing her hand at parting.

I don't understand. Is he my wife's keeper? And if he were? Such things do happen.

.   .   .   .   .

"But I shall have to do something with him"—and he turned to the obstinate visitor whose figure stung him though his eyes were turned away—"he can't possibly stand there all night. One of us must give way in this ridiculous quarrel. I really could tell him why I came to the farm. If only he weren't so arrogant. And so childish!" He pished, realizing the vast distance that lay between the lad's ideas and his own.

"Let him stand!" and he gazed at the ceiling.

At that moment there were steps in the next room. He raised his head to listen. Someone was coming to his door. Before he could think who it might be the latch was raised and the door opened, pushed violently from the outside. He sprang to his feet. Marusia stood on the threshold of his room.

She grasped the situation at a glance and went over to the boy with a decided step.

"What are you doing here?" she asked. Her voice was hard and slightly raised.

The boy drew himself up and stood eye to eye with the girl, ready for an unrelenting quarrel. But he could not get out the answer.

"Well, speak!" she repeated. "What did you come here for?"

He could not keep it up. Pierced by Marusia's menacing gaze he shrank, weakened, and dropped his eyes to the floor. He always felt a child in the presence of his sister.

"I came . . . I forgot . . . I wanted to ask——" he stammered with difficulty—"Monsieur Tadeusz . . . " he broke off and was silent, in terrible embarrassment. He did not know how to lie, and he did not dare to confess what he had come for.

"Well, what about Monsieur Tadeusz?" she went on mercilessly.

"Nothing!" he whispered, looking at the door. He went heavily over to it and stood a moment on the threshold.

"But remember, Marusia!" he tried to begin again—"remember!"

"Go away!" she ordered him shortly.

"I'm going. And if it's to be like this, I'd rather go away from the farm altogether," he burst out.

"As you like."

He went out, leaving the door half open behind him. The girl's eyes followed him, and when he disappeared she listened attentively to the dying sound of his footsteps. The tension did not leave her face till the door of the children's room creaked in the distance.

Then she sighed, half with relief, half sadly. Her face brightened and she raised her eyes to Tadeusz.

"Don't be surprised!" she said timidly. "I heard you two talking in such queer voices. What did he come to you about?"

"Oh, nothing special," answered Tadeusz quickly. "The boy has feelings about things and doesn't know how to take them. But he really means well."

"Did he offend you?"

"Oh, just a bit! but he disarmed me at once. Who knows if he didn't get the better of me—he did, for sure!" He recalled the whole course of the visit, which suddenly appeared to him in quite a different light. "But please don't go away!" he begged warmly, seeing her turn towards the door. "I would like to take this opportunity and have a talk with you."

"Today?"

"Today! now! I must go away from the farm tomorrow."

"Tomorrow? Already?" she cried painfully.

"Yes! I suppose I ought to have gone long ago."

Something like the stupefaction of a person roused from sleep immobilized Marusia's face.

"You're going away tomorrow? Tomorrow?" she repeated, pale as death—"for always? . . ."

"Yes!" he said emphatically—"for always. But we must

talk about what's to happen next. Courage!" He took her hand and pulled her towards the bed. "Please sit down and listen."

She surrendered without resistance, but also without the response with which she always yielded to his wishes. She left her hand lying limp in his and did not stir when the cloak slipped off her shoulders, uncovering her naked arm up to her neck. It was only now that Tadeusz saw that she had come to him in her nightdress, swathed about with a traveling cloak.

"I beg your pardon!" he drew back startled—"I didn't suppose . . . I didn't imagine you weren't dressed."

She did not move.

"It doesn't matter!" she answered calmly.

But from her bare back and neck crept a wave of scarlet that flooded her whole face.

. . . . .

That's how it was, word for word, gesture for gesture. And I, idiot that I was, did not realize for a single moment how immensely finer than myself was that girl. She saw through every word and thought of mine as through a pane of glass, and knew everything that I did not yet dare to think; gazing wide-eyed into the terrible future, she did not hesitate before the greatest sacrifice a girl's heart can make.

She was at once the moth and the flame—I was only an onlooker.

January 13th.

I've noticed for some time that even in my diary I don't confess to everything, passing over many thoughts and happenings which ought to be set down in it. There's nothing extraordinary about this, for it lies in the essence of human thought, whenever it goes off on the rails of self-criticism, to pass over knotty and burdensome moments. It's not to be wondered at. If life itself is a kind of acrobatics where we must vault over or avoid unpleasant and difficult obstacles— if we manage only in extremity to achieve a line of upright conduct—then how can thought, so evanescent and elastic, be expected to march with steady steps through the waste places of experience and memories? All the more that we can always justify ourselves by appealing to the possibility of resuming the thought or meditation on this or that *ab ovo*.

As I don't want to put off my self-justification till too late, and do want my diary to have a rather better form than the usual schoolgirl's journal, I must note down here a few of the Christmas incidents that ought to have been mentioned before.

They concern Helena. After that last "dancing" (horrible word!) I didn't see her again till Christmas Eve, and was not sorry. For our acquaintance had stopped at the point where you either say to a woman: "Come to me a little after such and such an hour," or you say nothing at all. So I said nothing and avoided meeting her to spare her the affront implied by that kind of silence. Klapa made it easier for me, for he didn't turn up once after that time when he came to my office and we went out to lunch together.

The Christmas holiday spoiled everything (you come to us and we come to you). We met the Klapas at the midnight mass, and when we separated outside the Church we, of course, expressed our mutual astonishment at "not having seen you for such ages." Damn this social politeness! What a heap of trouble in human relationships, what lots of little sins and big sins, what hosts of scandals have been brought about by that foolish doctrine: "It isn't done."

Ergo—a visit. It didn't matter much when they came to us, for our house was full of friends and relatives, and I was able to keep my distance with Helena, and even to pay her a compliment now and then across the table or the Christmas tree or the cake, and save the situation.

But when we returned their visit we came rather late, just as their guests were leaving, so that we found ourselves at once in our own little set, composed of Felix, the Klapas, and ourselves. The motorist wasn't there—he doesn't like Helena.

And behold Klapa, the angelic Klapa, remorseful no doubt at having entertained suspicions about me, simply falling upon me, and showing me a friendliness and affection that were quite disarming. When he had drunk a couple of vodkas, which was quite enough for his weak head, he actually grew witty and was quite amusing. He threw Helena at my head, taking no notice of my lack of enthusiasm or her evident alarm.

But that's nothing. At a certain moment he dragged me away from the table and whispered, as a great secret, that he had something very interesting to tell me, something that would amaze me. "A curio!" I thought, and *nolens volens* followed him into his study.

But what the professor took out of his desk was not a curio but a charming note-book, beautifully bound. I opened it—poems! in Helena's writing!

"What's all this?" I asked, pretending I didn't know what he was after. "A keepsake album, or what?"

"Nothing of the kind!" rejoiced Klapa—"Helena's poems, her original poems! Mind you, Helena writes poems."

"I should never have thought it."

"No, nor I, or I should have told you about it long ago. I found the book only the other day, at the hospital, not here. And I said to myself at once that I must show them to you."

"Why to me?"

"Well, of course, you're a connoisseur, a writing man. You understand one another best. Helena didn't want to give her consent, and, you know, I didn't bring it off. But after we met you in Church, I persuaded her and she agreed. But I had to promise I'd show the verses to you when we were alone, with no witnesses. Just cast your eye over them— I think she has talent, sir! Not only talent, she has something more than that. Do read one or two of them."

I opened the book reluctantly. Helena appeared to me ridiculous in the role of poetess.

Meanwhile, the very first poem, entitled "Between 5 and 7" (her regular hours of hospital work, unless I'm mistaken) struck me by its force of expression and an uncommon transparency of thought. The second—I don't remember what it was called—was less interesting. But when I read the page headed "You do not know me"—I broke out into a perspiration. It was poetry of the first water, and, as Klapa had rightly said, it was not only poetry. It gave me the impression that an invisible hand was unveiling before me the statue of a foundering man. For a moment I forgot where I was and whose hand had written those words.

"Splendid!" I whispered unconsciously, running over the poem again.

"Isn't it?" Klapa broke in eagerly. "You're reading 'You do not know me,' aren't you? When I came across that poem, do you know, I thought the earth was giving way under me. I simply couldn't believe that it was—Helena!"

"No wonder!" I had the greatest difficulty in keeping off the professor's garrulity, which depressed me dreadfully. "I find it very hard to connect these things with Helena. You're quite sure they're her own work?"

"Oh, absolutely. And now please tell me"—he fixed feverish eyes upon me—"how it can happen that a person with whom we are living intimately—you understand me, very intimately—whom we seem to know through and through, as they say, that—wait a minute—I can't put it into words! Well, that . . . firstly, a person——"

"You want to say that such a person's soul can be a riddle for us."

"Not only a riddle! A mystery, which we unconsciously make deeper the more intimately we seem to know the person. Which we drive farther into the pit by . . . by——"

"By the union of our bodies, amen!" And I got up, anxious to end the conversation.

"What did you say?" Klapa caught my arm.

"You heard, didn't you?"

"And you really think that?" Suddenly quenched, he stole a glance at me. "Well, in that case . . . really."

Klapa's confusion made me suddenly curious to hear his

last word on this question. Something whispered to me that Klapa had brought me here for a definite purpose which he would now like to withdraw.

"And what's your opinion?" I was already standing in the doorway leading into the hall.

"Oh, I haven't an opinion. I only thought—I supposed . . . that perhaps you and Helena . . . brother-spirits—it's obvious that you . . . but you're of quite a different opinion!" he broke off in a depressed way, as if afraid of his own words.

I arranged with Helena, in a few words, to come for a reading of the poems the day after tomorrow.

January 14th.

It was barely dawn when he got ready to start.

He hurried, kept forgetting things, kept dropping things. With hands that shook with impatience he wrestled with the tangle of his boot-laces, worrying about his tunic and cap and coat, though they were all lying to hand on the bench or the back of a chair.

"Quicker! quicker! it's time to go!"—he drove himself on, glancing time and again at the window, through which fell the glimmer of morning and the icy breath of frost.

Now and then his arms fell to his sides, and he stood motionless. The night still lurking in the corners of the room, the warm intoxicating night that made him powerless with its memories of past ecstasy, drew him backwards like an abyss. Out of its depths, from which he turned with shame and alarm, the last paroxysms of pleasure reached him yet.

And every time he looked backwards, the bewildering battle of thoughts, feelings, and impressions grew stronger, as did the mad instinctive voice that whispered incessantly:—

"Escape, escape, save her and yourself! Every moment is precious."

Ready at last, he reflected sorrowfully that he must say good-bye to the girl, must make an inhuman effort and explain to her that in spite of all that had happened his purpose was unshaken, was stronger than ever.

Where could he find strength to convince her, completely crushed and shattered as he was? How console her when he himself was near despair?

But . . . he must say good-bye. His escape from the farm would tear away the last ray of hope from her heart.

And what was there to be afraid of? She had given herself to him, had come to him in her nightdress; herself had shut his lips, herself had forced him by that compliant submission of hers in which, like the surface of a slumbering sea, all the strength of storm lay hidden.

Could anyone resist that terrible power?

He had merely stretched out his hand—why did he feel like a thief caught in the act of crime?

Throwing his knapsack on his shoulder, he glanced round the room. He knew he would never come back here. With an effort at calm and self-assurance, he went out, to stand still again with a beating heart because the door creaked as he pushed it open. The thought that someone might wake up in the children's room, that he might meet the boy at this moment, terrified him with the phantom of catastrophe. He crept stealthily to Marusia's door. Was she asleep? He listened, but there was no sound. Perhaps it was better not to disturb her? Perhaps he would really go away without troubling anybody.

But he mastered himself and knocked.

"Come in!" came the answer.

The deep calm ring of her voice did him good. He went in quickly, looking for her with anxious eyes. She was sitting curled up in a corner of the bed, with her feet twisted under her, wrapped in the same cloak and no doubt in the same nightdress. The strands of her loosened hair fell upon her shoulders. She looked like a penitent in the grey light of dawn. He thought she was crying.

But when he came closer and looked into her face, the eyes she lifted to him were dry and full of light, and the smile on her lips gleamed in the dusk, pale and calm as the glow of a sacrifice.

With a slight movement of her head she asked him to come nearer.

"Do you want to say good-bye to me?" she asked.

"Yes!" he answered quickly, coming up to the bed. And then he added slowly and distinctly: "I'm going."

"I know"—she nodded—"it's time."

"Listen to me!"

"I'm listening."

"It's what I wanted to say last night, what we began to talk about, what I came to the farm for, you understand. Listen . . . you must be mine."

"I am yours."

"No, not like that! You must be mine for always. You understand, don't you? my wife! Listen: I shall start to get

away from this country today, tomorrow, the moment I'm back in camp. And over there, at home, I shall put everything through. Don't interrupt me! I'm going to get a divorce! There's no other way. Then I shall come back here."

"*Yes . . .*"

"*Or else you'll come to me. That's even more likely. Anyway, it's all the same.*

"*Yes.*"

"*I shall write.*"

"*Yes.*"

"*I swear it.*"

Something like boundless pity flooded the girl's face. With a gentle movement, unrepulsed, she drew him to her. She clasped his head and pressed it to her bosom, like a mother, a sister, a lover.

"*I will do as you tell me," she whispered, "and I shall be yours till I die."*

The first rays of sunshine found him on the broad steppe highway. He walked quickly, and looked neither backwards nor at the road before him. He was blinded by the sun and by the tears running unheeded down his face.

. . . . .

Well, yes, it's happened. I foresaw it, I warned myself against it, and nevertheless I fell. And now I don't know what I'm to do next. For, if you like, it's nothing—an accident like a thousand others. But it's a bad business; you might call it an ugly business. Or, right out, an ordinary beastliness! I fitted Klapa with horns yesterday.

It took place in quite the classical way, and I'm certain

that if I had written a story on that subject beforehand, I couldn't have made up anything different from how it happened.

Shall I describe it fully, or limit myself to stating the fact? Oh, I'll describe it. Recapitulation of a thing of that sort makes it easier to look ahead, and I have a firm impression that various things are about to happen. It can't be helped! I won't turn everlastingly in this vicious circle. I'm out for trouble.

According to our arrangement, I went to Helena to read those poems. I must mention in self-justification, or rather for the sake of verity, that I really went to read verses and not for anything else. Helena's mysterious talent had made me curious, though I looked critically afterwards upon my first enthusiastic appreciation of her work. In any case, I wanted to convince myself that I had nothing against the "contact of souls," and my certainty that Klapa would want to be present at our meeting dispersed all idea of anything treasonable.

The situation I found when I got there confirmed this conviction. The Professor, delighted at my arrival, met me in the doorway, and Helena, very animated, with shining eyes and flushed cheeks, was in the study. She stood before me as embarrassed as a schoolgirl before her master. She looked pretty and charming, for innocence is very becoming to her.

"It's all right!" I thought, set at rest; and to show that I was ready to come into the *entente cordiale* we were making I kissed both her hands with more fervour than usual.

That was a mistake, of course—a bad mistake, for the

kisses made her tremble and drop her eyes and press her knees together convulsively, after her manner.

"Donkey!" I thought, "don't call the wolf out of the wood, or the nature out of a human being!" and I immediately began to talk. About poets, of course, and art in general, and creative work. At first lightly, and then more seriously—for it appeared that Helena not only writes unusual poems but can think and talk about art in an unusual way. I should never have supposed it.

It's a long time since I heard such an animated and sincere and interesting conversation. The Professor, carrying the discussion here and there into the sphere of knowledge and scientific creativeness, seconded us quite intelligently and very wisely. Really, when Klapa opens all the stops in his brain and lets in a little air, he becomes a dialectician worth listening to.

Unluckily, the stops in the Professor's brain started to shut down. Today, looking backwards at the extraordinary happenings of yesterday from a suitable distance, I'm certain that the Professor's plan was as follows:—firstly, to take me in to Helena; secondly, to facilitate the contact of souls and help to draw us together; thirdly, to leave us alone and go magnanimously away. If he had any fears or doubts about it, the atmosphere of our meeting completely dispersed them.

It's not to be wondered at, seeing I was quite deluded myself.

So at a given moment the Professor got up, bowed to us and declared with a disarming smile:

"Excuse me, dear people, but I've got to go to the laboratory. You'll take the opportunity to read your verses to him, Hela, won't you?"—he stroked Helena's head with that idolatrous respect for her which I've noticed in him since he discovered the book of poems.

"Unless you want to run away," said Helena, innocently enough and quite under the influence of our conversation.

"Of course not!" I answered cheerily. "I'll go through with it, I give you my word!"

I don't know whether I sent her a profligate look at this moment, or whether a devil leapt into her, but her eyes suddenly fluttered like a caught bird, and she grew deathly pale.

I went cold all over. In that one second we lost our balance completely and never got it back—and never shall again. The glance she sent me from behind Klapa's back as he said good-bye to me gleamed with a wild sensual determination.

What more? Klapa went, and we sat for a long time without exchanging a word, without even looking at each other. I confess that during this time I was thinking of various circumstances and horrible things such as if the blinds were far enough down, if the servants were out, etc. And the result of these investigations was quite satisfactory. I don't know if Helena had been expecting me with the definite resolve to fall, but everything was prepared for it. Even the couch was covered with a new rug, drawn very smooth. Perhaps it was only just so, as women do things—in case of anything happening.

But it was difficult for me to take the initiative. That decisive turn or movement or gesture which you make to possess a woman, even if she's in absolute surrender, isn't an easy matter at all. I've known men turn the world upside down to win a woman, and when the moment came for them to take her, they drew back and went off with nothing.

I behaved more or less like a schoolboy, begging her "nevertheless" to read me her poems. It turned out that the book was in another room. She got up and went out with the step of a somnambulist. It was a long time before she came back. . . . Perhaps she wanted to give me a chance to escape, or was deluding herself with the idea that she was getting composed. But neither of these things happened.

So she came back, trembling like a leaf, and began to read the first poem in a dead, stifled, toneless voice. I was obliged to interrupt. . . .

"Do let me have a try at reading them!" and I reached out for the book. She gave it me with her head bent on one side like a person expecting a blow.

That was the end of everything. Our fingers met somewhere on the binding, and the book fell from among them together with the contact of our souls.

In a moment I was at her side. She only had time to give one faint cry before she threw her arms round me in a delirious embrace.

Madness! Never in my life have I lived through such a storm as burst upon us. Nor such depression *post factum.*

When I came away she was lying on the couch half-naked, crumpled, nearly dead. Neither by word nor look did she say good-bye to me. She didn't care . . . nor did I.

But what happened if Klapa found her in that state? I passed his silhouette in the street as I came home.

January 16th.

There's a sequel. Today, at the office, at about eleven o'clock, I had a visit from two stiff and ridiculous gentlemen in black coats. One of them was Felix, and the other Klapa's assistant. They had come to represent the Professor in a matter I knew of. In spite of my low spirits, I wanted to give them a fillip on the nose apiece and fling them out of the door, with a good kick at Felix in a part whose very existence he had forgotten in that lofty moment.

Unluckily there exists a certain law that makes us mirror the monkey tricks and looks of those surrounding us. I got up, cleared my throat, and bowed.

"My seconds will call on you today, gentlemen." It was like an examination in the code of honour!

Then I ran round to my office colleague and to the motorist, asking them to be my seconds and warning them that they must accept without discussion all the conditions imposed by the other side.

January 25th.

The Professor and I are going to fire at each other at six o'clock tomorrow morning. All my life I've looked upon the code of honour and the duel as one of the privileges of the fool over the enlightened individual, and yet I'm going to fight and I feel that it must be so. The frightful hopelessness of transactions of this kind is closely bound up with certain inextricable situations in our lives. There's nothing to be done. If there's no other way to it, may a bullet sent skywards solve the question for me, Helena, and Klapa. For I'm not going to aim at the Professor's ribs—and even if Klapa wants to hit me, he can't shoot.

I'm miserable about all this, and my soul is full of crawling thoughts as blind as slow-worms. I feel that tomorrow will start a series of worries and misfortunes and hopeless regrets. I am stalked by the dark phantom of the future, and I can't and won't put up any resistance.

All day long I've been saying good-bye to Zosia. She doesn't know anything yet, but she'll know everything tomorrow for certain. Or perhaps she does know today, perhaps she has an inkling. Her meditative sadness, and the silent wonder with which she accepted all my humble attentions, have given me a lot to think about.

I'm sorry for her. She has loved me very deeply, and I have grown accustomed and attached to her. She made one mistake when she demanded a share of what no real man ever gives into anyone else's keeping—the treasure of his work and his creative thought—and another mistake when she wanted soul, heart, and body to be on an equal footing in our union. But she has known how to forgive—she would forgive me about tomorrow if I asked her. But I'm not going to ask her. So I speak about her love for me as of something that has ceased to be.

I keep out of Eva's way. For she is the last thing left to me.

February 1st.

I'm wounded. Klapa shot me in the leg. By accident, of course. There was a stone in the middle of the place our seconds measured out for us, and the Professor's bullet, fired at the ground, glanced off it.

I was so unprepared for getting hit (I distinctly saw the barrel of Klapa's pistol aimed at the ground) that I put down the sudden pain in my leg to cramp, and did not drop till they gave me the pistol for the second shot.

It's a moment I shall never forget. I saw before me, instead of the mangy little forest, a patch of bright sky ringed by men's faces. For they all ran up to me, and the Professor, too. And they were so kind and so upset and so radiating with brotherliness that I felt bound to justify myself.

"It's nothing, my dear sirs!" I made an effort and smiled —"it's only my leg."

"What? then I——?" the Professor was looking at me, badly scared.

"No, not you! it was that stone, look, in the middle of the field—perhaps you noticed it——" I gabbled, gazing fixedly at him, for his face was extraordinary, an open book where you could see the tragic sorrow and alarm at the bottom of his soul.

"Don't take it to heart so, Professor!" I cried out in something like anger, and then remembered that I had no business to talk to him like that. For they were ready to believe that I was taking advantage of the temporary superiority the bullet in my leg gave me over that broken-hearted man.

Our reconciliation—to speak exactly, our handshake—was like a bit out of a play. Klapa wanted to say something, but he kept it in, cramped by the presence of the others. He looked into my eyes and found nothing.

"You're an extraordinary man!" he whispered as he turned to go. "Nothing bowls you over!"

I think he's wrong about that . . . but no matter. We shall see.

I spent the rest of the morning after the duel at the motorist's, for it had been agreed there, on the field, that we would try to keep the whole thing secret. I don't quite believe it's possible, but we shall gain a day or two. My wound is trifling, and since it has been bandaged I can even walk without limping. It hurts, of course, but that's just where the self-control I've always valued so much in life comes in. The mastery of pain is a certain kind of voluptuousness; and it's such ages since I practised that sort of gymnastics that I'm quite glad of this rare chance of testing my strength.

Up to now I'm doing rather well, for Zosia is still revolving in the orbit of yesterday's moods. I put down my pallor and idleness and lounging in arm-chairs to overwork.

But I have arranged to sleep in my study in case my leg gets worse.

February 2nd.

How this damned leg hurts me! I could hardly get to the motorist's to have my wound dressed. Something's gone wrong with it, and the doctor has absolutely forbidden me to walk for a few days at least.

In view of this, the motorist is keeping me at his house. We're sending word to Zosia that we are off on a trip to the mountains. It's a sorry kind of blind-man's-buff and horribly cowardly of me. But they say that time, by delaying shocks, makes them more bearable.

February 3rd.

My leg has swelled up. The doctor says it's a slight local infection. If I can't walk by tomorrow, I shall go home and face the consequences.

February 6th.

Helena has poisoned herself. If it weren't for this temperature of 104, which I've had for two days . . .

February 8th.

They think I'm unconscious all the time, whereas I . . .

February 10th.

I'm better. And they haven't even cut my leg off.

February 11th.

I'm better. They say that misfortunes come in couples, but they might go further and say that one counteracts another. And Helena's suicide would have had a greater effect on me if it hadn't been for the gangrene which flung me outside of life and kept me unconscious during the worst days. Fate stages things in a strange way! That atom of poison lurking in the Professor's bullet proved to be a beneficent power that paralysed the horror of the drama about me and brought it to silence. Thanks to it I was turned from a criminal into a man deserving of pity; it threw me into

Zosia's shielding arms; it closed the opening mouth of public opinion before there was time to beat the alarm drum of scandal; it bound up wounds, dried tears, kept everyone from reflection—and when the sluices of thought were opened everything was over.

Neither I nor Zosia nor anyone else has courage now to look back and brood over the heritage of trouble, with a view to adapting ourselves to its consequences. It has passed over. . . . And we must begin to live again.

February 12th.

And yet there are changes. Other people have had to drink the cup of bitterness to which I barely put my lips. Zosia! . . . I look at her (for I'm beginning to look at things again) and I see, through her complete apathy, the apathy of one who is only just climbing out of the very depths of trouble, the beginnings of deep changes in her. Perhaps they are not the beginnings. I read in her regard a hardness that speaks of mature decisions, and her whole attitude towards me has the rigidity of a duty fulfilled.

She never speaks of what happened lately, and seems entirely taken up with the question of my health. But why have I no feelings for her beyond admiration at her devotion, a quite arid and reasoned admiration, without any of the affectionate warmth of gratitude?

February 20th.

The first normal day after all these weeks. Normal, in so much as outwardly it is like all the other three hundred days in the year. Apart from that it is harsh and pregnant with coming events. And it bucks me up for that very reason.

It began with the office. A concerted duplicity about the vague obsequious greetings of my fellow-workers aroused my vigilance at once and put me on my guard. There had evidently been some sort of a kick-up during my absence; or else the office felt entitled to pry into my personal affairs. Silent as the grave, I merely nodded to my second in the duel; and Michal, inclined to be garrulous over the morning's post, was badly snubbed. So that I was charged like a Leyden jar when my chief, who arrived earlier than usual, sent for me. In reply to his inquiries about my health I said I was feeling splendid. Before he could get in another question, I attacked him about the accumulation of arrears during my absence. I put forward one or two new projects. It was really because I wanted to avoid friction with the man, for I value him and like him, and am rather keen about the terms we've been on up to now.

But it was no use. I forgot that the chief has a young wife. They say that she once let him down, and though that's all over and completely done with it's not been forgotten. The chief's a most forbearing man in every way, but he's a Cato where marital fidelity is concerned.

"I must speak to you on a certain distressing matter," he said severely, hemming and hawing, as I took my papers off the table after finishing what I had to say about the work.

"Namely?"

"Namely about your duel and all the disastrous things involved in it. It's made a very great sensation in the town, sir!"

"I've no doubt of it!"

"Our institution, you understand, has come under everyone's notice through this business. I've had a lot of unpleasantness on that account; a lot of unpleasantness!" he repeated emphatically, staring at the mouth of the inkstand.

"Well, sir?" I hurried him on, feeling my impatience rising.

"Well, I can't conceive how you, a steady man with a family, in some ways such a nice man——"

I was furious.

"May I beg for a strictly business conversation, sir?" I interrupted rudely.

The chief rose to his feet, as sublime as a statue.

"Certainly!" he declared ceremoniously. "You may beg for immediate leave."

I went away to my room, but instead of writing an application for immediate leave, I wrote out my resignation. And I ordered Michal to take the paper to the chief, principally because I caught him listening at the door as I came out of the chief's office. There was no answer, and it was only towards the close of office hours that the chief summoned me again. The light in his eyes was unfriendly, but he had an amiable smile on his face.

"Please sit down!" he said, apparently absorbed in my report. "You misunderstood me."

"No!" I replied standing. "I only wanted to make the situation easier for you. And for the whole institution."

He pretended not to have heard me.

"I thought that your health——"

"It's quite good at present."

"Then you don't want leave?"

"No!"

"In that case I return this to you!" he handed me my document. "Kindly forget about our conversation today."

Thus I won the first and only open battle of the day. But I should be a fool if I did not see that this easy victory was really a defeat which will hatch future trouble. I have in mind the chief's liking for me, now probably gone forever.

A series of lesser encounters, of the guerrilla and skirmishing kind, awaited me at home.

First and foremost, a letter from Klapa requesting me to meet him in the park tomorrow evening.

"The life of my dead wife remains a tormenting mystery for me. You may possibly know more about her than anyone else, not excepting myself. You need not be afraid to come— if you don't want to tell me anything I shall bear you no grudge."

What a horrible prospect! That park at night, and that man trying to look into the soul of a suicide! But I must go. There are things one is simply bound to face.

Next, Zosia, who had a talk with me today for the first time. She too began with my health.

"I see you're feeling better already!" she said after we had finished dinner. "Your leg doesn't hurt you any more?"

"No! I feel a bit tired still, but it'll pass. I've spent my time quite normally all day today."

"Normally?"

"Yes!"

"You're a wonderful man, my dear!" she observed coldly, looking me straight in the face.

I was perplexed. "You don't understand me! I only meant that my health allows me to live normally again."

"Oh, is that it? And have you nothing to say to me? And don't you think," she went on, without waiting for an answer, "that before you return to your normal life a good many things must be cleared up between us? that you owe me something—if only a few words—if only . . . But what's the use of my saying all this?"

"Zosia," I replied with all the sincerity I could find in me at that moment, "what I might have to tell you wouldn't clear up anything, believe me. But all the same you have the right to demand whatever you like of me. . . . So if you really want——"

She shook her head.

"No! no! without any compulsion! You ought yourself——"

"Of course. But I feel helpless——"

"Well, what's to be done? Are we to go on living like this?"

"We may as well try! And if we can't——"

"And if we can't?"

"We'll think of some other way out."

"In that case," she burst out in an impulse of sudden frankness, "I don't mind telling you that I've been thinking about that for a long time!"

I said nothing, for I did not want to wound her by observing that I'd been thinking about it for a long time too.

February 24th.

My meeting with Klapa has taken a load from my heart. We believe too readily the writers who tell us that tragic experiences bring about a complete change in a man's soul, open new horizons of thought, enrich the feelings, etc., etc. The average man has only a certain limited quantum of endurance of pain, and when this is exceeded he ceases to react. When he has borne all he can bear, he cuts the sore place out of him and returns impoverished to his usual mode of life with all his habits and customs, these being stronger and more lasting than any shocks and accidents, even of the most terrible kind.

And so it is with Klapa, whose shaken mind is starting to seek the equilibrium so dear to him by formulating the reasons for Helena's tragedy. Incorrigible man! He can't stir without his "firstly." But there, we won't grumble! That harmless vice has enabled him to achieve this wonderful gesture towards an understanding with me, on the plane of a simple unhampered exchange of ideas.

We had a long and exhaustive talk, and as soon as I grasped what the Professor's aim was I did all I could to help him to achieve it as quickly as possible. In a frank and faithful account of my relations with Helena I traced the unfortunate two-sidedness or rather three-sidedness of her nature. I did not even draw back before a summary description of our last meeting. Of course I did not spare myself at all.

Today I admire my courage, or my cynicism, whichever you like to call it. But cynicism is sometimes rather stimulating, and I rendered the Professor an undoubted service, for he was strengthened and almost calm when we separated. As I looked at his retreating figure and noticed the new freedom and springiness of his bearing, I could not help feeling that the man will recover from the mystery of Helena's death a hundred times more easily than he could have endured the mystery of her existence.

Horrible thought! For when I think of her grave, that dreadfully lonely grave, I am completely overcome by terror and sorrow. That's how I shall lie some day.

February 25th.

"Why? . . . why was Daddy ill so long? . . . why is Mummy so sad? . . . why did that lady die? . . . why won't anybody tell Eva anything?" Why and why?

. . . . . .

Hungry, ragged, cold, stubbornly marching, he crossed the steppe on his way back to the town. A feverish haste burned in his brain and pulsed through his body, urging his limbs to unceasing strain and effort. The bracing difficulties of his tramp made him feel like a fish in water. Heedless of food, rest, and sleep, he gave no rein to his thoughts, and his mind went back to the farm only because it was a goad to spur him on. He was filled with glad hope and self-assurance when he saw how quickly figures and villages and encampments fell behind him.

For, if he could so easily defeat the wilderness, with only his legs to help him, why should he not conquer that other expanse beyond which lay the solution of the problem that tormented him?

Why should he not get through to his wife, break the bond that irked him, and even return to Marusia if need be? The war? The obstacles? The war was over now for certain, and if it wasn't . . . he would manage it in spite of the war. Every means would be fair, where love and faith and honour were at stake.

The extraordinary emptiness of the steppe gave him strength and courage. No one challenged him, no one asked who he was or where he was going. Here and there homeless dogs attacked him, but he easily drove them off with a frozen lump of clay. He became so bold that he went straight through the villages under the very windows of the district guards. And nothing happened. The few people he met looked upon him with amazement and a mixture of fear and aversion.

From this he concluded that no one on earth save himself knew what he wanted; that he alone had the courage to want anything more than to hide in some winter lair.

He went into hiding himself only under compulsion and never for long. Blizzard and cold and desert made him feel at his best. More than once he regretted being unable to prolong his march right away past towns, countries, mountains and rivers—to the goal itself. Only two points on the earth held his mind: one behind him—the farm; the other, far ahead—his home. The thought of any halts between them roused his impatience. What if the winter were twice as hard, what of hunger and footsoreness, if he might only work his lonely way on and on?

But he slackened his steps when he was still some distance from the town. A strange echo, that barred his way, came to him in the fitful gusts of wind. Time after time it struck him in the breast, evoking a deep and menacing response. It was so far off that he could hardly hear it, but it filled the air with moaning and made the earth tremble.

At his last night's lodging it throbbed suddenly with a loud roar that brought him to his feet, startled from sleep. His heart grew cold and he frowned as he listened to the thunderous noise. Cannon were being fired in the town.

He felt an angry impulse to make his way round that hateful place and push on without stopping, past people and their treacherous dwelling-places. But he pulled himself together. He had to go into the town, since his plan of escape demanded it.

He redoubled his steps, and by noon came into the confusion of a street fight. The method of the shortest cut tried in the steppe took him right through snaky lines of sharpshooters and over the crests of barricades. He dropped into side-alleys, sheltered from bullets in courtyards, and reached the camp at dusk.

In a few words he asked his companions what was happening. They overwhelmed him with an avalanche of news about revolutions born from the revolution, about conspiracies and insurrections, stormings, massacres, and frightful slaughter.

When he had heard them out, he shrugged his shoulders and went to bed. Next day he sought out Ignacy, who was

sheepish from fright, and asked him straight out if he would
escape to Poland with him at a moment's notice.

"You're out of your senses, man!" cried Ignacy. "Do you
know what's going on over there?"

"No, I don't," he answered, "and I don't think anyone
does. When we get to know, it may be too late."

"But they're killing everybody!"

"Have you been to see?"

"No, I haven't! and I confess I don't want to."

"Well, think it over till this afternoon. I'm absolutely
going to leave the camp tonight. In two weeks' time, in a
month at most, I must be home! And now good-bye—I must
go to the priest about something." And before the eyes of
his dazed companion he ran across the camp yard, climbed
over a breach trodden out in the wall, and disappeared.

.　　.　　.　　.　　.　　.

And I thought I should never sit down to this novel again.
But when life crushes me and I find myself alone in the
world and have no strength or desire for anything, a spirit
of revolt takes possession of me and I want to show what
I can do.

But it's a pity I haven't managed to avoid pose in that last
episode, for all my revolt. And that muddles up the part
where Ignacy is asked to join in the flight.

Rubbish! Ignacy, alias Felix, doesn't need to be explained!
He's the sort of man that nobody needs and nobody can do
without. If he's going to trip me up like this, I shall get rid
of him on the first stage of the journey.

February 25th.

Zosia hasn't been home since morning. She went off somewhere and took Eva with her. Is it just an accident, or the first step towards the parting of the ways?

Kunda sighed deeply as she cleared away the unusual places from the dinner table.

 .   .   .   .   .

He got to the presbytery without difficulty, for the street fighting had quieted down and it looked like a complete victory for the Reds. The ragged detachment of guards, tired of fighting or else busy chasing officers and "functionaries," paid little attention to him in view of his different uniform and spent figure.

But at the presbytery itself he came upon soldiers standing guard at the four corners of the building.

"Where are you going? You can't pass!"—a gloomy ruffian stopped him as he tried to slip through the door.

"Why not?" he asked, feigning stupidity.

"The presbytery is under surveillance, that's why!" cut in the Red Guard. "Who are you anyway?"

"A war prisoner. You can see for yourslf."

"A prisoner? . . . well yes, so you are. What do you want of the parson?"

Tadeusz, realizing that he would gain nothing by arrogance, took refuge in subterfuge.

"You see, comrade," he lied hastily, "we've some wounded men in camp. And it's the custom with us for the priest——"

"All right!" interrupted the guardsman. "Get along!"

He went into the audience room and, finding it empty and

silent, rang the bell twice. No one appeared, so he looked into the next room and discovered a servant cowering in the corner. He had the greatest difficulty in worming out of him the information that the priest was upstairs in his bedroom talking to a gentleman.

He ran upstairs, found the right door by the sound of voices, and knocked with energy.

"Come in!" cried the priest doubtfully.

He pushed the door open, but stood still on the threshold, checked by an unexpected sight. The man with the priest was Judge Szarota.

"Oh, I beg pardon!" he gasped without stirring. "I didn't know you were engaged, Father. At least, I didn't suppose ——" he broke off, looking from the priest to Szarota, both of them no less surprised than himself at the meeting.

The priest was the first to break the awkward silence.

"Come in!" he begged with forced politeness. "What brings you here at such a time? And how did you manage to get in?"

"That was nothing!" he waved his hand carelessly. "They let me through. I wanted to speak to you, Father, about a very urgent and rather confidential matter. Unfortunately" —he gave a sidelong glance at Judge Szarota, whose small eyes were boring into him obstinately—"unfortunately"—he ended, trying to appear indifferent—"I see that you are engaged."

"No, not that exactly!" answered the priest. "We were talking about one thing and another. Judge Szarota arrived a few days ago and hasn't been able to get away—these disturbances——"

"Father!" Judge Szarota interrupted. *"You may as well tell him. I came about Mademoiselle Radziejowska, and we were just speaking of her. You didn't suppose that, did you?"*—he smiled sarcastically at Tadeusz.

The smile and the words acted on Tadeusz like a challenge.

"Well, that's very lucky," he said in a hard voice, *"for I happen to have come about Mademoiselle Radziejowska too."*

"Ah," Judge Szarota seemed surprised.

The priest made a wry face. He got up from his seat, deeply worried, and glanced at the door leading into the next room.

"We'd better go in there," he sighed.

Tadeusz went up to the table.

"There's no need! I haven't any secrets. We can all three discuss it." He sat down sideways to Szarota, and went straight to the point. *"I wanted to ask you, Father, to take Marusia under your care."*

"But——" the priest lifted his hands.

"One minute, please. I ask it because I am starting to escape to Poland today. You needn't be so astonished. I'm sure I shall get through."

"And what has that to do with Mademoiselle Radziejowska?" hissed Szarota.

"I was just going to tell you. I'm running away so that I may be able to divorce my wife, come back here, and marry Marusia, or possibly get her and the children over to Poland. And except for you, Father," he went on, taking no notice of the priest's amazement and Szarota's uneasy movements,

"*I don't see anybody who could take care of Marusia during that time without any self-interest.*"

"*Very good,*" gasped the priest, "*but Marusia——*"

"*She'll wait for me, I give you my word for it. You needn't either of you have the least doubt about that.*"

"*Has she promised you?*"

"*Yes!*" he replied, rising to his feet. Although he had spoken in one breath, he felt as tired as if he had had a long exhausting conversation. He considered his mission done, and did not in the least want to enter into any further discussion or to answer the questions visible in the eyes and gestures of the priest and Judge Szarota. He bowed.

"*Please think over what I have told you, Father. You may not like it, but there's no other way out.*"

He put his hand to the door, and, if he did not make his exit, it was only because the priest amused him by brandishing his arms in an extraordinary fashion, as if waving him away or begging him to remain—there was no knowing which.

"*But all this is simply unheard of, my dear sir!*" cried the priest, his arms still working like a windmill. "*I can't consent to it. I must demand explanations; it's impossible for me——*"

"*I count on you nevertheless, Father!*" interrupted Tadeusz as he went out.

He was slightly irritated. Disenchantment undermined the triumphant knowledge that he had done what he had to do, and he felt bitterly disappointed. He had meant to come to an understanding without any of this violence. On his way to the priest, he had been prepared for an honest heartfelt *talk in which he might have been ready to confess everything. But the reality had been different. Some demon had sent that fool of a Szarota to turn the priest's head with his own hopeless affairs. It was all about his courtship, no doubt.*

The idea! Tadeusz laughed as he went downstairs. The tiresome picture of that hypochondriac calmed him now and reconciled him with reality. Hard luck! To this man he had nothing to confess. So after all he had done what he could. Now he had only to get away.

He went through the empty audience room with firm steps and was near the front door when he heard the sound of feet behind him, and someone called him. He looked round. Judge Szarota, very pale, was hurrying after him.

"Were you calling me?" he asked carelessly, but in a warning tone.

"Yes, you!" said Szarota, catching him up. "Wait a moment"—he laid his bony hand on Tadeusz's shoulder.

"Keep your hands to yourself!" cried Tadeusz, shaking him off.

"You needn't be angry! Only answer me one question."

"Please make it a short one, then. I'm in a great hurry!"— he opened the door and stood in it, waiting.

"You've just been there, haven't you?" hissed Szarota in his ear.

"Where?"

"Where? at the farm!"—he again gripped Tadeusz's shoulder spasmodically, piercing him with the unendurable gimlets of his eyes.

"Let me go!" shouted Tadeusz, possessed by sudden brutal anger. He felt tempted to strike his assailant right between

those piercing eyes and that hooked nose of his, and was tak-
ing his hand from the door to do it when the thought struck
him that a plain answer to the question would be a blow a
hundred times stronger, more painful, and nearer the mark.

"Of course!" he drawled with calculated vindictiveness;
"I've been there. I was there a month or two, I don't remem-
ber how long. In spite of all your tricks, you old spy!"

Szarota drew back as if stabbed by a feeling of abhorrence.
A twist of pain flickered across his face, but he mastered
himself and stared at Tadeusz with tranquil eyes that had
grown brighter.

"Then she is unfortunate," he said, marking his words,
"and you—you are a beast."

March 1st

There is a great quiet and emptiness about me. No one has
been to see us since my illness—I use "us" here out of habit,
out of vice, for it is only myself that keeps people off. How
glad I should be, in other circumstances, that nobody bothers
about me. But I miss people today. When I put everyone
against me like this and offend people and trample on them,
I wait until someone turns up who understands that I do it
only out of the despair of a heart grown savage, a heart in
which a thousand arrows are planted. That someone doesn't
come . . . and I shan't go out to look for him. And so the
ring of loneliness narrows about me.

.   .   .   .   .

He put his plan into execution that very night, and to-
gether with Ignacy, who consented to the escape with a

heavy heart, became a drop in the bewildered flood of people that poured itself over Russia in the dawn of the revolution. He got out of the town with an echelon of Red Guards chasing somewhere after the remnants of the counter-revolution. The Reds gave him a lot of trouble, and so did Ignacy; and even the train behaved badly, for it started off in the opposite direction to their homeward journey. Tadeusz, hanging on to the step of the one and only coach, cheered up his companion by saying that there was no harm in this, the chief thing being to get into the stream that rushed along the railway lines past torpid and blockaded towns, and let themselves be borne forward till the current flung them up on the shore they longed for. The theory proved correct, for at the first stopping-place the errant echelon wheeled round and began to rush in the opposite direction, passing the town under full steam. Then it halted somewhere and scattered to the four corners of the earth—whether in pursuit or flight or dispersal, God alone knew! But it left behind a couple of soldiers' overcoats—the best safe-conduct possible in those times.

On their next train they traversed an enormous expanse, nearly the whole of the steppe, right away to the foot-hills of the Urals. And there the train was held up by a band of Cossacks. Every tenth passenger was lined up and shot, but Ignacy was "one" and Tadeusz was "six," so that they got off with their lives. From this place they made their way to Orenburg. Ignacy routed out some kind of a dismayed Polish Committee to which he attached himself, saying he was fed up with adventures and would take a month's rest. This led to a quarrel, and the friends separated.

Tadeusz's further experiences surpassed his wildest dreams. He was caught into an incredible maelstrom, into a tangled million of moving currents of which every one rushed in a different direction and after its own fashion. Wherever these currents crossed they formed maddened whirlpools or left in their wake a stiffening lava—the overflow of the masses of people drifting up from every side. He overcame obstacles that defied all his preconceived ideas about the possibilities of resistance in the human body, and saw things that he had never imagined in his worst dreams.

At the beginning he persuaded himself that nothing of all this really mattered. And the goal he had before him—that one inevitable goal—seemed to sanction the indifference with which he forced his way on in the teeth of the horrors that faced him—people flung out of moving trains, women and children trampled down by crowds, old men begging vainly on the wagon steps for a morsel of food, every kind of bloody violence that cried to heaven for vengeance. For a long time the frightful excesses of freedom beat unavailingly at the powerful barrier of a heart absorbed with its own grief. But with time, when blow after blow fell upon him, when horror stared at him on every side and sleep was not to be thought of under the constant menace of sudden death, the dull incessant pain in his heart became like an incurable disease. He would not yield to doubt, kept himself rigidly in hand, the scaffolding of his will still held—but the weariness that possessed him was like the sleep of the dead.

That living part of his soul filled by Marusia began to freeze and harden like the castle of glass where the princess of the legend lay asleep. Not that he forgot her. At every moment, in every hard trial and need, his thoughts turned to her with longing. It was only that the distance between him and her dear picture was growing wider and deeper, only that a rampart of blood and fire and violence was rising up to separate them, only that her real shape was vanishing into the beyond.

He drifted on, stunned by reality, dazed with remembrance. Recollection brought him at times a spasm of grief that shook his stricken soul. But his store of inner strength was fast running out, and every fresh outbreak of feeling left him weaker.

When, at last, flung up by the wave upon the longed-for shore, he found himself lying in a field-hospital within the frontiers of Poland, he was overcome by utter weakness—utter nothingness.

·   ·   ·   ·   ·

Have I said enough to explain how it was that I never returned to Marusia? Is one conscious enough, through this, Tadeusz's Odyssey, of a suffering beyond all power to bear?

I endured so much. More than I have been able to get into this sentimental rhapsody of flight. There, among cruel experiences whose very description awakens abhorrence, was welded to my heart the cold and terrible armour that repels the world and men with its ruthless "Begone from me!"

March 2nd.

I have seen Szmid. I forgot to note down here that I had glimpses of him twice before.

Once on the duelling ground, when I was just preparing to fire—or perhaps it was when I was already hit. I had a hazy impression of the two black stars of his spectacles among the bushes, and I couldn't be sure if it wasn't fancy. But now I think I really did see them.

The other time Szmid passed me when I was talking to Klapa in the park. I wanted to stop him, but I was afraid to spoil the effect of our understanding, if such it may be called.

I sought him out myself today, without any difficulty, for he is lying ill in the cottage of the park guardian. God alone knows what ails him. He doesn't complain of anything, and you can't see anything wrong with him. "I'm ill," he says with a certain satisfaction. I've often noticed that conception of illness and behaviour towards it vary on every rung of the class ladder. These very poor people do not succumb to illnesses, but they are "ill." And so they get better or die without losing the balance of ill-luck between life, illness, and death.

But Szmid. I went to see him, deuce take it, because I'm so horribly lonely. Besides that, something attracts me to him. Szmid is the very voice of misfortune. I was curious as to what he would say to me after all that's been happening; and he was bound to know about it even if the black vision at my duel was only my fancy.

Szmid said:

"We're going through hard times now." (Szmid feels himself a fragment of humanity and often uses the plural when speaking of himself.) "People don't know what they want, Stach."

"Or perhaps they only know what they want."

"You've always got a clever answer. Well, people behave like dogs. Don't be angry, Stach, if that sounds coarse. But I've been lying here for several days and looking at that dog"—he pointed to a mongrel dozing under the cooking stove. "He's a funny creature! He smells out something over here, and then smells something over there. And before he's had a good sniff at this, he's off to sniff at that. He's got his soul in his nose, mind you. And at night he can only howl at the moon for being too far off for him to smell it."

"That's not his fault."

"I didn't say it was, for he's just a dog. . . . What were we talking about?"

"Nothing in particular; you were saying the times were hard. . . ."

"Aha! Very difficult times. The war is over and nobody has been able to get home yet. Some couldn't find their homes and others found them different from what they'd expected. So they wander about the world and get in each other's way. I've been afraid to go about the streets lately. I got ill at the right moment."

"How long have you been laid up?"

"About a week, I suppose. But if I could, and if it wouldn't be rough on Mikolaj, I'd like to lie up for a year. It's nice to have your own corner and your bed. Were you ever ill, Stach?"

"Oh, yes—but a long time ago, when I was little. . . ."

"Of course! Why should you be ill? You've got a bed without that. You've got a flat—that front room of yours, so sunny I was surprised. But the flat's nothing—you've got a kind, pretty wife and that beautiful little girl."

"Yes, I have."

"That's what I said. And you've got your profession. You can speak to the whole world. You've got a name. . . ."

"Well?"

"Eh, Stach! In your place I'd leave people alone and only have to do with God."

March 8th.

The best thing just now would be to go away somewhere. Not for long, and I don't want to run off altogether; but for a month or two. I should have time to think, and it would make it easier for Zosia. I should be out of people's sight. That sort of compulsory break-off is often the surest test of the reality of feelings and habits. Not to speak of getting freshened up, a thing I've been needing for ages.

But there's an obstacle, and a serious one. I've no money and no time. I was a great ass to refuse the offer of leave my chief made me. I might have been able to borrow something if I'd accepted it. And now I don't know what to do.

I'll have a shot at it, though; primo: a letter to my publisher to tell him my novel is nearly finished and that it's time to consider a further advance; secundo: a talk with my chief—private and confidential—with a request for advice, as he has a sensitive ear on that score.

So—two falsehoods *minorum gentium,* the contemplation of which makes me angry and ashamed. Damned bad luck! I've never yet had resort to that kind of life-rope.

.   .   .   .   .   .

~~In spite of his quarrel with Tadeusz, sealed by an "inflexi~~
ble resolve" to break with him for ever, Ignacy was not long
at Orenburg. The mania for imitation which was one of the
chief links binding him to Tadeusz proved stronger than
even the most wounding offences and the most resolute de-
terminations to be independent of him. The thought of his
friend, embarked on an impossible mission and yet not drawing back before it, gave him no peace till he started off into
the unknown. He safeguarded himself by documents and
~~permits from different committees.~~

      .   .   .   .

Have I gone out of my senses? Why all this spite? And
why Orenburg and Ignacy, anyway? The devil! I'll cross out
that bit!

March 12th.

I've spoken to Zosia about my possible departure. She said
indifferently that she had nothing against it, though she
couldn't understand how my going away would make the
situation any better. I should come back and it would be just
the same. She advised me to have a talk with the motorist,
who is going off somewhere or other.

      .   .   .   .

~~When Madame Kamila was summoned to the front by her~~
husband, who was seriously ill, she jumped at the opportunity of leaving the Colonel's adopted fatherland. She did not
believe the rumours of dangers and difficulties of travel or,
~~if she did, she believed also in her star with all the light-~~

mindedness of a woman who trusts in her own charms and talents and intuition.

The acquaintances she had made in various interesting circles of the town after breaking away from her husband's narrow home came in highly useful now for obtaining her permits for departure. Some of her former friends sat upon the all-powerful revolutionary committees, and these paved her way to the highest spheres of influence. She was given not only all possible permissions, not only a private coach to the confines of Soviet Turkestan, but even an ideal travelling companion in the person of a young Red staff officer sent on special business to Moscow.

So she started, the admiration of everyone for her cleverness, common sense, and energy. The officer proved a charming companion, not only on account of the powerful influence his "special" documents gave him over the entire area under Soviet rule. He was no more a Bolshevik than was Madame Kamila, and it was his career that took him to Moscow. He considered this acquaintance with the Colonel's wife, who could, "in case of anything," be useful as a witness that he wasn't such a frightful Bolshevik after all, to be one of the lucky moments in the complicated affairs of his life, and he behaved towards her with all the chivalry of a gentleman who knows whom he may need and when.

In these circumstances, and as Madame Kamila also divined all the possibilities involved in her companion's protection during the further stages of their journey, their alliance took on a more enduring aspect and was prolonged up to the first revolutionary-counter-revolutionary frontier. The terms they were on, though very familiar and abounding in mutual

~~confidences, never exceeded the limits of propriety; for the~~ officer put his career first, and Madame Kamila knew how to value the flower of virtue in the bouquet of her numerous qualities.

They arrived at counter-revolutionary Orenburg together, after changing their outward appearances, clothing, and documents. Madame Kamila found friends there and took steps to get new permits and safe conducts and coaches. They were just about to proceed on their journey when someone recognized the officer and gave him up to the Cossack authorities.

Unfortunately the events that followed are only known up to a certain point. The officer was shot, but before his death he accused Madame Kamila of being a dangerous Bolshevik emissary sent out as a spy to the Cossack stations, while he himself was a small and insignificant person compared with her. Madame Kamila had her first disappointment in the power of her charms when she stood before the court martial. She was condemned to death, but it is not quite certain if the sentence was carried out.

For there are "eye-witnesses" who are said to have seen Madame Kamila at the side of the Esaul Szkarupa, one of the most sinister figures of the White regime. A certain prison warden related that the detachment of Cossacks ordered to shoot her "borrowed" her before the execution. He knew nothing of what happened afterwards, but he heard ~~no firing. Others again~~

     ·   ·   ·   ·   ·

That's bad too. I'm making a screen of these unimportant figures to cover the transformation of Tadeusz from a

knight and a hero into an ordinary bread-eating man. It
doesn't help a bit, seeing that I find myself whistling at sight
of this "new" figure. Suppose I were to apply that same spiteful shrewdness I've been using for Ignacy and Madame
Kamila to Tadeusz? I shan't save the novel, but I shall at
least achieve—a heroic gesture!

.   .   .   .   .

~~In spite of his quarrel with Tadeusz, Ignacy did not stay~~
long at Orenburg. He felt something like remorse at having abandoned his friend. The mania for looking after
people which was one of his chief links with Tadeusz now
found a fertile field to graze upon, and joined with his innate feeling for heroism (thus he spoke of himself) to torment him until he started off into the unknown. With the
safe-conduct of a "loyal refugee," won after endless appeals
~~to the committee.~~ .   .   .

March 14th.

I don't know what made Zosia advise me to have a talk
with the motorist about my going away—he doesn't give me
the impression of intending to go off anywhere. Perhaps he's
only thinking about it, as I am—or perhaps. . . . Well,
it doesn't matter. The worst of it is that we were unable to
come to an understanding, not only on the subject of the
journey, but about various other things that have cropped
up between us.

The trouble was a certain small detail that I noticed in a
corner of his study at the very beginning of our conversation.
Eva's "Teddy," that beloved, petted Teddy, plucked completely bare by a too-loving hand. When I saw him, put

down to sleep as Eva puts him, in a strange house, my heart felt as cold and empty as though something had gone out of my breast to sit by that dozing Teddy—something that was mine no longer and that was turned away from me.

So Eva, taken out of her home by Zosia, goes there. It doesn't matter so much that Zosia goes to see the motorist; it would be difficult for me to forbid it (and I somehow believe they are both quite innocent, and I somehow think they don't yet know what to do . . .) but Evka. . . . I've never drawn Eva into the orbit of those possibilities of which the emigrant Teddy showed me the menace and sorrow.

Nevertheless I brought him home with me, to the great embarrassment and wonder of the motorist. I meant to give Eva a scolding, but when I got home she was in bed and asleep, with her hands under her bright head. And she sighed so deeply through her dreams that I had to throw Teddy into bed with her.

.   .   .   .   .

After a few days in hospital he felt well again, but he did not get up, prolonging his illness by every sort of malingering. He was in no hurry. All the enthusiasm with which he had started from his prison-house, all the ruthless obstinacy with which he had fought his way through the chaos of incredible trials, all the mechanism of haste which he had used against everything assailing him and against the lurking menace of return, suddenly died down and gave place to something like cowardly laziness and pusillanimous indifference.

It was in vain that he cheered himself with the thought

~~that by arriving where he was he had accomplished every~~thing, ~~that the meeting he had before~~ *him with his wife and* ~~their clinching discussion would be merely an easy finale.~~ . . .

March 20th.

Awful day! No leave and no money! My publisher wrote by return that the publishing conditions are too bad at present to allow of his making advances except in the case of work that is quite finished and given in. "And then, of course, only if it is suitable for publication!" The idiot! I wrote back, also by return, that unusual producing conditions oblige me to hand over my manuscripts only to such publishers as can advance me money before the work is finished. "And then, of course, only when they can publish the book in accordance with my demands."

It was all an octave lower with my chief.

"There can be no question of leave, my dear sir," he said; "we are simply submerged in work, as you know better than anyone."

"But you yourself offered me leave a short time ago!" I opposed, for I was wild.

"And you yourself refused it!"

"Because I felt it to be insulting."

"And I feel your present demand to be, let us say—well, presumptuous, going too far. . . ."

For the first time since I've been in the service I constrained myself to humility.

"You haven't quite understood me. I only wanted to ask . . . I was in such a position . . ."

"I can do nothing for you!"

I felt like a beaten dog. If anyone falls into my hands to-day, I shall bash his face in.

March 21st.

Someone did fall into my hands. The victim was Felix, but it was I who had my face bashed in. Yes, brutally, ruthlessly, and with vigour. It quieted me down at once. In the twinkling of an eye I forgot all about leave and money and even about Zosia—about everything.

For Felix brought me news from Marusia's steppe. Someone who hasn't yet had the pluck to get away from there, one of the thousand grey figures of the war, a man whose name I remember though I have forgotten his face, writes thus (I am copying his letter exactly, for I took it from Felix and kept it) :—

"I don't know if you still remember me, but we were once together in the prisoners' camp at Troick, in barrack 8. We exchanged addresses then, and I am taking advantage of it now, for all our efforts to get into communication with Poland by other means have come to nothing. If you get this letter, for God's sake do something to help us to return. The whole world has forgotten us, and yet there are still quite a lot of us here. We are living in the most abject poverty, in conditions we never dreamed of in our prisoner days. There are women and children among us, and even an old friend of yours, Madame Szarota with her son. Her husband was shot not long ago. She asked to be remembered to you. ——Signature."

And here I sit over that letter with an inconceivable chaos in my mind. I don't know whether to be glad or sorry,

whether to curse or bless fate. What am I to do, what can I
do? This unexpected news, so very probable—what am I
saying?—true, essential, infallible—alters and shatters everything. Marusia is alive! It's a strange ordering of fate that
she should make a sign just at this moment of my life.

But . . . a son? Whose son is it?

March 24th.

I'm off to Warsaw, to raise hell in responsible circles on
the score of that handful of castaways left to their fate in
Turkestan. Whatever may come of it, I simply must do
everything in my power for Marusia to return to Poland. I
hope to be able, at least—at last—to pay the debt that has
been weighing like a nightmare on my conscience. And afterwards—we shall see. I must look into her eyes, hear her voice,
touch her hand—for I can't remember and am afraid to
dream.

It's a horrid business that I've been obliged to borrow the
money for my travelling expenses from the motorist, but
Felix says he's absolutely stony. When I took it I had the
impression that it was the first instalment on Zosia.

I left a card at the office to say that I've been called away
for a couple of days on urgent private affairs. They can do
what they like about it.

March 27th.

Well, the first act's finished! I think the row I made in

Warsaw won't blow over without something being done. I ran from one office to another like a lunatic, and a lunatic of the worst kind—cold, lurking, inexorable. Mr. "Vice" himself (the memorable person of the banquet) could not get out of my visit. He received me loftily, it is true, and talked nonsense about reasons of State not permitting the Republic to continue its repatriation policy on account of the doubtful elements coming in from Russia. But I quieted him by declaring that I would move heaven and earth through the Press for a foot of soil to be found in the motherland for her most necessitous sons. He promised to send a special order by the next courier, and I'm sure he'll do it, for in one of his secretaries I discovered a comrade from the days of war, imprisonment, and revolution; he will keep the august statesman up to the mark.

So the first act is, I say, ended. What next? I am struggling with the thought whether to give Marusia a sign of life from myself, or not. Difficult problem! If she doesn't know that I abandoned her simply from weakness of will and spirit—if, having had no news from me since we separated, she supposes me dead—the news may be a heaven-sent blessing to her in this dark hour of her life. But if she knows— if that son is mine . . . if Szarota was capable of such great devotedness—devotedness which must have killed, by force of contrast, all recollection of me—if she has cut me out of her memory, which she had a perfect right to do . . .

No! I can't risk it. Felix shall write the letter, and not to Marusia, but to that man he knows. And he shall bring in a few words about me, just that I am living.

Only I don't know whether Felix's disinterestedness about

Marusia, a disinterestedness that safeguards me against any possible blunders on his part, is sincere.

March 28th.

Felix wrote the letter humbly word for word as I dictated it. He is depressed, for he is in love with Zosia. Zosia likes the motorist better. Felix wants to annoy Zosia by facilitating my communication with Marusia, for he isn't sure whether Zosia, preferring the motorist, doesn't happen to be in love with me. Felix is terrified, besides, at the thought that he produced his play without contemplating the possibility of Marusia's return. I'm sorry for Felix, but he's too insignificant to worry about.

March 29th.

But what about myself and my novel now? Of course I can't write another word of it. It was a mistake from the very beginning, for it never entered my head that the end of it might be played out in my actual life. And anyway I wrote it without conviction. I keyed my nerves up to the effort, and gave way now and then to a paroxysm of the recollections that form the better parts of the manuscript. Looking at the thing calmly, I see that I was only deluding myself when I said I should finish it. It was largely a question of ambition, and, what is worse, one of money. I never liked the book as a whole, and I don't suppose I should ever have published it even if I'd been able to get it done. There's nothing for it but to roll up the manuscript and put it at the bottom of the cupboard, underneath the archives, in the burial-place of unfinished writings and failures.

All the same, I can't help regretting six months of work wasted. That's a long time at my age, for I'm getting near the turning-point of a man's creative powers. If only I could start something new. If I could achieve a single idea, a single impulse, a mere stirring of that chaos of feeling where solid particles of thought are born and circle and hover and struggle for space till they rush downwards carrying everything before them. But there's nothing. Nothing whatever. All that I had in me, bad or good, right or wrong, I have put away today among the archives.

I've a bad time ahead of me now that my haven of work —that port outside of life, calm in hours of storm, stormy in days of stagnation, independent, invincible—is shut away from me.

There's nothing but life itself left. Nothing but life.

I am locking my bureau. I shall only be able to hover about it now, and I'm going to be terribly lonely.

March 31st.

But something must be done, something actual, for this living under one roof with Zosia has become absurd. I haven't the faintest idea how one begins to take steps (so-called) towards divorce. Probably by finding a lodging for oneself. A pleasant state of things! A couple of more or less decent rooms with a kitchen cost 1000 dollars nowadays. A sum beyond my wildest dreams. Of course a bachelor's room would be much cheaper, but I must reckon with the possible return of Marusia.

For even if she shouldn't want to hear my name—if she

couldn't forgive me—oh! what's the good of deceiving myself? I believe that she loves me and will forgive me everything if she comes. And I . . . I am longing for her with that
eternal longing for the love of womankind, all-embracing,
immeasurable, deep as the sea. If only she would come soon!

April 5th.

I don't know what's going to happen. For the first time
in my life I'm as weak and poor and helpless as a child.

I went to call on someone I know today who has a house
agency bureau, and is a barrister as well. I shan't write anything about the house difficulty, for a flat continues to cost
1000 dollars . . . but his advice, those lawyers' tricks connected with a divorce or a separation . . . Abominable! I'm to
persuade Zosia to admit things that are untrue and abhorrent, to facilitate a separation for me? Never!

And Eva? According to the letter of the law she would
remain with her mother, it seems. I never supposed it was
like that. And I could never imagine life without that kiddy.
She's my only luxury; the one inconsequence, the one weakness that I'm not ashamed of and don't try to conceal.

April 11th.

For the last few days Zosia and I have been out-bidding
each other in displaying our affection for Eva. I got cheap
credit at one of the toy-shops and made the most of it. They
have splendid things there. I discovered a rabbit the other
day that plays, gets in and out of his basket, and pricks up
his ears.

I also recollected that, as a writer, I get a discount on books. So I draw on that too.

The first time I came home with new trophies for Eva's palace of wonders (which means her toy corner), Zosia seemed surprised and even quietly delighted.

But that state of things didn't last long. The very next day she began a counter-offensive and brought home a huge bear such as I'd been fruitlessly hunting the town for. I shouldn't be a man if I hadn't thought it was the motorist who gave Zosia the money to buy it. Whereas it wasn't. A pawnticket for her bracelet (a souvenir of the early days of our married life), a ticket that I came across by accident, revealed the source of the money.

Apart from the toys, we devote all our leisure to the child. She in the morning (it's a queer thing, but since I went to the motorist she doesn't go there with the child any more), and I in the afternoon. We have tried playing all three together, but it didn't answer.

I don't know what will come of it, for this race between two parental egoisms has no sense whatever. I suppose that Eva will put an end to it herself. She isn't half so delighted with this unexpected shower of favours as you would think. She studies us carefully with her wise eyes, and I've noticed since yesterday that she is anxious. She cuddles up to me with a kind of nervous passion, but she doesn't forget her mother, and goes into the next room to her, time after time.

I must say this for Zosia, that she shows amazing pluck and tact over the whole business, and avoids everything that might reveal the meaning of our silent competition.

Only she has fits of stifled, heart breaking crying at nights.

April 12th.

How are things going with Marusia? I heard from the Ministry yesterday that all the necessary steps have been taken to facilitate the repatriation of our people in Turkestan. So that there are hopes that the matter will be carried through quickly, since correspondence with the Moscow delegation shows that all the necessary materials were collected long ago, in spite of much trouble with the local authorities. The report of the delegate to Turkestan was enclosed in the letter. I am requested to read this and forward to the Ministry my opinion of the people to be evacuated, "of whom a detailed list is appended."

The report is dated January 1st. I went through it thoroughly, but did not find the news that interested me most nearly. Not a word about Marusia, and no mention of Judge Szarota in the list of the living or of the dead.

But there is mention of the priest. "These people," writes the delegate in the paragraph about the remnant of the Polish colony, "are deprived of spiritual care, as the parish priest was arrested at the very beginning of the revolution and no one knows where he was sent. I consider it my duty to draw the attention of the delegation to the personality of this chaplain . . . etc., etc."

I can guess the rest for myself. When the priest was sent away Marusia had no one to protect her, and this must have been almost as soon as I left her. It was a chain of misfortunes, for her father lost his life very soon after, killed by an assassin's bullet on his way home from the front. If, with that, she was expecting a child, and if it is true that the

Sarts and Kirghiz turned Bolshevik and destroyed the European settlements on the steppe (as I have heard from various sources) —if—but these are questions that are frightful to investigate.

What must have been the changes in Marusia's soul when she was faced with such terrible trials? I sometimes think that all the hopes that stirred in my heart at the news of her return will be shattered painfully by my having to meet someone new and strange. And if she has lost her beauty, the beauty of a wild-flower torn from the soil a hundred times?

April 19th.

My life is falling to pieces, quickly and completely. There was a fresh scene at the office—it's the last one, I think.

It is my duty as a diarist to mention that the leave I granted myself to go to Warsaw three weeks ago caused a nasty quarrel with my chief. I didn't write about it at the time, as nothing positive came of it.

It was only today that the sequel took place. And it was the controller, verifying our consumption of coal, who provided the pretext.

It was like this: heaps of slack grow up year after year in our coal-cellars. This slack, which is State property, is given back every year to the coal-merchant, who in exchange supplies our porters with a certain quantity of coal (a metre of coal for three metres of slack). Of course all this has been done on the quiet, on the strength of my authority and thanks to the discretion of the chief, who pretends to know nothing about it.

This year we had a new intendant, who was no sooner in his post than he put before me a "plan for realizing" the slack. I didn't agree to it and ordered the stuff to be given for the porters, as usual. He gave it, but he entered it into the expenditure book. Now the controller's come, and as I've had one or two cuts at him by letter, he has a spite against me. So he's taken this up. That's all. No one can imagine the disgust with which I've noted this down in my diary, which, after all, cannot be merely a chronicle of absurdities.

But I must just mention the finale. I was ordered to sign the report of the matter, and the chief went absolutely solid with the controller over this. So I signed it, adding a few words to say that the quantity of slack was not exact, as two or three kilograms of it had been left in the lungs of the porters who work at sifting the coal. Hurrah! *e pur si muove!*

Only it's a pity the thing has happened at such an awkward moment. At present the office is my chief source of income, and if they give me the sack I don't know what I'm going to live on, or how I shall provide for Zosia and Eva— or help Marusia if she comes. Shall I go in for journalism or what? I could of course easily get out of it by some bureaucratic swindle or other—for instance, some demonstration that the "sums" for the slack (*nota bene* about a hundred and fifty zlotys[1]) were remuneration for extra hours of work —but there's something about this business that makes me stiff-necked.

April 21st.

However . . . my office activities are suspended. The pre-

[1] About $17.05.

cipitate controller rushed off with the report to his head office, and the head office, shocked by the comment I had appended to my signature, ordered my immediate suspension
from duty pending investigation, etc.

The chief locked himself into his room and the document
liberating me from my duties was brought to me by Michal,
whose air and figure were as incredibly "official" as if he had
never taken part in the sharing of coal sums. I was just going
to give him a few acid words when he looked cautiously
round and whispered mysteriously into my ear:

"There's a delegation here, sir, of our office servants, behind the door. Perhaps you——"

"What do they want?"

"I don't know. Something or other. It's about that coal
slack. Must they go away?" He jumped back prudently,
noting my movement of impatience.

"No! Show them in!"

They came in. Zyla and Gnojek, the seniors, in the van,
and after them the rest of the delegation—that is to say,
every man Jack of our porters. Bonk, Klocek, Wontorek,
Figlas, Cienciala, and Dyl.[1]

Zyla, who likes to orate, came up to my desk, but his
tongue clove to the roof of his mouth.

"In the name of——" he began, and stuck.

"Cut the cackle and get on with it."

"We, the office servants, sir . . ."

"Well, what do you want?"

There was a silence, and then Zyla's hand, holding a roll

[1] Literal translation of these peasant names: Fibre and Muckyman; Beetle,
Turnip, Woodblock, Edge, Joker, and Plank.

of money, was laid on my desk. Zlotys and two-zloty pieces, of course.

"What's all this?" I turned round and stood face to face with the delegation.

"Well, you see, sir, it's for that coal!"

Two courses lay before me: to yield to emotion or to get into a temper. I chose the second.

"Go to blazes!" I shouted, and went out of the office, slamming the door after me.

Nothing will make me give in now. The delegation of the office servants has filled me with extraordinary fire. . . . The devil! I have allies among people yet.

April 22nd.

I have! a string of my office colleagues came to me today. One with advice, another with words of sympathy, a third with a knife into the chief and the controller. Everybody has something to remind me of; money lent in a black hour, or intercession with the chief, or leave—I can't understand myself when I found time to do it all.

I sent the lot of them packing, for human gratitude has in it something that makes you weak and powerless. How much easier it is to live among the hard-hearted.

April 26th.

I'm simply going out of my mind from sheer boredom. I was yoked to two ploughs and they're both at a standstill. I prowl about my room like a wolf in a cage. God alone knows what thoughts come into my head. They run into thousands, and they're all equally sterile and hopeless and murderous. I must do something, I absolutely must do something. . . .

I've been for a big walk into the country, some thirty kilometres there and back. And I brought home, in addition to enormous fatigue, a load of unexpected impressions. Thoughts strange and immemorial have driven away all the unrest of the day.

First, it's spring. A few steps beyond the turnpike gates of the town it is spring. Flowers bloom. The wind blows across the fields. Birds float and sing overhead. The earth breathes warmth, and the young branches of the trees are swelling towards the sun. The insect bursts through its dead chrysalis—the beast leaves his winter lair. Everything yields to the one eternally recurring law—we alone wander about in the labyrinth of towns that we ourselves have built, blind, deaf, unfeeling.

Then my young days. The foot-path is not yet grown over by which I used to go to my first meetings with a girl. The rock of my youthful dreams still stands as it stood in the heart of the forest, and you can't see that the arch of trees has grown any higher above it. The same lop-sided inn stands at the cross-roads, and the old wooden bench is there still, and the table, and the mug of milk on the table. The plains and the hills, the streams and the meadows and the copses, the old oak with four letters carved on it, and even the hole in the fence we weren't allowed to get through—nothing has changed, for it's only a flash of time since I was there last. But in that flash I lost the treasure of youth.

Then the meaning of life: we are out to conquer the world, but there's less and less room for us in the fortresses we've built of our booty and plunder. We wrest from nature the secrets of her most puissant laws; we change the face of the earth; in our struggle for independence we stake our existence, and that of the generations to come, upon one card—but before we have taken a single step forward, the pulsing time-beat of nature tells us that everything is over.

April 27th.

I went to the motorist today to ask him if he could put off the date for the repayment of the money I borrowed from him when I went to Warsaw. I wasn't obliged to do this, for no date had ever been specified, but I hate the feeling of dependence a debt gives one. Especially that kind of debt.

I knew in advance that the motorist would only laugh at my scruples, but I never expected him to offer me a larger loan for settling my "worries"—and I'd never have believed that I should promise to accept it if the need arose.

I feel I must explain myself here. It's my opinion that matters have taken what I may call a negative turn between Zosia and the motorist. Either he's declared himself and been sent packing, or else—which is more likely—he came to pieces when his naïve and childish first love for Zosia was confronted by the necessity of solving the hard riddles of reality.

There are no actual foundations for my idea, but—my motorist is changed. His face has something bitter about it, and he behaves like a child with a splinter in its finger. And I'm sure he doesn't see Zosia now.

Marvellous are Thy works, O God! That man, a daredevil, a hero, a conqueror—they tell extraordinary tales about his crazy courage—is as helpless as a child when he comes in contact with ordinary people and circumstances. I imagine how much he suffered and how greatly he was amazed, when he was forced to examine the thread that binds Zosia and me and all of us, the actors and supers of the drama he has been drawn into by accident, following his heart's desire.

I don't know how far he has got, though all the signs show that this process of change has only just started in him. For the moment he is taking refuge in flight. He has a good ally in the shape of a new car of the latest sporting pattern.

When he took me to his garage and showed me his new model in detail, his eyes shone with the old heroic fire and his lips smiled enthusiastically. I've never heard such ardour in his voice.

He described the engine with special emphasis, extolling the simplicity, accuracy, "honourableness" (*sic*) of every one of its parts.

"You get no surprises!" he said, leaning against the hood, when we had finished looking the thing over, "no surprises, mind you! And what harmony! Every part of her does its bit, and the whole thing is a lovely job. She's as powerful as a dragon and as gentle as a child. Clever, too. If you want her to go beyond her strength, she warns you; if you over-strain her, she lets you know. She never startles you."

"And yet accidents happen."

"Not her fault, old man. Only once in a thousand times. And if it is . . . then it's plain sailing. It very seldom happens"—he slowed down thoughtfully—"that you come

through if the brakes refuse to act, for instance, or the steer-
ing-rod snaps."

"Are you off anywhere?" I hastened to change the subject.

"Oh, rather! I'm thinking of a long trip. Look here!" he
ran his finger over a map on the wall, mentioning tracts and
towns and kilometres.

"Are you going in a party?"

"No!" he answered shortly. "Alone!"

Well, be off, my friend, if there's no help for it. I'm only
afraid you won't get away from yourself by it. You don't
know what an expedition lies before you. In these wild zigzags of yours across the world you're going to take your road
for the first time over the commonplaces of life, just as we
others take it every day. Our way may be less frantic, but
it's every bit as long and quite as complicated.

April 28th.

I'm only going to jot down the most important events of
today, for they are very numerous, and I haven't time to go
deeply into them.

First of all, I asked the motorist to let me have a room in
his villa instead of lending me more money. He has given
me two, with entrance hall, kitchen, and bathroom; quite independently, as he expressed it, of the cash which he continues to hold at my disposal.

Next, I had a talk with Zosia, proposing that we should
try living under separate roofs for a time, while keeping up
our meals together. She assented, with the stipulation that I
am to pay her expenses only until she has found work of

some kind, which may be any day now. At Zosia's request, to which I immediately agreed, we did not speak about Eva. Felix has undertaken to find Zosia a job. So perhaps?—no, let's go on.

I was summoned to the office, where they offered me, pending the clearing up of a certain matter, a resumption of my duties under supervision and with less authoritative powers. I refused categorically, whereupon I was ordered to send in my resignation. Which I did, for I'm simply fed up with the whole business.

Then I went to two newspaper offices to ask for work, and got taken on as a *feuilletoniste* at one of them. That's really the nastiest thing that's happened to me today, for the way the editor received me and my colleagues greeted me was full of that spiteful sympathy for the man who's done for himself. The pay is middling, and the prospect a down-hill one. But I shall get up again.

April 29th.

I'm in my new lodging. Moved into it by stealth with a suitcase for all luggage, so that Eva might not notice anything. Don't feel up to much. Spent most of the day at my old quarters, playing with Eva and begetting an idiotic story for the paper. (It went very badly.) Zosia was only at home for dinner, for she is out a great deal after that job. She looks pretty bad. Eva is off colour too. She either didn't notice my flitting, or else she thinks one shouldn't mention it. The second, more likely. She looked at us so inquiringly, with the corners of her mouth drawn down. And every time

I smiled at her she seemed cross and half-mournful. We shall have to be awfully careful with her, for she has her mother's inflexible reserve and my temperament and sensitiveness.

Kunda called her a "poor orphan" during dinner today. If she ever says anything of the kind again she'll have to look out for another place.

May 9th.

They don't like my short stories. The editor accepts them as if it were a favour, and the colleagues read them at their desks with ironical comments. It's no wonder, for I know what they're worth better than anybody. If only I weren't obliged to sign them with my full name—that name which, as the editor says, is their chief value. I'm digging my own grave. Perhaps I never was a real writer?

I'm getting used to my new lodging by degrees. There are times when it has a certain charm for me, something like a smile of youth at my bachelor solitude. I catch myself dreaming—of Marusia, of course. I wish she would come; I should like my heart to beat again with fear and impatience before our meeting, I should like to see—Oh! Eva's coming in! . . . she's paying me her first visit today.

May 10th.

A telegram! Felix has brought in a telegram that he got today from Baranowicz. It says:—

"We are at Baranowicz. Send Monsieur Stanislaw's address." And it is signed: "Jerzy Radziejowski."

May 11th.

I am waiting. Waiting, filled with forebodings and anxious thoughts. All the conclusions Felix and I came to yesterday, discussing that telegram till late at night, seem doubtful and improbable. Of course Jurek could sign the telegram even if it was sent by Marusia. There are a thousand arguments in favour of her choosing her brother to speak for her. ... Shame, uncertainty ... fear of putting herself forward— all that would be so characteristic of Marusia. Or Jurek might have come on ahead with his younger sister. . . . He might have ... but I'd have liked it a hundred times better if the telegram had been signed Marusia.

Felix has started for Baranowicz—he proposed this himself, and I had to agree to it, for it's better for me too to have someone to speak for me—and he promised to wire me how things are directly he arrives. He may summon me there. . . . So I'm all packed up ready in a fever of impatience. There ought to be a telegram by this time. Suppose I start without waiting for it? Suppose Felix, who disappeared so mysteriously from our horizon when he had the first news about Marusia, has given up all hopes of Zosia and is digging a hole about my feet? What demon urged me to consent to his being a go-between?

I'd better go, and not wait for the telegram. But perhaps our trains would cross? It's enough to drive one mad!

May 14th.

It's three days since Felix left, and there's no news. If they don't arrive by this evening or give any sign of life, I shall go to Baranowicz.

Today Eva brought me a daisy-chain.

May 16th.

Jurek has come, with my son Staś. . . . Marusia is dead. They took her out of the train the day before they started. A few hours later, in the cholera barrack, she died. She found time to write a letter, and to entrust the child to Jurek and both of them to God. I haven't the courage to open that letter.

May 17th.

"My dear Stach:

"God is showing his mercy to us by taking me, for no one needs me. If you still remember me, pray for me. Staś is your son. I believe you will love him and care for him, although he bears another name. I married to save the child from shame. I have no grudge against you. I love you, Stach, in the hour of my death as I have loved you all my life.

"Your Marusia."

My house is like a tomb. I have locked my doors; no one shall come in here. Even Eva was turned away today.

Loneliness and desolation. . . . My poor little son . . . and Jurek.

The second day is passing and not one of us has had the courage to open his lips. We seem to be suffocating in the silence of the grave.

May 20th.

My son is three years old. He is small and thin, and his face is full of stony terror. I don't know if he can talk and I don't believe he knows what it is to laugh. He regards me obstinately with eyes that are neither Marusia's nor mine nor human at all. They are the eyes of misfortune calling upon God for vengeance.

Jurek is a grown man now. He is tall and very handsome, with a head that looks as if it were cast in bronze. Two premature furrows running from his nostrils to his mouth give his face the stamp of tragic experience and are balanced by a vertical slash of decision down the middle of his forehead. And Jurek says nothing. Sometimes he looks at me hard, almost threateningly, as if challenging me to ask him about the thing that hangs between us, crushing and heavy as a stone. And I am afraid to ask.

Every evening we sit opposite one another looking at the floor. Every evening fear shuts our lips.

I have sworn to myself that I will ask him tomorrow.

May 23rd.

Jurek has gone away. He left an hour after our talk. A frightful headache drove me out of doors, and when I came back he had gone. He never took the clothes I had got ready for him, nor anything for his journey, though I know he had hardly a penny in his pockets.

But about our talk. It started for no particular reason. I was standing at the window after breakfast, looking out at

the spring day. There's a bush in the garden that made me
think of the farm in the steppe. I began to dream about the
past, and I was just going to call Jurek to look at that bush
when suddenly his voice, hard and level as the strokes of a
hammer, hit me. Jurek started to speak, taking up the story
of Marusia from the moment I left her.

They did not stay long at the farm after my departure.
A revolt broke out among the natives and drove them from
their home. Barat turned out a traitor. The farm was
burned down; Jurek set fire to it himself when they left.
They went to the town and found none of their friends there.
The Bolsheviks had taken the priest off somewhere. Madame
Kamila had vanished like a stone in water. It was fortunate
that they did not hear of their father's death till later. For
Marusia was simply in despair.

The only person who looked after them was Judge
Szarota. They did not give themselves up to his care at once
—he, Jurek, did not like Szarota, nor did Marusia. But
something happened to Marusia that Jurek did not understand at the time—and she married Szarota. Jurek broke
with them all and went off to get work. Where? It didn't
matter. But since I asked him why, he would tell me. He
believed in me, believed in my return, in my honour . . .
he was young, he cared for me. How he regretted his opposition later on.

Marusia wasn't happy with Judge Szarota. It wasn't his
fault—he was a good man, very unselfish. But he hated the
Bolsheviks. His convictions were unshakable. He took part
in counter-revolutionary conspiracies, and was arrested soon
after Marusia's son was born.

From that moment their life was very hard—they were together again, for Jurek returned to his sister. Marusia divided her time between her imprisoned husband and her child. She was in prison too for a time, suspected of being a go-between for Szarota and the counter-revolutionaries. Little Staś fell ill, Marusia's health completely gave way, and, even he, Jurek, went down with typhus. I asked about Irenka. Oh, she lived with them for a short time and then broke away—got to know some young commissar and married him, and had a "beastly" civil wedding.

Judge Szarota was shot in the end, after a trial that lasted two years. Then they resolved to come back to Poland. They got false passports. Jurek didn't want to wait till that gentleman from the Polish delegation came to Turkestan again. They were already in the train, waiting for the day of departure, when Marusia fell ill with cholera. Perhaps she caught it from the well at the railway station, or perhaps from the cakes they bought, in the absence of bread, from the Sarts. She had been ill for so long that it didn't take much to finish her. She had got very thin and weak—they said it was after the baby.

She was taken out of the train to the cholera barrack, where she suffered horribly and died in torments. There was no priest, so he, Jurek, had made the sign of the Cross over her before her death. And it would be hard for God not to accept her among his saints! She came to herself for a time before she died, for she had begged the doctor to give her something calming. It was then that she wrote the letter and made Jurek swear to deliver Staś, our son, into my hands.

What they went through afterwards was beside the point.

Staś was very ill on the journey; they thought he was dying. He was unconscious when they reached Baranowicz. Then he got better, as I could see. That was all. Jurek had kept his word to his sister. He had done what he had to do.

And he went away without saying a word, leaving only a laconic note behind him:—

"I'm going to Warsaw to earn my living. Please don't try to find me out. Good-bye, Jerzy."

May 24th.

Good-bye, my young hero! I can see you wandering among millions of strangers, a comer from a far land, the returning son of prodigal fathers. The motherland will be long in learning to value the treasure of virtue hidden under the armour of your honour. They'll pay you little enough for your laborious hands, your unbowed neck, your open forehead! Not yours will it be to know kin and kind, recognition in high places, friends' advice. Poisoned with misery and pride, you will choke down the bitter bread of humiliation; and in your lonely wanderings you will be snared a hundred times in the trap through whose villainous gate that reptile of yesterday—the coming citizen and favourite of fortune—crawls out upon the wide arena of life.

But you will come through everything with your lion's heart and heroic shoulders. The fighting blood and bone of you was bred in the winds of the steppe, where mother nature lashed you and set beasts of prey about your path. And what you have seen is more than the masters of the world, the snobs and Philistines of our time, have dreamed in long alarming nights. The day will come when the wave that strikes you and carries you away will lie conquered at your feet.

I wish I could see your smile on the day when your soul uncloses for the world and for men of good will.

May 30th.

I'm quite alone now. Zosia and I separated this morning.

I went to talk to her about little Staś—and found her door shut. After I had knocked three times Zosia came. She let me into the hall and asked what I wanted in that house.

The question was such a surprise that I didn't know what to answer. I felt injured. The usual egoism of a suffering man who cannot understand that other people suffer too.

I turned on my heel, but Zosia detained me almost by force. White as the wall, she got out through her clenched teeth:

"You! Don't you dare to imagine that I'm thinking about myself!"

"What do you mean?"

"Don't you know? Why haven't you brought that child to me?"

I was still unable to understand.

"Staś? That was just what I came to talk about."

"You needn't. I know everything. I have thought it all out. I've written you a letter."

"Give it to me!"

"No! I'd rather say it! Listen. I can take that child in here. But I won't have you! I won't! How could you behave

so to that poor girl?" she burst out, wringing her hands and
threatening me by turns.

I don't know what happened to me, but I answered, very
stiff and hard:

"Whatever there was between her and me remains between me and God."

"You've a lofty way of expressing yourself."

"As you like! I can't give up the child, for that was her
last wish. And if you consider that we can't go on meeting
each other in these circumstances of course I'll adapt myself
to it. We can discuss Eva by letter. Have you anything more
to say to me?" I was standing with my hand on the door-
knob.

"Yes, I have!" she answered in a suffocating voice. "You
are a bad man, Stach!"

We separated without shaking hands.

June 1st.

Nevertheless Staś is going to be able to see Eva. Once at
my place, once at Zosia's. We came to an agreement about
this through the intermediary of Felix, who in some inexplicable way has turned up at Zosia's side again. Never mind
that! I am grateful to Zosia for her generosity which, to
speak frankly, I never expected. But we are the worst judges
of those nearest to us.

Today Staś and Evunia are to meet for the first time. At
my place. I've abandoned all my pride and borrowed money
from the motorist to fix up a children's corner. I shall get
my pay at the newspaper office tomorrow, and perhaps I

shall give him some of it back. Could anyone believe that I
go on writing horrible articles about the theatre and the
municipality and the trams?

June 3rd.

It's a dreadful thing, but I—don't love you, my little son.
I took careful stock of you during your play with Eva yesterday. You are a poor, distrustful, reserved little savage.
You didn't smile when Eva, in the kindness of her heart,
gave you her adored Teddy to play with—you pushed her
away when she tried to put her arms round your neck. You
only know the words "Go away," "I won't," and "I don't
want."

And yet I don't know if you will find in all your life a
sweeter and better comrade than your elder sister. She bore
everything and forgave you everything as soon as she knew
you were a "poor darling."

Oh, Eva, Evunia! How much courage and self-sacrifice
you bring to the task of mending the broken threads of our
home life!

When they had finished playing today, my daughter invited Staś to come and see her, kissed me, and then stood in
the doorway, thoughtful and undecided.

"Daddy!" she said softly, "may I ask you something?"

"Yes, you may."

A moment of silence—and then:

"Aren't you coming to us, Daddy?"

"No, dear."

Silence again . . . a sigh and a whisper:

"Perhaps you'll come? Why aren't you good to me, Daddy?"

June 4th.

Felix, our go-between, came today with plenipotentiary powers from Zosia. It was about the formal putting through of our separation, within the bounds of existing possibilities. I told him in advance that I agree to everything Zosia wishes, but it turned out that her terms are unacceptable.

She proposes: first, that I should take over our flat, as she is going to move somewhere else (what does that mean? there aren't any flats to be let in the town); second, the furniture, and all the house contains, except her clothing, underlinen, and a few trifles, are to remain with me (that's absurd, of course; the lion's share of the sticks are her property, brought into our home in her dowry), third, she is to earn her own and Eva's living herself—I shall only have to pay for schooling and possible exceptional expenses connected with her education (ridiculous! it all ought to be mine); fourth, I can see Eva every day, but never in her flat (that's the only point I have nothing against).

I don't know what has prompted Zosia to conditions so magnanimous, and at the same time so humiliating for me. The fact that Felix brought them gives me an unpleasant suspicion that this whole business may be a blind for some kind of far-reaching understanding with him. Of course, I've nothing to go by. The lofty and yet modest air with which he dictated the terms doesn't mean anything. It's rather a case of a generous action on Zosia's part, intended to shame me, "the bad man." But I'm writing nonsense, for anyone can detect the suffering and self-denial that speak through Zosia's terms.

But I can't accept them. Whether I'm a bad man or a good one, I can be generous too. I shall send her a suitable answer by letter today.

June 5th.

Yesterday evening I made a discovery about Staś that touched me frightfully. I hadn't taken my eyes off him for two days, startled by the devastation that his experiences of revolution have wrought in the child's mind. And I couldn't catch him at a single childish movement. There was nothing but a dull gloom, the ostensible submission of a caged animal broken by sporadic flashes of alarm. The nurse whom the motorist has routed out somewhere makes no difference, nor the garden by the garage, nor Eva's visit, nor his return of it.

Until yesterday evening, as I have said. I put him to bed as usual; he shut his eyes at once, as usual, and fell asleep —or didn't fall asleep, taut as a string and quite motionless. I put out the lamp, lighted a night-light, and went and lay down in the next room. I couldn't get to sleep. The utter silence reigning in Staś's room alarmed me. For I know all the stirrings and tossings and sighs of a child going off to sleep. I know the music of its breathing as it sleeps. There was nothing of this with Staś. He lay in the next room as still as a dead child.

I don't know when it was, but I had been in bed some time when I heard the rustling of bed-clothes being pushed back in the next room, and the sound of bare feet on the floor a moment later. I held my breath. Not only out of curiosity, for I was encompassed by a superstitious fear. I could have sworn just then that a ghost was drawing near my door and that I should see it. Meanwhile Staś came to a standstill on the threshold, turned towards my bed. I couldn't make out his face, but his whole figure, stark with caution, showed that he was looking at me and listening to see if I was asleep. My immobility quieted him, and he shut the door nearly to and went back.

Then I got up, and went very carefully on tiptoe to the door. I could see through the chink into the room. Staś was kneeling beside his bed on the bare floor, and making strange movements with his hands upon the wall as if he wanted to climb up it or to scratch it. I couldn't imagine what he was after till I caught the whisper of a prayer. Staś was praying. But in what a way! With desperate alarm, with fever speed, with the wildness of appalling grief.

I don't know what such a prayer can mean, but if it is heard in heaven God Himself must weep with all His angels.

I didn't close my eyes all night. Early in the morning I hunted through my war "archives" and got out a picture of the Madonna that I found one day in the prayer-book of one of my colleagues who died in prison. I had kept it because there was a striking resemblance to Marusia in the Madonna's face.

And when Staś woke up I nailed the picture above his bed and went away at once.

Staś came up to me today for the first time and leaned against my knee and looked into my eyes for a long, long time.

June 8th.

I've sent away the nurse. She called Staś "possessed," a "half-devil," and deuce knows what. Who knows if she doesn't beat him when I'm not there? I shan't get another, for really Staś is a terribly difficult and repellant child. Even Eva is beginning to sigh impatiently during their daily games.

I shall look after the child myself.

Zosia has written back to say that she will communicate with me for the future through the lawyer, as she cannot consent to my answer. It seems that she has some new propositions to make.

June 9th.

Eva hasn't been to see us today. Is that how Zosia's "new propositions" are going to look?

June 10th.

Eva is ill.

June 12th.

They say that Eva may be in for scarlet fever.

I went to see some doctor friends at once, and was told that this is certain to be a home diagnosis as, with the exception of a few imported cases, there is no scarlet fever in the town. Doctors always have their "with the exception of." I am tormented by a supposition which I dare not express.

June 13th.

Yes! Eva has scarlet fever—in a very severe, and they say a very unusual form. She evidently caught it from Staś. It's my fault! I ought to have asked Jurek more about the symptoms of that mysterious illness Staś had on the journey. In any case I ought to have put the child under medical supervision for a time . . . or have waited a while . . . but what's the use of tormenting oneself when it's too late?

I am fighting against horrible forebodings. It's hard to believe that the most innocent creature under the sun should have to answer for my sins.

June 15th.

The motorist has gone off to fetch an old friend of his who is a splendid doctor, the director of a children's sanatorium in the mountains. The motorist says he is a perfectly angelic man and a miracle-working doctor. So I feel a bit less anxious. This doctor is to stay with us, so that I shall have first-hand information about Eva all the time.

Staś has never once asked why Eva has left off coming. He's an utterly weird child. When I caught him at his prayers that evening, I thought it would be the beginning of my fondness for him . . . But now I'm very much afraid I may be going to hate him.

June 16th.

That doctor won't be able to come until the day after tomorrow, if then, for he's down with flu. It's enough to drive one mad! I can see that things are going badly at home with Eva, but nobody will tell me the truth about her illness.

I keep running over and looking at Eva's window. The blinds were pulled up this morning, but now they are half drawn. And there's a most uncanny movement about the house. Every minute someone goes in or comes out. Felix, Klapa, some man with a beard and another man in big spectacles. I know that man. It's a doctor from Helena's hospital.

Szmid put in an appearance about noon, with a bunch of white roses. He walked to and fro under the windows and made me wild with anxiety. When at last he turned into the house, I wanted to call out and keep him back. . . . A superstition! He came out a minute later without the flowers, very alert and cheerful, and the blinds were drawn up again.

The motorist has been to see Eva twice today, and he says that the disease is taking a "normal" course—a thing I may find out for myself. Zosia has nothing against my visiting Evunia during her illness.

But I can't go there. People in my state of mind can only bring bad luck. And I haven't the courage to go. I haven't courage for anything.

June 20th.

I try to escape from myself by taking Staś for walks. We go along the river hand in hand. And some recollection from years ago comes into my head involuntarily—a blind fiddler led by a small child. Which is the more helpless of the two, and which of them leads the other?

So Staś and I walk beside the river. We dawdle along the embankment together; together we stop to listen to the plashing of the water, our eyes dwelling upon the monotonous procession of ships and boats and barges. Nobody knows us there, nobody asks us anything; this strangeness of the things about us and the rhythm of movement are very soothing.

And now and then I feel as though a current of understanding and brotherliness were flowing into me from Staś's cold thin hand. But not always. When we pass under Evunia's window on our way home, I grip my son's fingers in a spasm of anger.

June 21st.

The doctor from the mountains can't come, and I have decided to call in a specialist and have a consultation of doctors today. They say that Eva's case is normal, but when the consultation was decided upon and I proposed we should call it for tomorrow, the motorist said quickly: "Better today." And from "today" it became "at once." They are there now. In a quarter of an hour or so I am to have a full report. They shan't put me off with humbug any more.

The best thing for me to do now would be to go down to the river, but unfortunately something drove me away from there this morning A freight train laden with cargo for a ship came slowly along the embankment. I meant to hurry by to avoid the tumult it would cause, but Stas tugged unexpectedly at my hand. Greatly surprised, I stopped and asked him what he wanted, but he didn't answer. His eyes were fixed very hard on a half-open freight car. The train came to a standstill, and workmen went up to the car with handbarrows.

Staś flung himself backwards.

"Mummy!" he whispered with quivering lips.

I carried him home in my arms, crying as if his heart would break.

June 23rd.

This can't go on. Eva is very ill. The doctor says that though her constitution is good she hasn't much stamina and is unusually delicate. So that the crisis, which is due in a day or two, may bring in complications of an unexpected kind.

I'm not going to wait and see what that cautious diagnosis means. So Staś and I are moving into my old flat in a few minutes. In view of possible complications, I must be on the spot. I don't suppose that Zosia will . . .

.   .   .   .   .

.   .   .   .

.   .   .   .   .

July 3rd.

I seem to be waking out of a lethargy. I have come back from the bottomless pit and hardly recognize the earth I live on. The spell of things lost and found again encompass me. I am dazzled by the white page of my open diary, and I write as if for amusement, watching my pen's enigmatic movements as it makes letters into words and words into thoughts. A broad strip of July sunlight comes in through the open window, and I know for a certainty that it's a bright summer day outside. I feel the blood pulsing in my temples. Nothing can happen to me now.

But that's enough for today.

July 5th.

This diary must soon be brought to a close. It came into being as a harbinger of storm, so it may as well disperse with the storm that is over. But it shall first catch the last echoes of the thunder.

The day I took Staś and went back to my old home, Eva's illness took a very disquieting turn. I knew it when I found my room full of people talking in whispers. It was evident that no one was expecting me, for when I appeared a sudden silence fell. But I felt the weight of the eyes that rested upon me.

Then Kunda came and took Staś away, and someone opened the door into Evunia's room.

I went straight up to her bed without greeting anyone. She did not know me. Her eyes were misty, her lips black with fever. . . . But I won't recall it.

.   .   .   .   .

I don't know to what or to whom we owe Evunia's recovery. The doctor from the mountains, who turned up just as the crisis started, earned my undying gratitude. When I looked into his blue eyes, through which one seemed to see to the bottom of his serene soul, I began to feel more hopeful. He did not put on any clever airs, nor try to calm me down, nor make any stipulations, but set to work at once. For two days and nights he was in the house practically all the time. Zosia and I took it in turns to help him, so that there were always two people at Eva's bedside. And it all ended happily.

Oh, yes! the doctor, when I thanked him for his wonderful devotion (for after all I'm nothing to him, and there are plenty of sick children in the world), answered that he had read my books, and that somebody ought to show gratitude for them.

And I thought that my writings were merely a handful of words scattered on the wind.

.   .   .   .   .

The picture of the Madonna which is so like Marusia is still hanging above Evunia's bed. It was Staś who brought it into her room at the most critical moment of her illness; we had almost forgotten his existence during those awful days, and Kunda took pity on him and looked after him. I don't know up to now where he slept and what he did and what he had to eat.

He came into the room and up to Eva's bed without looking at us, clutching that picture in his hands. We were all— I and Zosia and the doctor—silent and stony under an awful menace, for Eva was just dropping off to sleep and we did not know if she would wake again. The doctor said everything depended on that sleep, and we were afraid to stir, afraid to breathe.

And yet not one of us had the courage to keep back that child as he stood by his sister's bed with his eyes fixed upon her. And drove the sleep away from her eyelids. And forced the holy picture into her helpless fingers.

Evunia woke up. She looked at Staś through her half-open eyes, and then her gaze dropped to her hands and her lips curved into a slight smile. Staś nodded his head and went out of the room.

My heart was wrung as I looked at the picture, trembling in Eva's fingers. Would it drop out of them, or not? . . .

I thought—no, I would have sworn—that everything depended on the picture at that moment.

It did not drop. Evunia fell asleep smiling, though you could hear Zosia's stifled sobbing from a corner of the room. My own eyes must have been wet. Only the doctor looked quietly at me, nodding his head like Staś.

I didn't know how it would be with Eva, but I felt calm and in some sense relieved.

I felt that between these two children and God's mercy, under the spell of the Holy Virgin's picture, some great understanding had come about which counted more than the care of us three despairing people.

July 10th.

I've heaps of things still to do. I feel like a captain who has come to port after storm, and whose ship, overstrained, damaged, unsafe, must start next day upon a further voyage.

And my divorce from Zosia? Neither of us says a word about it, and, judging from the way things are going between us now, neither of us wants to open the subject. If I were not so cautious and didn't have this indefinable newly acquired fear of life and people, I should say that the question of our divorce has completely fallen through and will never crop up again.

Staś and Evunia! It's they who solved my problem—our problem, perhaps—without asking anyone's advice. They have become great friends. I don't know who told Eva that Staś is her little brother, but that's what she calls him, and she's very affectionate and emphatic about it. While he, just as quiet and mournful as ever, looks at Eva as though she were a picture and follows her everywhere like a shadow.

Their attitude towards the holy image, now hanging on the wall between their beds, is one of solemn respect not unmixed with a certain familiarity. Eva, who is always superstitious, declares with the utmost seriousness that she was just going to die, only "God didn't let her." Staś assents with a manly nod of the head. I'm sure he'll never tell her where he took that picture from. I'm beginning to notice a lot of resemblance between Staś and Jurek.

Jurek: as soon as I've pulled myself together I shall have that boy found. He's the biggest anxiety of my life at present.

Letters—three. They all came some days ago and I only opened them today. My newspaper office, my Government office, and my publisher.

The first leaves me cold: the sack! I threw it without regret into the waste-paper basket.

The second leaves me cold, too, though it is very nice: a request that I should take up my office job again with rehabilitation. I must write and tell them very politely that I'm not coming back. Nothing attracts me there now. What if I did pass for an exemplary Government clerk in my own and perhaps even in other people's opinion, seeing that I always despised my shop and everything connected with it? No kind of work is worthy of a man unless it's bigger than he is.

Third item of news: a kindly smile from fate. The first edition of my two last books is sold out, and my publisher is disposed to issue a second. He encloses the contract for me to sign, and a cheque.

Whatever made me think I had a lot of things to settle?

July 14th.

I've taken a cottage in the mountains for the summer. It's not much of a place, but it's away from people and near to nature. Something's drawing me back to nature again.

It seems I've met everyone's wishes, for our household has become very jolly. We are packing up in a great hurry. Zosia, who is always so tidy, has turned the house upside down, even moving the furniture out of its usual place. I help her for all I'm worth. I want this trip to wipe out all traces of what's been happening lately.

In the intervals of packing we discuss our summer holiday. Zosia asks if it is nice and quiet where we're going, and I say it is. And if there are meadows with flowers, and I say there are. And if we shall be able to have a peep at the farmyard and work in the garden, and I say that there's a garden, and flower-pots in the windows, and a hen-roost, and birds in the trees, and simply everything that we've got to get to know again and grow fond of again so as to be able to live again.

Evunia tells Staś marvels about the mountains and forests and the bridge that the torrent carried away, and about a mushroom that was too big to go into the saucepan, and about a cow with one horn and a cock that pecked a hawk to death. Staś listens attentively and doesn't quite believe her, but his eyes shine with enterprise. Dazzled by the fountain of his sister's fancy (damn it! Eva is coming out with a talent for literature!) he tried to throw something into the treasure chest of their impressions on his own account.

"And I"—he interrupted her yesterday—"I've seen a camel!"

It was like a thunderbolt. Eva's face grew blank.

"Have you?" she stammered, amazed.

"Yes, I have! he had a head like a sheep and a neck like a goose."

Here Eva burst into frantic, indescribable laughter. Staś seemed hurt for a moment and then joined in with all his heart. I should have laughed too if I hadn't caught, in Staś's voice, a likeness to his mother's.

July 15th.

It hasn't been quite so jolly today.

Felix came in to say good-bye this morning. He's off to the border provinces to take a master's job in a new school for boys. He's been thinking about this for some time, only there were obstacles—circumstances and illusions—in his way.

But now his mind is made up. One must begin to live "seriously" sometime.

"Seriously!" he repeated, looking me in the eye as if he feared I shouldn't agree with him.

We had a long talk and really understood each other for the first time in our lives, I think. We found heaps to say and were both amazed at the way our views harmonized. We separated very good friends.

Whatever becomes of Felix, I'm bound to miss him at times. Nothing bad ever happened to me through him. He was often of great use to me, and he did all the dirty work of my life eagerly, under the delusion that he was merely walking at my side. He never satisfied me, but he never failed me either. He was always the one to be sacrificed, and he has swallowed the bitter pill of failure in my place more than once. He had virtues that weren't virtues, and defects one couldn't take offence at. Everyone knew him through and through, but nobody could say what he really was; for he always went in another man's shadow.

Now he's trying to set himself free, and I think he's on the right road. Those distant provinces—it's the first sacrifice he's conscious of making.

Good-bye and good luck, Felix! The beginning of strength lies in the first renunciation.

But what's going to happen to the motorist? He's been in to tell us that he's starting on his crazy expedition tomorrow. He stayed only a few minutes, saying he was out to test his new car. He was very sure of himself and in better spirits than ever, and yet he made an uncanny impression on me.

In the moments when he wasn't smiling all over his face he had an ill-boding look that made me turn cold.

I'd give a good deal for that man not to go away.

July 16th.

Zosia has a splendid idea—for me to go with the motorist. It came up while we were discussing yesterday's visits over tea. Zosia, it appears, is just as worried as I am about the motorist's trip. For us both to have forebodings. . . . Hang it all! I must run round to him or he'll be starting.

(Undated.)

I'm writing at one of our stopping-places, on the last leaf

of my diary. We are *en route*. The motorist himself doesn't know where we are bound for, for he's quite abandoned his original idea and has put himself into the hands of God. Fate has queered his plans in another way, besides, by giving him one more passenger—Szmid. We met him somewhere at a cross-roads on his annual trek among his old schoolfellows who have homes in the country. We took him up under the pretext of giving him a lift over the first stage of his journey, and he turned a bit crusty and put up some resistance. Once he contrived to give us the slip at a place where we were putting up for the night. But it ended in his giving way, and he has now surrendered his soul, as we have, to the demon of speed that is carrying us across the world with perfect, imperturbable, and soothing uniformity.

I may even say that Szmid is taking the lead in our adventure. Although he's blind, it is he who decides which way we are to go, where we shall stop and for how long; and it's marvellous what instinct—the instinct of the tramp—he reveals. He's absolutely unequalled as a companion, for he has no needs of any kind and seldom opens his mouth; if he does speak, it's always to the point, and his utterances have the ring of an amen.

Today, for instance. We climbed out of a dusky labyrinth of ravines and hillside valleys on to a great hill, and crept along its crest at a foot pace. The view on every side was magnificent. It was one of those places where we see the face of the earth in a full, unknown beauty—just as the birds and tree-tops see it.

The car throbbed and rocked and panted upon the rough road. The sun was blazing overhead, and an aimless wind scattered the heat with a freshness breathing from the shadowy gorges or blowing from the glassy sky.

We looked at Szmid and waited for him to call a halt, but he kept us going till we got to a place where the road started downhill. And there, under a rocky cliff that shut off the long line of hills like a bastion, he stopped us.

"I think there's high ground on the left here," he said, as we got out of the car.

"There is."

"Let's go up."

The cliff wasn't easy to climb, and turned out to be higher than we thought it from below, but the view it gave us was so immense and beautiful that it made us sad. Everything—forest, meadow, homestead, mountain, valley, river—grew small, melted into the distance, lost its limited sense and meaning, was drowned in space and swallowed up by sky. The abandoned car lay against the slope at the foot of the rock, as helpless as a turtle.

We sat with our backs to one another, as though each of us were taking a separate slice of the world for his own possession. Nobody said a word, but our thoughts, running off in different directions into the far distance, collided with each other and started fighting.

Szmid was the first to turn his head.

"Is it pretty here?" he asked.

"Yes, very."

"Is the earth below us?"

"Yes."

"And nothing but sky above?"

"Nothing but sky."

"Then I've been here before," he murmured. After a moment he added with a sigh: "It's good when a man remembers what God's world looks like."

The motorist got to his feet. "A man," he said with a passion of revolt and resentment, "knows how his own world looks and doesn't need God for it."

Szmid was silent.

"Do you hear, Szmid?"

"There's no man without God," Szmid replied.

THE END

4688